PENANCE

David Housewright

PENANCE

A Foul Play Press Book

THE COUNTRYMAN PRESS
WOODSTOCK, VERMONT

First Edition

Copyright © 1995 by David Housewright

Library of Congress Cataloging-in-Publication Data

Housewright, David, 1955-
Penance/David Housewright.—1st ed.
p.   cm.
"A Foul Play Press book."
ISBN 0-88150-341-X
I. Title.
PS3558. 08668P46   1995
813'. 54—dc20   95-20830
                                                 CIP

Published by Foul Play Press,
a division of The Countryman Press, Inc.,
PO Box 175, Woodstock, Vermont 05091-0175

Printed in the United States of America.
10 9 8 7 6 5 4 3 2 1

For Renée

ACKNOWLEDGMENTS

Special thanks to Dale Gelfand, Laura Jorstad, Lou Kan–nenstine, Alison Picard, Judith Marie Strobel, Michael Sullivan and Renée Valois.

ONE

I STARED AT my reflection in the interrogation room's two-way mirror, not caring at all who might be staring back. I looked like hell: eyes bloodshot from lack of sleep, stubble giving my face an unwashed look, hair sticking straight out above my right ear, pillow hair. I was wearing a sweatshirt that proclaimed the Minnesota Twins' victory in the 1987 World Series, blue jeans and white Nikes, no socks. Still, it could be worse. I could be wearing the blue-striped shorts the cops found me in when they busted down my door at 6:00 in the A.M. Instead, they let me dress before hustling me out of the house and into a squad. I thought of grabbing my drinking jacket—my blue nylon windbreaker with POLICE spelled out on the back in huge white letters—but I doubted the detectives would appreciate the irony.

One of the detectives was parked in a metal chair, leaning back against the wall just to the right of the mirror, watching me from under heavy eyebrows while trying to appear menacing. His name was Casper and he was bald and pale like the ghost. He did not speak, had not spoken since he and his partner installed me in the interrogation room. I watched him watch me until he folded his arms across his chest and sighed heavily.

"Not bad," I told him and laughed. I had used the same technique myself, often in that same room, letting Anne Scalasi question the suspect while I lurked behind her. She was the friendly, compassionate, understanding big sister. I was the Prince of Darkness. We were pretty good, she and I. We had a ninety-eight percent clearance rate when we worked Homicide together. Conviction rate? Well, we could only catch them. We couldn't help it if courts let them go.

I was still chuckling when Casper's partner entered the room carrying a file folder. His name was Martin McGaney and in direct contrast to his partner, he was tall and black with a mustache and hair cut short. He glanced at Casper, who continued to stare, and then back at me. McGaney was relatively new to Homicide; he had filled the slot that opened when Annie was promoted. Casper was a six-year veteran of the division, yet McGaney was already acknowledged as the better investigator. When I first met him, his rookielike enthusiasm and undisguised adoration for his boss were almost laughable. He had settled down nicely since then.

"You know your rights," McGaney reminded me with a practiced scowl.

"Anne Scalasi," I said.

"Lieutenant Scalasi is far too busy to hold the hand of every suspect we bring in for questioning."

"Did she say that?"

McGaney did not answer.

I looked at the mirror, tried to look beyond it. She was back there, watching. I could feel her. And for the first time since the detectives wound the cuffs around my wrists, I was frightened. Anne Scalasi was the highest ranking female officer in the St. Paul Police Department, the newly promoted commander of the Homicide unit. She was also my best friend. When I was lying flat on my back in a hospital room a couple months ago, several pounds of bandages wrapped around my head, she kept a vigil at my bedside, holding my hand like a lover. Later, members of the staff would comment on how beautiful my girl was. Only she wasn't my girl. She belonged to a cop who worked the Midway District and to three kids who seemed much too old to be hers. Still, I expected her to come to my aid. The fact that she didn't could mean only one thing: I was in deep shit.

"So, Taylor, tell me," McGaney said. "Where were you Saturday night?"

"I was holding up a liquor store in Nordeast Minneapolis."

That caused Casper to push away from the wall, the front legs of his chair thudding heavily when they hit the floor. "Smart ass," he said between clenched teeth.

"Check it out," I told him. "I'll bet you fifty bucks someone robbed a liquor store in Nordeast Minneapolis Saturday night."

McGaney glanced at the mirror and then back at me. He smiled. "You amuse me, Taylor."

"Hey, if I can bring a little sunshine . . ."

"Where were you Saturday night?" McGaney repeated.

"Let's cut to the chase, fellas," I said. "First you tell me what happened Saturday night and then I'll decide if I'll tell you where I was."

"We ask the questions," Casper told me.

"Hey, pal, don't mess with me. I've been to the circus before."

A few moments of silence passed while we all thought it over. Finally, McGaney asked, "John Brown, remember him?"

"Vividly."

"When was the last time you saw him?"

"At his sentencing."

"You said you were going to get him when he got out."

"No, I didn't."

McGaney read from the file he opened in front of him: "Your exact words were, 'It doesn't matter, six years or sixty. I'm a patient man.'"

I had to shrug at that. It sounded like something I might have said.

11

"Brown was released from Stillwater a while back after doing four of six for criminal vehicular homicide."

"Was he?"

"You didn't know?"

"I haven't been keeping track."

"Bullshit," Casper said. "Man drives drunk, kills your wife and kid, you vow vengeance in fucking open court and now you say you just forgot about it?"

"I didn't forget about it. I just decided life was too short to spend it waiting to murder the guy."

"You carry a nine-millimeter, don't you?" McGaney asked. "A Beretta?"

"No."

"Ha!" Casper snorted. He was getting to be a real chatterbox.

"I haven't carried for a couple months; I intend to let my gun permit lapse."

McGaney thought about it. "Shooting those guys, going to the hospital yourself, it must have messed you up pretty good," he said.

I turned my head away at the reference. Yeah, I was messed up. I was also angry, frustrated, embarrassed and more than a little ashamed of myself. But I did not want the cops to see any of that.

"Where were you around midnight Saturday?" McGaney repeated.

"Are we back to that?" I asked.

"Let's bust 'im," Casper urged, continuing to play his part.

"What charge?"

"We don't need a charge, smart mouth. We can hold you for a free thirty-six."

"Gee, a day and a half in county. How will I ever stand the strain?"

McGaney studied me for a moment and then said, "At midnight Saturday a person or persons unknown shot John Brown at close range with a nine."

"In one ear and out the other," Casper added.

"He was sitting behind the wheel of a four-by-four in the parking lot of a strip mall on West Seventh Street," McGaney finished.

News of bloody murder doesn't usually faze me. I've seen too much of it. Yet, I admit to being shook over Brown's death. For some reason I expected the sonuvabitch to live forever.

McGaney leaned in close. "Now, Taylor, *you will* tell me where you were or *I will* put you in a cell and by the time you get out, I'll have your license for obstruction."

He probably could, too. The Department of Public Safety, which regulates private investigators in Minnesota, is always happy to accommodate local constabularies. However, telling the truth was going to be tricky. Between 7:30 Saturday night and 4:15 Sunday morning, I was losing twelve hundred and fifty-five of someone else's dollars playing Texas Hold 'Em in a hotel suite in downtown Minneapolis. I'd been hired by a bookie named Randy who lost six thousand bucks in the poker game the week before. Six K wasn't much to Randy; it was the principle of the thing, he kept telling me. He was convinced there was a mechanic working the game but he didn't know who. He hired and staked me to find out. Twelve players sat in and left during the evening. Most of them were occasional players, guys with a few extra dollars in their jeans and a Steve McQueen attitude. A few were hustlers, a couple were professionals. None of them were likely to admit to a cop that they were gambling—gambling is illegal, after all. Well, maybe one would . . .

"Heather Schrotenboer," I said.

"Who's she?"

"She's a student at the University of Minnesota; she's working toward a master's degree in psychology. I was in a hotel suite with her from about eight until four in the morning."

"Discussing the conflicts between Jung and Freudian theory, no doubt," Casper said.

"Are they in conflict?"

"You were with her the entire evening?" McGaney asked.

"Yes."

"How convenient."

"Isn't it, though. Almost like I had it planned."

McGaney abruptly left the room. I watched him leave, averting my eyes from the mirror, embarrassed by what Anne probably thought of my confession.

"I thought shrinks used a couch," Casper said.

"We had a couch," I replied, feeding his assumption.

When McGaney returned just minutes later, he surprised me by saying I was free to go. "Ms. Schrotenboer confirmed your alibi," he said. *Why would he take her word for it,* I wondered. Especially over the telephone.

"That's it?"

"That's it."

"What the hell . . . ?"

"Beat it," Casper added.

"Don't leave town," McGaney warned.

"Don't leave town?" It was a stupid thing to say and only TV cops say it. Legally, I could go anywhere I pleased and McGaney certainly knew it. No, it wasn't a warning. He was trying to tell me something. But what? He gave me a hint as I brushed past him.

"And I expect you to call when you learn more about Brown's murder."

He didn't say "if." He said "when."

I hailed a cab on Minnesota Street and gave the driver directions to my house in Roseville. The driver was Laotian—after California, we have the largest Hmong community in America—and he drove ten miles over the speed limit with two fingers on the wheel, all the while assessing Sunday's Vikings loss. "Football? You call that football? I don't call that football," he kept repeating in a thick, Southeast Asian accent.

While he rambled, I tried to reason it out. The cops go to all the trouble of dragging me to the station at the crack of dawn and accuse me of murder just to release me a short time later on the say-so of a woman they spoke to on the telephone? Something else: Cops don't like it when private investigators become involved in ongoing criminal investigations; hell, they don't like private investigators, period. So, why did McGaney all but order me to investigate John Brown's murder? And where was Anne Scalasi? There was an odor to this. It smelled like . . .

"Shit," the driver said. "The Vikings haven't been worth shit since Bud Grant retired."

"How long have you been following the Vikes?" I asked the driver when he pulled onto the horseshoe driveway that curved in front of my house.

"Seventeen years," he answered. "Since moving here from Muong Son."

I gave him a nice tip but no sympathy. The Vikings have been breaking my heart for a lot longer.

I stood naked in front of the mirror, dripping water all over my bathroom's linoleum floor, noting with distress my thinning hair and wondering how much longer it would hide the scar above my right ear. Like most men, I'm terrified at the prospect of growing bald. I can see myself years from now in a scene from a Three Stooges short: I'm wearing a toupee, Curly points at it and screams, Larry knocks it off and Moe shoots it.

The telephone rang and grabbing a towel I answered it in my bedroom, half expecting to hear Anne Scalasi's voice. Wrong. It was Heather Schrotenboer.

"Are you all right, Taylor?"

"Fine. How 'bout yourself?"

"I got a call from the police . . ."

"I know."

"They wanted to know if I was with you Saturday night. I said I was, but I didn't mention anything about the game. They didn't ask about the game, so I didn't say. They just asked if I spent the night with you in a hotel. I said I did."

"You did good."

"They probably got the wrong impression."

"Probably."

"Are you in trouble?"

"Not anymore."

Heather was small and blond and although she was twenty-four, she looked like a high school girl. When I met her she was wearing a blue cap that said Top Gun and smoking long, thin, shiny cigars. When I asked her why she was in a hotel room filled only with men playing what is largely a man's game, she flashed an elfin smile and said, "Field research."

"Why did you need an alibi?" she asked over the telephone.

"It's a long story," I told her.

"I'd like to hear it. I have a class in fifteen minutes but could I come over tonight and talk?"

"More research?"

"Something like that," she answered.

Water dribbled down my bare legs and soaked the carpet under my feet. I tightened the bath towel around my waist and said, "Come on over." I gave Heather my address and a few simple directions.

"I knew you were a dangerous man when we met," she said and chuckled.

"Yeah," I told her. "You better be careful."

TWO

I FOUND A meter with twenty minutes left on it near the public library and walked the two blocks to the Ramsey County courthouse in downtown St. Paul. I was looking for Cynthia Grey. Grey had represented John Brown four years ago. Since then she had become one of the best-known defenders of drunk drivers in Minnesota, often appearing on local talk shows to trash our DWI laws. I found her number among the eleven thousand, two hundred and twenty-one listings of attorneys in the Minneapolis and St. Paul telephone books. Her secretary said she was at the courthouse. It was Monday morning; all the weekend drunks were entering their pleas.

News of John Brown's tragic demise rattled me, but it didn't exactly break my heart and I had no real interest in finding his killer except that the St. Paul Police Department seemed anxious that I do so. For that reason I decided to give it a day or two. Besides, except for my chore for Randy, I was between jobs. I had just helped an insurance company catch a ring of crib burglars that specialized in antiques. The thieves targeted their victims by reading obituaries in the newspapers—they would call during the funerals and if no one answered, go burglarize the house. They would then take the antiques and sell them at flea markets across the Midwest. Armed with a list of stolen items, I'd haunted the markets in Iowa until I came across a dealer who admitted to buying some of the merchandise. With his help, I backtracked the burglars to Minneapolis. There were four of them and they were all now under indictment in U.S. District Court in Des Moines, charged with about two dozen counts of interstate transportation of stolen property. One of the victims whose heirlooms were actually recovered, an elderly woman with clear blue eyes, sent me a gross of chocolate chip cookies in gratitude. They were pretty good, too; I've been living off them for nearly a week now.

The courthouse, which also houses St. Paul's city hall, was built in 1932 and has been in a constant state of disrepair ever since. I waited outside the revolving glass door as a team of workers sporting white hard hats came out of the building, looked up, then glanced at a blueprint that one of them unrolled like an ancient scroll. Across the street, a man wearing a blue ski jacket with red lining watched us over the top of a newspaper.

I found Cynthia Grey on the eighth floor, just outside the courtroom where citizens arrested for driving while intoxicated made their initial appearance. She smiled as she accepted the enthusiastic thanks of one of her clients. Her smile had all the sincerity of a beauty pageant contestant. I stood about twenty feet away on the other side of the corridor, arms folded, and waited.

"Don't forget, Tony," she interrupted him at last. "We have a deal."

"Oh, yeah, sure, absolutely, no problem," Tony told her, still shaking her hand.

Cynthia fished a white business card from the pocket of her jacket and handed it to him. He took it reluctantly. "This is the name of the woman who runs the treatment center,"

Cynthia said. "She's expecting you to call. So am I."

"I will, I will, I promise," Tony said.

"If you don't call her, don't ever call me again. And, hey. Next time take a cab."

"Oh, yeah, absolutely. Thanks, Miss Grey. No kidding. Thanks a lot."

Tony turned and headed for the elevators, shoving the card into his pocket as he went. Cynthia watched him go. She sighed deeply.

"A lot of lawyers don't want to dirty their hands doing drunken driving defense," she said. "I was the same way. At first I took the cases because I was just starting out and I needed the billings. I didn't like it, but I did it. I don't struggle with it anymore. Now I realize that any time an accused drunken driver with an alcohol problem comes into my office, it's an opportunity to get him some help. I'm doing the right thing. I believe in what I'm doing."

She looked directly into my eyes. "That's what you wanted to know, isn't it?"

"It answers a question I've nursed for a long time," I admitted.

Cynthia Grey had shoulder-length brown hair with matching eyes, slim features and long legs largely hidden by her black pleated skirt. She wore a matching black blazer over a white collarless blouse, a white handkerchief peeking out of the breast pocket. Her leather briefcase was brown. She stepped halfway across the corridor and stopped. I met her there, my hand outstretched. She took it. Her hand was soft, yet there was nothing soft about her grip.

"Good to see you again, Officer Taylor."

"Ex-officer Taylor," I corrected her. "I'm a private investigator now."

"Ahh, that's right. I've been reading about you. Tell me, how many men have you killed now? I lost track."

I winced at the question, considered a four-letter-word reply, thought better of it and said, "I need information concerning one of your former clients."

"I have no former clients."

"I want to know what John Brown's been doing the past few months, where he's been staying."

"Where he's been staying? All things considered, you're the last person I would give that information to. I might tell him you're looking for him, though, the next time I see him."

"Well, hopefully, that won't be for a good long time."

"What's that supposed to mean?"

Before I could answer, a man in a rumpled gray suit appeared at the end of the corridor and shouted, "Hey, Grey!" Cynthia turned toward him. "You might want to wander up to sixteen. One of your clients is standing on the ledge; says he's gonna jump."

Cynthia dropped her briefcase and ran as best she could in heels to the elevators. I retrieved the briefcase and followed. She was waiting for the courthouse's notoriously slow elevator when I reached her side. I took her arm and directed her toward the staircase. She went up the stairs quickly, reached the sixteenth floor and walked instinctively to the prisoner holding room. She was barely winded; I was sucking air. A small crowd had gathered outside the room, afraid to enter. Cynthia pushed through the gawkers. I was right behind her.

The holding room was essentially a conference room with large, old-fashioned windows befitting the age of the courthouse. A prisoner had opened one of the windows and crawled out onto the twelve-inch ledge where he squatted, looking down and holding onto the bottom of the window for dear life. Cynthia moved toward him. I attempted to go with her, but she put a hand on my chest and shook her head.

"Hi, James. How you doin'?" she asked as she approached the window.

"I'm not going to jail!" the prisoner screamed.

"Certainly not," Cynthia agreed.

She leaned on the windowsill. I watched her mouth move but could not hear what she said to the prisoner, although she seemed to use his name a lot. She talked to him for what seemed a half hour, but when I glanced at my watch, I realized it was only a few minutes. After a few minutes more, the man slid back into the room and slumped in a chair next to the conference table. He was crying and shaking quite a bit. Cynthia closed the window and turned her back to it.

"Trust me, James," she told the man. He nodded and covered his face with his hands.

I waited for Cynthia in the back of the courtroom. James had composed himself well enough to enter a guilty plea to misdemeanor domestic assault charges, but broke down again when the Ramsey County sheriff's deputies laid hands on him to take him back to the detention center across the street.

"You said I wouldn't have to go back to jail," he shouted at Cynthia as the deputies led him away.

Cynthia packed her briefcase without comment while a trio of suits crowded around, waiting to take her place at the table.

"Buy me a drink," she said as she went through the courtroom doors, brushing by me without stopping.

Cynthia Grey ordered a double Scotch, neat. She stirred it with her finger and turned the glass slowly clockwise, widening a circle of moisture on the table top, but did not drink; she dried her finger on a napkin.

"You did well, getting that guy off the ledge," I told her.

"Thank you."

"What did you say that convinced him to come in?"

"I told him we would work things out," Cynthia said. "I told him it wasn't as bad as it seemed. He has a lot of criminal things pending, including a felony assault charge, and he's spent a lot of time in custody—over two weeks. Some people can't take jail. Not even for a day."

"Did you tell him he wouldn't have to go back to jail?"

"That's what he wanted to hear."

"I would have wanted to hear the truth."

"You would have wanted to hear anything that would have gotten you off that ledge."

Cynthia picked up her glass, regarded the contents thoughtfully, then returned it to its place.

"What exactly do you want, Taylor?"

"Are you going to drink that Scotch?"

"I haven't had a drink in seven years and two months," she replied.

Yeah, I figured it was something like that. I hailed our waitress and asked her to remove the Scotch and bring the lady a designer water with a twist of lime. Cynthia did not protest. I felt slightly guilty for staying with my Summit Ale and slightly superior for having conquered my own drinking problems without resorting to abstinence.

"You still haven't told me what you want," Cynthia reminded me.

"I want you to tell me what you know about John Brown's activities since he got out of the joint."

"So you can kill him?"

"I don't know quite how to tell you this except to come right out and say it: John Brown is dead. He was murdered Saturday night."

Cynthia fell back against her chair like someone had pushed her there, mouth agape, eyes wide. I knew what she was thinking.

"Yeah, the cops thought I did it, too. Only I didn't. To prove it, I'm going to find out who did."

Enough time passed for me to finish my Summit Ale while she worked it through. Finally she said, "Brown's dead?"

"So they tell me."

"And you're going to find his killer? You of all people?"

"I thought I'd give it a day or two, until a paying customer comes along."

She thought about it some more.

"I guess it wouldn't do any harm," she sighed and then said more clearly, "I was informed by Corrections three months ago that Brown was paroled to a halfway house in Minneapolis. That's all I know. I haven't seen or spoken to him in four years. He wouldn't answer my letters or return my phone calls. Apparently he thought I should have done better by him. He's probably right. I didn't have enough experience back then. If I defended him today, I'd probably get him off—at least get him a shorter sentence."

"There's a happy thought," I told her.

"In this country, the law . . ."

"I'm not interested in the law," I said, interrupting her lecture, my voice calm. "And I gave up on justice a long time ago. What I need is an address."

She gave it to me.

"A private investigator, an ex-cop: If not justice, if not the law, what do you believe in?" she asked as I wrote the address into a small notebook I carry.

"I'm not sure I believe in much of anything," I said. "Like a lot of people, I make it up as I go along. Mostly, I guess it's a matter of what I can live with."

"If everyone felt that way . . ."

I pushed myself away from the table.

"No, wait, please," Cynthia said. I waited. She looked down at her hands. "I apologize that I never got a chance to tell you how sorry I am about your wife and daughter."

"Thank you," I answered and in a half moment relived their deaths at the hands of John Brown, who was so drunk he couldn't tell the difference between red and green. He served four years, four lousy years. It should have been life. Now

23

this woman was saying she wished she could have gotten him off. Well, it was her job, I suppose.

"It's getting to be a long time ago," I told her. Yet that's not how it felt.

"Is it because of what happened to your family? Is that why you quit the cops?"

"No."

"What then?" she asked, her eyes wide and glistening.

"It's not something I discuss with my friends much less . . ."

"The lawyer who defended . . ."

"Strangers," I said interrupting her, completing the thought.

"Have dinner with me tonight," she said.

I was jolted by the invitation and answered too abruptly, "No."

"How long are you going to resent me for defending Brown?" she asked.

"Until hell freezes over."

I have nothing against lawyers. After all, a sizable portion of my income is derived from law firms—gathering evidence, investigating witnesses, checking testimony, recovering stolen property, that sort of thing. And if many of the lawyers I work for are jerks, well, a buck's a buck. But this wasn't business. This was personal.

Cynthia gave me a regal nod, but I didn't leave. I sensed that offering the dinner invitation had been an effort for her and now I felt I owed her something in return. So I told her, "Taking the jumper off the ledge the way you did, that took guts. I admire you for it."

She nodded.

Then I ruined it all by adding, "But that little contest with the Scotch? Really, Counselor, that was one of the dumbest things I've ever seen."

"If you say so," she replied curtly.

I let it go at that.

I left the tavern and made my way toward the public library, hoping I wouldn't find a parking ticket jammed under my windshield wiper. Along the way I noticed a man pretending to examine a watch in a jewelry store window, a newspaper tucked under his arm. He was wearing a red ski jacket with blue lining—*the old reversible jacket trick,* I told myself, smiling.

THREE

IT WAS JUST A house, a large, old Victorian that needed paint in a ramshackle neighborhood where most of the homes could benefit from a little maintenance. There was no sign, no address plate, nothing to indicate who lived there. That was probably the way the residents wanted it. If the locals knew who their neighbors were, no doubt they would organize to force removal of the halfway house—there's nothing like adversity to bring a neighborhood together. The more enlightened among us, of course, would accuse the locals of everything from shortsightedness to discrimination to hypocrisy. But then, none of us would want a halfway house for convicted felons next door, either.

I parked on the street and followed the crumbling sidewalk to the porch. The front door opened before I could knock and a tall man with a prison pallor stepped outside, followed by a cloud of cigarette smoke and the faint aroma of coffee, extra black.

"What do you want?" he demanded, startling me, moving in close, giving me a good look at a mouthful of decaying teeth.

"I want to play point guard for the Minnesota Timberwolves, but I'll settle for speaking with the administrator." I backed away and dug in my pocket for the photostat of my license.

He glanced at the ID. "Smart ass," he said.

"People keep calling me that."

"Fuck you."

"C'mon pal, no trouble for either of us, okay? Just tell the guy who runs the place . . ."

He poked me in the chest.

"Don't do that," I told him.

"I don't like you," he said and poked me again. I tried to swipe his hand away but caught only air as he quickly pulled it back. He gave me a playground-bully smile and said, "You wouldn't last fifteen minutes in the yard."

I believed him. I took another step backward.

"You're a fuckin' pussy. I'm gonna kick your ass."

I took still another step backward and went into a free-fighting stance, weight evenly distributed, feet at forty-five-degree angles. I took a chance and kept my hands low. My left leg began to tremble slightly with anticipation. Or was it fear? It always does that, even when I'm just sparring, my groin protected with a fiberglass cup, my hands and feet encased in foam rubber.

I'm not a big man. I barely passed the minimum height requirement for a police officer in St. Paul and several veteran officers refused to ride with me for fear they'd continually have to save my ass from various surly and much larger miscreants—small cops are challenged a lot. During my second week on the job, a dis. con. dribbled my head on the asphalt four times before I subdued him with the butt of my Glock 17. Soon after I began studying a combination of judo, karate and aikido. I pulled eighteen separate muscles attempting to master the basic kick and what I did to my hands, plunging them in and out of pea gravel to toughen their edges, I'm amazed my wife ever allowed me to touch her.

Still, I learned fast. I do not have a belt; I have not attempted to earn one. Nor am I interested in the virtues that martial arts are supposed to instill: control, courtesy, discipline, respect. I am interested merely in survival. When I had first approached the *sensai* at Dragons, my *dojo* in Minneapolis, he asked me why I wanted to master the arts. "So I can beat the hell outta people without getting hurt myself," I answered. He looked at me like he felt sorry for me. He told me the arts must be used only as a last resort; he told me, "When hand go out, withdraw anger; when anger go out, withdraw hand." I have tried to live by that philosophy ever since. Mostly, I've failed.

"Pal, I'm the last guy you want to dance with," I warned the convict. He didn't believe me. He grabbed the lapel of my sports jacket. I grasped his hand with my left and pushed up on his elbow with my right. When his back started to arch, I pulled down hard on his hand and pushed the elbow straight up, flipping him on his back, his head thudding loudly on the porch floor. Nothing to it. If the PI gig didn't work out, I could always get employment as a bouncer at a high-class strip joint.

"This wasn't necessary," I told the convict calmly, listening to his pain and applying more pressure to his shoulder joint whenever he tried to move. "This did not need to happen."

Eventually, another man appeared at the door. "Stop it, stop it!" he screamed in a high, effeminate voice.

"Are you the administrator of this facility?" I asked.

"Yes."

I released the convict and stood up. "Hi. I'm Holland Taylor."

He ignored my outstretched hand and demanded to know what was going on.

"Nothing," my attacker told him, massaging his shoulder.

"I told you what would happen if there was any more trouble, J. T.!" the administrator yelled.

"No trouble," I said, taking J. T.'s side. "We were just putzing around. I was showing him a karate hold."

"Yeah," J. T. confirmed. "Thanks," he said and retreated into the house, still kneading his shoulder. The administrator watched him go, not believing a word of it.

"Holland Taylor," I repeated.

This time he took my hand. "Elliot Seeley. Now tell me what really happened."

"Nothing much," I said. "He merely took exception to my looks. He's not the first."

"I'm truly sorry," Seeley said and I had the impression he was. "J. T. has had a difficult time adjusting, more difficult than most. He's been in and out of prison nine of the past eleven years; I think he's more comfortable inside than he is outside. Anyway, that's my problem. What can I do for you?"

I showed him my license. He wasn't any happier to see it than J. T., but at least he didn't poke me in the chest.

"I'm looking for information about John Brown."

"What kind of information?"

"When did you see him last?"

Seeley sighed heavily, like he was repeating a story that already bored him. "Saturday night, about six-thirty."

"Where was he . . ."

"He left here with Joseph Sherman in Sherman's four-by-four," Seeley said, anticipating my question.

"Wait a minute . . ."

"They said they were going to meet a man about a job. I didn't believe them, but I didn't stop them. And no, I haven't seen or heard from Sherman since, and no, I can't say where he might be hiding."

"Who is Joseph Sherman?"

Seeley sighed again. "He was one of our residents. He was paroled to us about three weeks ago after doing six in Oak Park Heights. He and Brown roomed together while they were here."

"What was Sherman in for?"

"Criminal vehicular homicide, same as Brown."

"Tell me about his vehicle?"

"It was red."

"That's it?"

"I don't know cars. All I know is he bought it a week after he got out with the money he made in prison." Seeley shook his head in disgust. "He was paid seven bucks an hour, plus commissions, plus bonuses, plus college courses to do telemarketing work for companies like 3M. I guess he was a superb salesman. He walked out of the Heights with a check for sixty-eight thousand dollars and a bachelor's degree."

I was just as annoyed as Seeley. "Who says crime doesn't pay?" I asked, slipping the notebook from my pocket. "What can you tell me about him?"

"Mr. Taylor, I've already told you more than I should; I hope you understand."

I tried to protest.

Seeley said, "Why don't you ask the police? They know everything I know."

"The police?"

"The St. Paul police," Seeley repeated. "I told the two detectives everything when they were here."

"When was that?"

"Early Sunday morning."

"The cops . . . a salt and pepper team named McGaney and Casper?"

"That sounds like them."

"Sunday morning?"

"I'm sorry. If you want to know anything more, talk to the police."

I slapped the dashboard of my Chevy Monza, then apologized to her. She had served me faithfully for fifteen years and one hundred sixty-two thousand miles; she didn't deserve the abuse.

The first step in any murder investigation is always to contact the last person to see the victim alive. The last person to see Brown alive was Joseph Sherman. Brown was killed in

Sherman's vehicle and now Sherman was missing. *So why aren't the cops looking for him,* I wondered. Why did they bust my door at 6:00 in the A.M. if Sherman was such an obvious suspect? Why did they drag me to the stationhouse only to let me go a couple of hours later?

"The cops are messing with me," I told the Monza. "And this BS about Annie refusing to see me . . . All right, I'll play."

I fired up the Monza and steered her toward downtown Minneapolis. A blue Ford parked several car lengths behind me pulled out at the same time. I nearly lost him at the light and had to slow down so he could catch up.

"Come along, officer," I muttered. "I haven't got all day."

FOUR

THE TELEPHONE was ringing as I unlocked my office door and I caught it before my answering machine kicked in.

"So, who is it?" Randy asked after he identified himself.

"How you doing, Randy?" I asked.

"Oh, I'm hurtin', man. I'm hurtin'. I don't think I can take much more of this," he moaned. Randy hates for people to think that he is actually making money at his chosen profession and over the years I've discovered that his physical pain increases and decreases in direct proportion to his winnings. Considering his extreme discomfort, I guessed that Randy'd had a pretty good weekend.

"Did you finger the mechanic?" he asked again.

"Yeah, no problem."

"Who is it?"

"Do you really want to know?"

"What the fuck? That's why I hired you, man."

"What I meant is, would you be satisfied with your money back? Your money and the money I lost?"

"You lost money? I didn't hire you to lose money."

"Aww for crissake, Randy . . ."

"I want his balls! I want 'em served up with eggs and hash browns!"

"Then I won't give you the name."

The way Randy carried on, you'd have thought he was going to have a heart attack; I almost asked him where I could send flowers.

"I don't goon, Randy, you know that," I told him when his ranting finally subsided.

"Who's askin' you to? I got guys to do the heavy work."

"Here's the deal," I told him. "I'll get your money back. I'll put the fear of God into the mechanic. And you can keep my fee."

Randy paused to think about it. "How long have I known you?"

"Twelve years, ever since I busted your Super Bowl party."

"Okay, 'cuz of them twelve years I let the mechanic walk; I figure you got your reasons."

"I do."

"But I want my money and I want it by Friday or I'm gonna send my guys to talk to you."

I was so frightened I hung up the phone without saying good-bye.

Every man and woman in America leaves little threads wherever they go. They leave them in computer databases when they are born, apply for a driver's license, graduate from school, get married, get divorced, buy on credit, make airline reservations, stay at a hotel, apply for life insurance, order freshwater pearls from the Home Shopping Network—hundreds of little threads that when woven together produce a garment of who and what they are. In fact, it is virtually impossible not to become the subject of a record. The average person is on fifty databases at any one time and nearly all of them are readily available to someone with a personal computer, a modem and a telephone. Like me.

Most threads of information are stored in public files gathered by the government that I can access simply by signing on as "anonymous" and using "guest" as a password. Much of this information is contained in private databases such as those of credit bureaus that I can access for a fee. It isn't easy, of course. Locating banks of files that actually contain relevant information often requires as much detective work as investigating a dozen flea markets in Iowa. I often have to drag one database after another until I find the name I'm looking for. Or the Social Security number, our de facto standard universal identifier. Still, given time, I can usually gather enough bits and pieces to assemble a reasonably complete sketch of an individual, everything from date of birth to high school locker number.

I know PIs who conduct entire investigations by computer, never leaving their offices. There's a guy in Texas who does nothing but skip traces; he can run one in about ninety seconds. Other agencies specialize in background checks, verifying an individual's personal history for five hundred bucks a pop. Mostly they run these checks for businesses, pre-employment checks. Yet more and more they run them for single women who want to investigate their male friends and for fathers who worry about their daughters. All in all, it's a great time to be a private investigator: Nobody trusts anybody.

Still, I don't think relying exclusively on a computer is smart. You simply cannot get everything you need on-line and the facts you do generate often come without the nuances that give them true value. For that you need personal contact. You need to interview a witness, conduct physical surveillance, engage in waste retrieval and analysis. Otherwise, it is too easy to be deceived, too easy to come to the wrong conclusion.

I parked myself in front of my PC and thought it over, trying to decide where to begin. Above the computer hung a newspaper article I had framed in silver. HAVE PC—WILL TRAVEL, the headline read. Just under the headline was a photograph of me, dressed in a trench coat and fedora and leaning on my PC. The story was all about how I squashed the hostile takeover of a much-loved local firm. It was fairly simple, really. I merely followed the Social Security numbers of the CEO, CFO and president of the hostile company to a series of secret bank accounts in Nevada and Nassau, where they had squirreled away nearly fifty million bucks. My discovery, which generated considerable interest from the FBI, SEC, IRS and several other organizations with impressive-sounding initials, effectively killed the acquisition and earned me a twenty-five-thousand-dollar bonus (still unspent) from a much-relieved board of directors. It also earned me a lot of attention from the local media.

I made the papers again a few months back, only I haven't seen them. I was in the hospital at the time. Anne Scalasi saved copies; she assured me they all claimed I was a hero. I took her word for it.

I glanced at her photograph on my desk. She was dressed in blues, her hat hiding a wave of brown hair, the bill shading hazel eyes. The photo was taken the evening the St. Paul Saints won the Northern League minor league baseball championship. We had donned our uniforms and snuck into Midway Stadium, pretending to be security. A photographer who works for the *Pioneer Press* sports department took the picture for me; Annie doesn't know I have it.

Annie's photograph was next to Laura's. Laura, my wife. All golden hair and blue eyes. Laura had worked in advertising as an art director; the photograph was taken when she won a gold push pin or some damn thing at a Twin Cities advertising club awards show.

She and Anne had not liked each other. Anne dismissed Laura as being frivolous, questioning her occupation, her hobby of collecting antique dolls and toys, her interest in fashion. Laura found Anne obsessive, preoccupied with "the hunt," placing her job above all else including her family. Anne called Laura "the artiste." Laura referred to Anne as "Kojak." They never spoke except to send messages to me.

The evening Laura was killed she had asked Annie to tell me that since I was working late, she would take Jennifer to her swimming lesson . . .

Poor Laura. The man who killed her was given a lousy thirty-six-month sentence. Thirty-six months for her and thirty-six months for my daughter, to be served consecutively. And then he did only forty-eight . . .

Wait a minute! The usual sentence for criminal vehicular homicide is twenty-one months per count. John Brown was sentenced to a total of thirty months more because public outrage over the case generated by the Mothers Against Drunk Drivers—and by my being a cop, some say—compelled the judge to ignore the state sentencing guidelines. On the other hand, Joseph Sherman did six years for criminal vehicular homicide. Assume he was a good boy and walked after serving two-thirds of his sentence. That means the judge originally gave him nine years. Who the hell did he kill?

To find out I dialed up VU/TEXT, the database of the *St. Paul Pioneer Press,* and instructed the computer to drag it for any local or state story containing Sherman, Joseph's name. Up popped a menu containing eleven items in chronological order. I pulled the text of the last item, the most recent article. The headline read:

DRUNK DRIVER PLEADS GUILTY
IN REPRESENTATIVE'S DEATH;
SENTENCED TO NINE YEARS

Dynamite. A clipping service would have taken a week and five hundred dollars, yet I had everything I needed in thirty seconds for a fraction of the cost. I prepared a manila file folder, labeling it "Brown, John," and noted all pertinent information culled from the newspaper articles chronologically on a yellow legal pad.

To start from the beginning, Terrance Friedlander had been

running for his eighth term to the Minnesota House of Representatives. The minority party, anticipating defeat, offered only token resistance, specifically a young, unknown attorney whose political experience consisted solely of writing nasty letters on behalf of the Department of Transportation. The lawyer's name was Carol Catherine Monroe . . .

"So, that's how she got her start," I mused, noting the name on the yellow sheet.

With less than three weeks remaining in the campaign, Friedlander held a twenty-three-point lead in the polls. Yet, he was still out there pressing the flesh, distributing flyers door-to-door, flyers with his smiling countenance under a red, white and blue banner that read VOTE FOR TOMORROW; people actually glad to see him, happy to shake his hand, asking, "What's this new tax bullshit, Terry?"; "Hey Terry, you're not gonna let 'em move the airport, are you?"; and Terry smiling back and saying, "Not to worry, not to worry," until he went to cross the street and the car was on him, seemed to swerve toward him and wham! he was gone.

The car was a '74 Ford LTD, pale green with a black hardtop, witnesses said, license plate FAU 367. They found the car in a northern suburb, parked in the lot next to the Babe Ruth baseball diamond, the driver's door open, the engine running, the front seat reeking of cheap whiskey. They found the driver—the "alleged driver," the newspapers said—in his apartment three blocks away at 1237 Glendale Street. He was sitting in his kitchen, a liter of vodka on the table and two dead soldiers on the floor, when they came for him. His name was Joseph Sherman, and he claimed he didn't know what the cops were talking about, claimed he hadn't left the apartment all day. However, he had a long history of alcohol abuse and three DWIs to his name and when the assistant Hennepin County attorney offered criminal vehicular homicide instead of third-degree murder and second-degree manslaughter and a half dozen motor vehicle felonies, Sherman jumped at it.

The paper hadn't much liked the plea bargain, but the CA's case was circumstantial; no one could actually identify Sherman as the driver of the car—one witness was even convinced that a woman was behind the wheel. But then the judge ignored the bargain and dropped the gavel on Sherman for nine hard. That made just about everyone happy except Sherman and who gave a damn about him?

1237 GLENDALE STREET was the address of an aging apartment complex that boasted an indoor swimming pool, sauna, storage facilities and thirty-two moderately priced units, half of which had a wonderful view of Interstate 694. The other half looked out on the lot where I parked my car. I stretched after closing the door, hiding my eyes as I glanced at the blue Ford parked across the street.

I checked the directory. The caretaker, D. Ladner, was in apartment 101. D stood for Dorothy but after I introduced myself Mrs. Ladner insisted I call her Dot. At first she assumed I was looking for an apartment and told me, "Sorry, no vacancies." Then I handed her my card.

"Wow, a private investigator! Just like Rockford!" she exclaimed.

"Exactly," I lied.

"What can I do to help?" she asked, all set to rush to the closet for her trench coat and .38. The woman watched way too much television.

"I'd like to talk to you about your tenants."

"Is it Foley in two-oh-two? Last week I saw him holding a handkerchief to his nose; that's what happens when you use too much cocaine, isn't it? You get nose bleeds?"

"Could be he picked it a little too close," I said, dampening her enthusiasm.

Dot thought about it for a moment—who else among her tenants could be a criminal?—then she remembered herself.

"Please, please, c'mon in, don't stand in the hall," she said. The apartment was simple: bedroom, bathroom, kitchen, living room/dining room combination, with windows on two sides. The carpet was green; the furniture old—"antiquey," my wife would say. The TV was tuned to a soap. "All My Children." Dot turned down the volume but did not switch off the set.

"Who are you after? A drug dealer?"

"How long have you been caretaker here?" I asked in reply.

"Eight years. I moved in right after my nephew bought the building, my husband's sister's boy, Kevin. He gave me the job after my husband passed. I have a picture . . ."

"Perhaps later," I said, wondering whose picture she was going to show me, the husband or the nephew. "Did you know Joseph Sherman?"

"Oh, him," she replied, obviously disappointed. "The police were asking about him the other day. I was hoping you were here about something new."

"The police were here?"

"Sunday," she replied, glancing at the soap—Erica Kane was in bed with someone. Fetching lass, that Erica Kane. "They were St. Paul police," Dot continued. "Very pleasant."

"Short white guy, tall black guy?" I asked as the soap went to commercial.

"Yes," Dot replied, then corrected me. "The tall officer was a person of color. We don't call 'em blacks no more."

"My mistake. What did you tell them?"

"They asked me if I had seen Joseph Sherman around here and I said I didn't."

"So, you did know Sherman."

"Uh-huh. I didn't like him, though. He was an alcoholic and I have no time for alcoholics. My cousin Ruth's boy Jerry was an alcoholic and he was no good, I can tell you. He caused Ruth plenty of heartache and then he killed that politician—Sherman, not Jerry—and the reporters came 'round." Dot shook her head. "I was all set to testify at his trial. The prosecutor wanted me to tell how he was always drunk and causing trouble with the other tenants, only then there wasn't a trial. I was kinda disappointed, you know? I had plenty to say."

"What kind of trouble did he cause?"

"The tenants were always complaining that he had his TV on too loud."

"What else?"

"Some tenants saw him stagger when he walked, needed to hang onto the railing to get upstairs. This is a respectable place. Anyway, the last I heard of Sherman he was doing hard time in the slammer."

"Slammer?"

"That's what you call prison, isn't it?"

"Among other things," I agreed.

"Yeah, the heat busted him for whacking the politician with his ride," she added, showing off her TV vocabulary.

"Sure."

The woman nodded at me just like one of the actors in "Dragnet." "He's out, you say?" she said.

"Yes, ma'am," I replied in the clipped manner of Jack Webb, who knew as much about being a real cop as your average finishing-school debutante.

"Think he'll be coming back for his stuff?"

"Stuff?"

"Clothes, furniture; it's in storage."

"Storage?"

"In the basement."

"Show me."

Dot took a large ring of keys from a hook in her kitchen. I followed her out the door and down the steps into a huge basement. She moved quickly, without speaking, as if on a mission. She walked me past a dozen or more room-sized lockers with large wooden doors, finally stopping at one with BUILD- ING stenciled across the front. She bent to the padlock. She had trouble springing it open.

"After he was convicted, we moved Sherman's belongings into the storage room and waited for someone to claim them. No one did," she said while she worked the lock. It wouldn't open. She tried several other keys without success.

"Let it go," I recommended at last.

Dot nodded.

"Who were Sherman's friends in the building?"

"What friends?"

"Didn't he have any friends?"

"Not here."

"You sure?"

"As sure as I can be."

"Who were his neighbors?"

"There's only one tenant left who was living here when Sherman was."

"Who would that be?"

"Meghan Chakolis."

"Which apartment?"

"Three-eleven."

"Which was Sherman's apartment?"

"Three-twelve."

"Ms. Chakolis live alone?"

Dot nodded again. "Ever since her husband left, about six years ago."

"Where can I find Ms. Chakolis during the day?"

"The State Capitol."

"The State Capitol?"

"She works for the government."

"What does she do?"

"I have no idea."

Parking at the State Capitol is a joke, so I pulled into the Sears lot across the street and walked through the store, so the security guards would think I was a customer and not make me move my car to a parking lot that cost money. It made for a longer walk, but I didn't mind. The air outside was crisp and clear—autumn in Minnesota. It's one reason I remained here when my family moved to Fort Myers in Florida.

The driver of the blue Ford followed at a discreet distance. It was the sloppiest tail job I had ever seen. Either that or I was supposed to see him.

The State Capitol Mall is like an oasis in the depressed area that is Rice Street–University Avenue, an area that is making a big comeback thanks to the efforts of its residents, but which still has a long way to go. The State Capitol Building itself is sprawling, ornate and white; if you're looking for grandeur and sheer elegance in your government buildings, this one would do nicely, with Greek columns, high, arching windows and a massive dome topped with gold. Above the enormous front doors a team of golden horses pulls a golden chariot. Forty-five steps lead to the doors—I counted them years ago while on a grade-school field trip. In the summer about a hundred thousand people will loll on the grass in front of those steps and listen to the Minnesota Orchestra play the "1812" overture while Fourth of July fireworks explode overhead. In the winter the grass is covered by sheets of snow virtually undisturbed by tracks.

The State Office Building, located on the left side of the mall, is nearly as big as the capitol and perhaps more imposing, with slate gray stone and a red-tile roof. The State Capitol Building has a museumlike quality; the State Office Building looks like people actually work there. The members of the House of Representatives are quartered in the State Office Building, the state senators in the Capitol Building, rank having its privileges. The two buildings are connected by a long underground tunnel wide enough for a golf cart but not much else. Nobody wants our legislators to actually go outside, to be exposed to the elements.

A security guard wearing the navy blue uniform of the State Capitol Security Force sat behind a small desk just inside the State Office Building's main entrance. He gave me a look, but it wasn't hard. He didn't ask my name, he didn't ask where I was going, he didn't ask if I had any C4 in the heels of my shoes. The security force officers are mostly door shakers; they're licensed to carry guns but they don't. This is the people's building after all and all the people are welcome. Still, people's building or not, the State Capitol and support buildings can be awfully intimidating to visitors, as if they were purposely designed to remind us that the citizens sheltered there possess great power and influence and the rest of us do not. Moving to the information desk, I reminded myself that George McGovern once ran a motel in Connecticut.

Meghan Chakolis was tall for a woman, maybe five-ten, five-eleven, with black hair cropped short in the style of Pete Rose. She had quick, green eyes and spoke with the irritation of some small thing gone wrong. I found her exactly where the receptionist told me she was, in the Information Office of the House of Representatives, located in the basement of the State Office Building. She nodded when I introduced myself as if she were expecting me. She agreed to answer my questions but not in private; she motioned for her co-workers to gather around.

"I'd like to speak to you about Joseph Sherman," I told her. She visibly relaxed with the words.

"Is that all? I thought you wanted to talk about Carol Catherine," she said, and her co-workers drifted away.

"Carol Catherine Monroe?" That was the second time the politician's name had come up during the investigation.

"Ever since she announced her candidacy for governor, everyone wants to talk about her," she answered while motioning to a chair. "Mostly they want dirt."

"Do you have any?"

She didn't answer.

"Good for you. How long have you known the representative?"

"Since college," Meghan replied.

"Are you working on her campaign?"

Meghan shook her head. "Not this time. The House Information Office is a bipartisan organization. As director I am not allowed to become involved in any election campaign, local or otherwise," she said, then returned to the subject. "Isn't Joseph Sherman in prison?"

"No, he's out. And he might be involved in a murder. Did the St. Paul police speak with you?"

Again Meghan shook her head, repeating the word "murder" as if she never heard it before.

"The police didn't contact you?"

"No, of course not. Why would they?"

"Standard procedure. Man just out of prison, on the run, he tends to look up his friends."

"Mr. Taylor, I assure you, Joseph Sherman and I were not friends. He was merely a neighbor."

"Tell me about him."

"There's nothing to tell."

"Most drunks love to talk . . ."

"He didn't talk to me. Sherman lived across the corridor, that's all. I'd see him a few times coming or going, nod, make a remark about the weather—nothing more than that. After he was arrested an assistant county attorney deposed me. It was my impression that he wanted someone to say disparaging things about Sherman on the witness stand, only I couldn't tell him anything I haven't just told you. I had no interest in Joseph Sherman or his problems. I didn't feel sorry for him. I didn't feel anything toward him at all."

"That's interesting," I told her, and I meant it.

"How so?" she replied, ready to defend her coldheartedness.

"My impression is that you and C. C. Monroe are friends?"

"Carol Catherine's friends never call her C. C."

"I'll keep that in mind."

"Why? Are you her friend?"

I ignored the retort and continued my supposition: "You lived across the hall from Joseph Sherman. Joseph Sherman was convicted of killing Terrance Friedlander, thus making it possible for your friend to be elected to the Minnesota House of Representatives. Yet, you had no interest in him at all."

"Is there a point to this?"

"Like I said, I find it interesting."

Meghan Chakolis reached behind her, picked up a telephone and slammed it down on the desk in front of me.

"Call the local TV stations; tell them what you find interesting. Fifteen minutes of fame comes cheap these days," she said. Then she threw me out of the office.

FIVE

C. C. Monroe's campaign headquarters was located on Rice Street within easy walking distance from the State Capitol. I took my own sweet time getting there—no sharp turns, no speeding through yellow stoplights, staying in plain sight of the blue Ford.

Headquarters was an abandoned women's clothing store with posters on the windows urging citizens to VOTE FOR THE FUTURE, VOTE MONROE FOR GOVERNOR. A row of four cafeteria tables and metal chairs looked out the windows onto Rice Street, a dozen push-button telephones spread out over the tables. Another row of tables with telephones lined the far wall. Between them was a low platform. Hanging from the wall behind the platform was an American flag, the Minnesota state flag and a poster of C. C. Monroe looking washed out next to the real thing.

Carol Catherine Monroe, surrounded by TV lights, cameras, microphones and a dozen or more reporters all shouting out questions, stood alone on the platform. She was the only person in the crowded room who noticed when I walked in; everyone else was watching her. She smiled at me, and I smiled back.

Good Lord, she was pretty—photogenic, as the man said.

The camera loved her, loved her aquamarine eyes, loved her butterscotch hair, unblemished skin, thin waist and long, curvy legs. Which helped explain why the newspapers, weekly tabloids and magazines printed so many pictures of her cutting ribbons or delivering addresses, why such a high percentage of her sound bites made the evening news. That and her sharp tongue. When a member of the opposing party criticized her health care plan because of the expense, C. C. laughed and shouted, "Put another quarter in the jukebox, baby, 'cuz we've heard that song before." Not exactly "Where's the beef?" but for weeks afterward even the local ballplayers repeated the line.

"At least St. Paul's mayor paid child support," C. C. said in a clear, unwavering voice, answering a reporter's question. "He did not abandon the child as so many other men have in similar situations. He did not run from his responsibility. For that I think he should be commended. As for the rest, fathering a child while married to another woman, keeping the existence of the child secret"—C. C. shook her head just enough for her long, butterscotch hair to brush both cheeks—"I have no comment. If the people of Minnesota believe those actions make him unfit to govern this great state, they will say so in November. I leave it to them. I will say this, however: For *The Cities Reporter* to print the mayor's personal income tax information without his consent is the height of journalistic irresponsibility. I think the media have a lot of soul-searching to do."

One reporter in the back corrected her, reminding C. C. that *The Cities Reporter* did not print the mayor's income tax records but merely asserted that the reason the mayor refused to release them, unlike the governor and herself, was because they would prove he was supporting an illegitimate child.

"That kind of hair-splitting rationale might impress First Amendment scholars, Mr. Sheehan, but the people know an invasion of privacy when they see it," she scolded him.

Sheehan grinned and recorded the quote in his reporter's notebook.

"Beautiful," I said, not even thinking about C. C.'s looks.

A woman of about twenty turned and shushed me, her index finger pressed to her lips. A man stepped next to me, his mouth curled in a snarl. He also was young, tall and blond, with a thick neck and a too-tight sports jacket that threatened to rip when he flexed his muscles—the result of too much time in the weight room, I reckoned. He reminded me of Arnold Schwarzenegger in *Conan the Barbarian,* only with better teeth. I smiled at him. He didn't smile back.

C. C. continued to excoriate the media for "gutterizing" the campaign, to the applause of her supporters and indifference of the reporters until Sheehan asked if "family values" weren't important, especially given the importance of the office for which she, the governor and the mayor were contesting. C. C. allowed that they were. Then, Sheehan continued, wasn't it the responsibility of the media to print the mayor's story?

"To me, the timing of the whole thing makes it sorry journalism," she said. "This isn't a campaign story. It is a campaign rumor story. It has allegations, but no proof. Should it be printed? Probably—on the day after the election."

"You say that even though it may very well get you elected?" Sheehan asked.

C. C. paused, took a deep breath and answered, "It is the people who will elect me to office, Mr. Sheehan, not your newspaper. Especially not your newspaper."

More applause. And why not? C. C. Monroe was putting on a clinic: "Politics 101—How To Exploit Your Opponents' Personal Problems Without Looking Like It."

"Impressive," I said.

"Isn't she?" the young woman replied, not knowing sarcasm when she heard it.

"Do you believe these allegations will be a major topic of the debate tonight?" another reporter asked.

C. C. hesitated, looked reflective, then answered, "I certainly hope not. The League of Women Voters organized the debate and public television agreed to broadcast it so that the voters could hear our positions on the key issues. That is why I entered the campaign as a third-party candidate, to force the other candidates to focus on the issues—issues like health care, poverty, our schools, women's rights. I would be greatly disappointed if these allegations distracted us."

The young woman announced to me, "Representative Monroe is going to be governor. The first woman governor in the history of Minnesota."

"Sure about that?" I asked her.

"Who's going to stop her? The governor? Golly, he had to go through seventeen ballots just to get the endorsement of his own party."

Golly? Did people still use that word?

"It's amazing the good things that happen to C. C.," I said as if I actually knew what I was talking about.

"What's that supposed to mean?" Conan asked.

"First Joseph Sherman, now this," I answered.

The young woman flinched visibly, as if someone had pricked her with a pin. Conan crowded in close, giving me a good whiff of his mouthwash.

"Whaddyawant?" he asked.

"I would like to speak to Representative Monroe."

"Try again," Conan said, nudging me toward the door.

I feinted right and curled left, stepping around him, and addressed the young woman. She had seated herself behind the cafeteria table she used as a desk, stacked as it was with a pile of campaign brochures, a thick message pad, two number-two pencils and a telephone switchboard. Below the table were two boxes, one on each side of her chair, which she used for file drawers. She nudged one with her foot as I handed her my card. She took it reluctantly. When she read it, her face became a black and white photograph, all the color

drained out. I don't know why. It merely read: HOLLAND TAY-
LOR, PRIVATE INVESTIGATIONS and listed my office address and
phone number. There were no bullet holes, no bloodstains.

The young woman showed the card to Conan, who glanced
at it over her shoulder. "He's trying to cause trouble," he said.
"I'll take care of him."

I held up one finger when he came toward me. "If you so
much as breathe on me, one of us is going through the window." Before he could decide which one, I pointed at the TV
journalists who were now packing up their gear. "What kind
of trouble do you think that will cause?"

Conan hesitated, then looked at the young woman for help.
She ran her hand through her short brown hair. "I'll get
Marion," she said.

I smiled at him when the young woman left her post at the
reception desk. "What do you bench? Two-fifty?"

"Screw you," he said, apparently insulted.

We both watched the receptionist snake through the crowd
and tap the shoulder of a rather shabbily dressed woman
standing next to the platform. Surrounded by several campaign workers, she watched and listened intently as C. C.
spoke casually with the boys and girls of the press who did
not seem to mind at all that just moments before she had
impugned their integrity. She looked about fifty-five, slightly
shorter than me and a good seventy pounds heavier, with
mousy hair, a bit of a mustache and poorly applied makeup.
She was not attractive, probably had not been attractive when
she was young, and now didn't give a damn. She took my card
from the receptionist, asking a question while she read it.
The receptionist pointed at me and the older woman nodded.
She said something and motioned with her head toward a
closed door about as far away from the reporters as possible.
The receptionist gestured for me to follow her. Conan didn't
like it, but he did nothing to block my path.

Behind the door was a small office, a temporary affair decorated with a government-gray metal desk and chairs and a dozen or more boxes and stacks of campaign posters and stickers. "Ms. Senske said to wait here," the young receptionist informed me and left.

I waited alone for fifteen minutes, searching the office to pass the time. There was nothing personal in it, no photographs, no mementos. Finally, the woman entered the room, startling me.

"Mr. Taylor, I'm Marion Senske," she said, closing the door behind her. Her manner was brusque, bordering on open hostility. I didn't mind. I make my living visiting other people's lives. I visit them at the worst possible times, when they are strung out on fear and doubt. I don't expect good manners.

"Miss Monroe will join us in a moment."

"Thank you," I said, without being sure what I was thankful for.

"May I see your identification, please?"

She examined it like she was searching for some telltale sign of counterfeiting, actually holding it up to the light. "How long have you been a private investigator?" she asked, tapping the laminated card on her thumb. She had no intention of returning it.

"Four years," I admitted. She didn't applaud. "Would it help that I was a police officer for ten years?"

"In St. Paul?"

"Yes."

"Excuse me a moment," Marion said and withdrew from the office with my business ID. She returned ten minutes later and handed back my property.

"I verified your credentials with my friend in the police department," she said. "Apparently, you're well thought of."

"By whom?"

"Lieutenant Anne Scalasi," she replied, emphasizing *lieutenant*.

"Anne Scalasi?" I repeated, trying hard to mask my abso-

David Housewright

lute astonishment. I don't think I did a very good job of it. Marion double-clutched before settling into her chair.

"What are you doing here?" she asked after a brief pause.

"I'm looking for a man named Joseph Sherman."

"Who's Joseph Sherman?"

"Murder suspect."

Marion leaned toward me. "Who did he kill?"

"I think he killed a man named John Brown."

"Never heard of him."

" 'John Brown's body lies a-mouldering in his grave'?" I recited. Marion was not amused.

"What has this to do with us?"

"Has Sherman contacted Miss Monroe?"

"Certainly not."

"Mind if I ask her that?"

"Yes, I do."

"Tough," I said.

Marion sprang to her feet. I flinched, gripping the arm of the chair, feeling like the spectators around the lion cage who take a step backward whenever a big cat approaches the bars—safe but stupid.

"Carol Catherine Monroe is a gubernatorial candidate," Marion intoned carefully, as if the words could conjure a magic spell.

"I can ask her in private or I can ask her in public," I said.

"You still haven't told me what Sherman has to do with us," Marion said, reclaiming her seat if not her composure.

"If Joseph Sherman had not killed Terrance Friedlander, C. C. Monroe might still be working for the Department of Transportation."

"Oh God, now I remember," Marion muttered to herself, then said aloud, "If Sirhan Sirhan had not killed Bobby Kennedy, Richard Nixon might be working for the Department of Transportation. Now, for the last time, what has this to do with us?"

"Damned if I know," I admitted, recalling the receptionist's reaction to Sherman's name.

Marion Senske settled back into her chair and brushed the tiny hairs above her upper lip with an index finger, studying me like a chess player regarding an unexpected move. "Lieutenant Scalasi didn't send you, did she?"

"We haven't spoken recently," I replied carefully.

Marion nodded her head and smiled. "I understand," she said. That made one of us.

I was going to ask a question—as soon as I could think of a good one—but the office door beat me to it. It flew open, followed by the sound of a half dozen voices and a woman I recognized as the former anchor of a local TV news program whose ratings and career went south a few years back.

"Excuse me, Marion," she announced. "You wanted to see C. C.'s closing remarks for tonight's debate as soon as I finished writing them."

Marion took the sheet of paper the woman offered and read it quickly. "This is too long. She only has two minutes."

"C. C. can read this in two minutes."

"She's not supposed to read it. She's supposed to be speaking from the heart. Excuse me, Mr. Taylor," Marion said and hustled out of the office into the hubbub beyond, the former anchor following closely behind. After a moment I followed them to the door and looked out. C. C. Monroe was reading from the paper, Marion and the anchor timing her with wristwatches. I closed the door and returned to my chair.

"Annie, Annie, Annie," I repeated softly as I searched the ceiling. "What are you up to?"

None of us had been particularly pleased when Anne Scalasi came to the Homicide unit; each of us had different reasons why. One guy didn't like it because she was a woman—well, actually, a couple of guys. Another detective took umbrage that she was an outsider, that she was coming from the Bureau of Criminal Apprehension; he thought promotions should come from inside the department. Me? I wondered—aloud, I'm afraid—how anyone without street experience could be worth a damn in a murder investigation. I think I also said something derogatory about Angela Lansbury, but memory fails.

The day she arrived, even before she had time to set photos of the husband and kids on her desk, Tommy Thompson had dropped a file in front of her. It was the Micka case. "See what you can do with that," Thompson told her.

"Sure," she'd answered. Most of the detectives snickered behind their hands. I was pissed. Elizabeth Micka was a floater we'd discovered in the Mississippi six months earlier; we couldn't clear the case and it annoyed me no end.

The facts were these: Elizabeth Micka was twenty-four years old. Her body was discovered on the St. Paul side of the Mississippi River by a couple of kids playing hooky from school. She was wearing a bra, cutoff jeans and two cement blocks attached to her body with wire. The ME claimed she had died of strangulation.

Elizabeth had last been seen cutting grass by neighbors late on a Saturday afternoon—she was housesitting for her parents, who were on a six-week vacation in Europe; one couple remembered she waved at them from the inside of the attached garage when she put the lawn mower away. We searched the house four times, videotaped every inch. There was no sign of forced entry, no struggle. We found the white shirt her neighbors remembered she'd been wearing. It was draped over a chair in her bedroom. And we found about one hundred grains of sand behind her bedroom door.

Anne had studied these facts and all the others we had gathered, including transcripts of every conversation we had with the nearly two hundred people we interviewed. She studied them for three days. Then she announced, "It's the lifeguard."

"What lifeguard?" I asked.

"The lifeguard you interviewed."

"I didn't question any lifeguard," I insisted.

Anne checked her notes. "Seventeen-year-old neighbor, lives five houses down, works as a lifeguard in the summer at Lake Josephine, likes to pump iron."

I recall being angry. "What's his motive?"

"Elizabeth used to baby-sit him when he was a kid."

"That's a motive?"

"Unrequited love, detective. That's the motive."

I don't recall what I said then, but I don't think the words "Good job" passed my lips.

Anne broke it down for me. "Elizabeth," she said, "was strangled. Manual strangulation is a very personal method of killing someone. And the killer did not want the body found. Both facts indicate the killer not only knew Elizabeth, he had some personal attachment to her. Now, add these facts to the equation: The killer was not very sophisticated, otherwise he probably would have known that the gases that emanate from a decaying corpse would force the body to the surface of the river even with two concrete blocks attached to it. But he was organized—the blocks, the wire, getting the body down to the river. He was strong. And he wasn't afraid of water. In fact, I'd bet water was a natural element to him. After all, he could have buried her. Most people, that's their first choice."

I thought it over, tried to find a flaw, couldn't, decided to dismiss her anyway. "You've got it all worked out," I said contemptuously. Then I saw it. "The sand. The goddamn sand!"

"I wonder if he saved anyone from drowning that day," Anne said.

"Let's ask him."

We did. Anne, with her sympathetic smile and a demeanor to rival any grade-school counselor, held the kid's hand and brushed the hair out of his eyes and asked simple questions until he spilled his guts. The kid confessed (had been wanting to confess for six months it seemed) that he had been infatuated with Elizabeth ever since she was his baby-sitter. While riding his ten-speed home from the beach, he passed the Micka house. He was surprised to see Elizabeth mowing the grass; she had moved out years earlier. He decided to say hello, remembered that Elizabeth's parents were in Europe and changed his plans. While she was in the backyard, he slipped through the open garage into the house and made his way to her bedroom. He waited. She came into the bedroom, removed her blouse in preparation for a shower, draped it over the chair, saw him and screamed. He tried to make her stop, clutched her throat. It was all a terrible mistake.

The kid pleaded to man-one. The judge gave him fifty-four months and some psych time at the security hospital in St. Peter. I apologized to Detective Sergeant Anne Scalasi—a difficult thing for me, but man, she was impressive—and offered to buy her a steak dinner. Only Anne doesn't eat red meat and turned me down. I got her drunk instead.

Marion Senske returned to the room. "Sorry for the delay," she told me, circling to the far side of the desk. "You were saying that Anne Scalasi *did not* send you to me."

"Now that I have had time to reflect on it, I believe she did," I decided.

Marion smiled, actually smiled, if only briefly. "It would seem Lieutenant Scalasi has extremely well-developed political instincts," she volunteered. "Well-developed, indeed. She appraises the situation, recognizes the risks of personal involvement, then seeks to minimize them by moving in the most discreet manner possible. Yes, good instincts. Perhaps we can work together one day."

Have you ever felt like you were invited for drinks while everyone else was staying for dinner?

"Lady, I don't know what in hell you're talking about," I told her.

Marion studied me again. I began to feel like a laboratory rat. I promised myself I would give her a slow count to ten, then I was gone. I reached seven when she asked, "Are you discreet?"

"Yes. It's a job requisite."

She studied me some more. This time I got up to nine before she said, "I discovered long ago that the odds of a secret becoming known increase exponentially with the number of people who share it. Three people already share this one."

"That's it, I'm out of here," I announced and pushed myself upright.

"Tell him," a warm voice spoke behind me. I turned in my chair to see C. C. Monroe's radiant smile. She stood with her back against the closed door, wearing an oversized black-and-cream sweater with a roll neck and padded shoulders. Her skirt was black and pleated; it swished when she moved toward me. I liked it a lot. When a reporter asked C. C. early in her career why she didn't wear the traditional navy blue suit of Minnesota politicians, she answered, "I wasn't aware I was supposed to. I didn't take political science in college."

"I am not convinced it would be prudent to tell him anything just yet," Marion Senske said.

"He's here to help," C. C. replied. "You are here to help aren't you, Mr. . . . ."

"Holland Taylor," I said, extending my hand. She shook it without hesitation. "It is a great pleasure to meet you," I told her. I'm always gracious to prospective clients; it's only after they hire me that I become surly.

"I am Carol Catherine Monroe," she said, proud of the fact. "Please sit, Holland."

I sat.

"We could use your help and if you give me your word that nothing you hear will go beyond these walls, I will tell you why."

"You have my word," I told her.

"Oh God," Marion moaned from behind the desk.

Carol Catherine Monroe had been going nowhere fast until the day Terrance Friedlander was killed. She told me so herself, told me frankly while sitting across from me, our knees occasionally touching.

"The truth is, I didn't have a snowball's chance in hell of beating Friedlander," she confessed.

Friedlander was much loved in his district. The kids who played on his bantam hockey team called him "Mr. Terry." To everyone else he was just plain "Terry." He had won seven consecutive elections to the House by increasingly larger margins and it was said that whoever ran against him was a damn fool. Well, C. C. Monroe was not a damn fool. But she was bored silly shuffling papers for the DOT. She had been doing it for two years, since passing the bar. So she volunteered to oppose Friedlander, hoping that after the election the political contacts she'd make would help her move out of the Department of Transportation and into a more meaningful office, like the Pollution Control Agency or attorney general's office. Since no other candidates were forthcoming, the party leaders shook her hand, patted her head, whispered "Good luck," and got the hell out of there.

Then Friedlander was killed.

C. C. had not really wanted to go to the House of Representatives, had had no idea what she would do when she got there. Yet once she arrived she discovered, or so she said, "there was so much to be done, so much that I could do. I think it was good that I wasn't a real politician, that I wasn't beholden to special interests. I could see the possibilities."

She had also seen that she needed help. So C. C. enlisted the aid of Marion Senske, a private-practice attorney well known for her feminist activities who had lectured C. C.'s law class years before. Under Marion's tutelage, C. C. soon became a star of the local women's movement, preaching Marion's doctrine that "Women are not to be dismissed or taken lightly anymore. They have power. They can make an impact."

C. C. was outspoken and she was quotable, although the words were nearly always Marion's. Plus, she had great legs; her obvious sex appeal always guaranteed a larger share for the TV news programs and talk shows she appeared on. So that particular year, when the governor, who was running for reelection, and the mayor of St. Paul, who was trying to unseat him, turned into a couple of mudslinging Neanderthals who didn't give a damn about women's issues—galvanizing issues like poverty, education, child care and world peace—C. C. was the logical choice to carry the feminist banner into battle as a third-party candidate. "Beauty versus the Beasts," one columnist called it.

Still, no one had expected her to win, least of all C. C. Monroe. It was merely hoped that her presence in the race would force the governor and the mayor to address women's concerns. Only the governor's popularity was at an all-time low. Even his most ardent supporters on the Iron Range where he grew up—the Slavs, the Czechs, the Poles who worked the taconite mines—freely conceded that the governor's third term in office was probably one term too many and were loath to give him another. Then there were the allegations that he was too cozy with the construction industry, a major contributor to his campaign. Two days before C. C. entered the race, *The Cities Reporter* broke a story accusing the governor of having an affair with the construction industry's comely chief lobbyist; it ran photographs of him leaving the woman's townhouse, supposedly after midnight. The governor, his ever-patient wife at his side, denied the allegation, claiming it was a vicious lie, saying it was based on false and misleading information. Before she resigned from her job and disappeared from view, "The Other Woman," as she became known, also denied the allegations—I love that word, "allegation." What was it Jesse Jackson once said? "I not only deny the allegation, I deny the allegator."

In any case, the minority party quickly called for a formal investigation by the state senate, suggesting that impeachment might be in order. The senate, which was firmly controlled by the majority party, blocked the move. So, the minority party demanded a criminal investigation by the attorney general's office. Only the AG was also a member of the majority party and he had political aspirations of his own. Rumor had it that he offered the governor a deal: He would squash the investigation if the governor would agree to withdraw from the race and allow the AG to replace him on the ballot. This raised questions not only of propriety, but also of finances. Who would get the cash in the governor's well-funded campaign chest if he withdrew? The AG? The governor vowed no. Technically, the money was his to do with as he pleased once his campaign debts were paid, and he said he would sooner donate it to the Reverend Sun Myung Moon than give it to a backstabbing opportunist like the attorney general. Besides, he was the party's nominated candidate and he was not going to withdraw.

Meanwhile, the mayor's popularity had dropped like a stone. This is Minnesota, after all. We don't like tattletales and nearly everyone believed the mayor was responsible for the mud dripping from the governor's face. As a result, squeaky-clean Carol Catherine Monroe picked up a quick twenty percent of the voters in the newspaper polls when she entered the race and after a month was running dead even with the major candidates— plus or minus three percent, of course. More importantly, money was pouring in. It started as a trickle: five-, ten-, twenty-dollar bills from her admirers. But when it became apparent that her candidacy was legitimate, the trickle became a flood. Well-heeled donors and national PACs thought nothing of writing out sixty-thousand-dollar checks—the state limit for individual campaign contributions. And they bothered little over C. C.'s position on the issues. They cared only that she win and remember them afterward.

The receptionist was right, I decided after listening to the update. Carol Catherine Monroe could very well become the first woman governor in the history of Minnesota. Unless she, too, made a mistake. A mistake of biblical proportions.

"I had a boyfriend," she began.

C. C. started pacing the office, reading her own campaign slogans off the posters on the walls. Marion continued to sit behind the desk, looking down, shaking her head.

"His name was—is—Dennis Thoreau," C. C. added, casting a furtive glance at Marion. "We were in love. At least I thought it was love. I was much younger then. Anyway, when we were together, we made a videotape." C. C. said the videotape showed her in bed, showed her in various stages of undress, mostly with Thoreau, both of them playing to the camera, filling the lens. I had only one question.

"Why?"

"I don't know. I thought it would be fun, kind of kinky; a lot of couples are doing it these days."

"Really?"

C. C. was angry now. "Haven't you ever done something stupid, Mr. Taylor? Something you regretted, something you knew you would regret even while you were doing it?"

I recalled jumping off the roof of my father's house while holding a bedsheet over my head, only I reminded C. C. that I wasn't a member of the Minnesota House of Representatives at the time.

"Neither was I. I wasn't running for anything back then. I was still with the DOT. I still belonged to myself, not to the women's movement. Anyway, it's done. Now my boyfriend, my ex-boyfriend, is threatening to release the tape to the media unless we pay him ten thousand dollars. I doubt if the news stations would run it . . ."

"They'd love to acknowledge it exists, however," Marion said. "Show a few discreetly cropped stills."

C. C. nodded. "Especially Hersey Sheehan. It would be like winning the Triple Crown: first the governor, then the mayor and now me. *The Cities Reporter*. It's a rag."

"It claims to be an alternative to traditional newspapers like the *Minneapolis StarTribune* and *St. Paul Pioneer Press*," Marion said. "So it prints what the other papers won't touch. It's the only way it can stay in business."

"They should sell the damn thing at supermarket checkout lines," C. C. said.

"If they could, they would," Marion added, and then they both grew quiet, as if contemplating the possibility.

"So what do you want from me?" I asked when I became bored enough.

Carol Catherine Monroe looked at me expectantly with eyes that were wide and moist, with full lips slightly parted. The look said, "Help me." Or maybe I was projecting. Stick her on a bar stool and put a cocktail in her hand and it might mean something else altogether.

"We want you to deliver the money, get the tape and run the bastard off," Marion Senske said. "Isn't that why Lieutenant Scalasi sent you?"

"I thought I was here to get a line on Joseph Sherman," I said, not believing it at all. Sending me after Brown to help Monroe? Anne Scalasi, my Anne Scalasi, could never be this devious.

"I told you, we haven't seen or heard from Joseph Sherman," Marion assured me.

I looked into C. C.'s aquamarine eyes.

"That's true," she said. "But," she added in a halting voice, "even if you did come for another reason, couldn't you, wouldn't you, do this one little thing for us? Please?"

Ahh, what the hell. Since I was already in the neighborhood . . .

C. C. had not seen or spoken to Dennis Thoreau for six years. Their relationship ended while she was running for her first term in the House. The reasons she gave me for breaking up with him were vague. "It just didn't work out," she said.

According to C. C., Thoreau appeared at campaign headquarters one afternoon just to say hi. He said he was moving back to St. Paul after spending some time in California. They had a pleasant conversation, reminisced about old times. The next day they did lunch. Over the next two weeks Thoreau visited headquarters frequently, even worked the phones a few times. C. C. had actually considered resuming their relationship.

"The man could charm the fish from the sea," she said.

"Humph," Marion grunted.

Then Saturday morning, Thoreau called C. C. and just as pleasantly as you please demanded ten thousand dollars in tens and twenties.

"I thought he was joking at first. I even laughed," C. C. said. "Only he wasn't joking. He told me he would make copies of the video and send them to all the TV stations and newspapers if I didn't give him the money. I told him he was insane. I told him I had friends in the police department. I told him never to call me again. When he started to laugh, I hung up. Then I talked to Marion."

Marion Senske shook her head and looked at C. C. with quiet disgust. C. C. pulled her butterscotch hair across her mouth like my daughter used to do when she was caught misbehaving.

"He called back an hour later," Marion added. "He asked if we had come to our senses yet."

"Did you speak to him?" I asked the older woman.

She shook her head and gestured at C. C.

"Should we pay him?" C. C. asked hopefully.

"It's always easier to pay," I told her. "Until the price becomes too high."

"Your job is to make sure the price doesn't become too high," Marion told me.

"I get four hundred dollars a day plus expenses. I also like my clients to sign a standard contract stating that I am acting on their behalf and that . . ."

"Nothing in writing," Marion insisted. "I'll pay you cash. Right now. But we've never met. You don't know me and Carol Catherine is someone you've only seen on television."

"All right," I agreed. It wasn't the first time a client had made such a demand.

Marion Senske fished a bulging number-ten envelope out of a drawer, a thick rubber band holding the contents inside, and slapped it down on the desktop with so much force it seemed like the entire room shook. "I want the videotape," she said emphatically. "Don't give him the money until you get the tape."

"Should I count it?"

"Do what you think is best," she told me and took her purse from the desk's bottom drawer. In it was another envelope. From that one she withdrew four one-hundred-dollar bills and handed them to me. I put the bills and the envelope in the same inside jacket pocket, the one over my heart.

I asked her about the money, whether it could be traced. She assured me that it could not.

"Candidates are required by law to report the sources of their income, all of it, along with all expenditures of one hundred dollars or more if the money is spent directly on an election campaign. However, no law requires a candidate to disclose where the money goes if it is not spent on an election. We simply list the expenditures in the 'noncampaign expense' category. We could use it to pay our water bills if we wanted to. It's all perfectly legal."

"I'm sure it is," I told her. "Where can I find Mr. Thoreau?"

Marion handed me a piece of paper with an address on it. I put it in my pocket and moved toward the door. C. C. took my hand as I started to pass. She held it lightly and then kissed it. "Thank you, Holland," she said.

I don't like the name Holland; Holly is worse and I have often bad-mouthed my parents for giving it to me. Yet, the way she said it . . .

I knew I was being used. That's okay. All my clients use me. That's why I get the big bucks. The question was: Was Anne Scalasi using me? I tried hard not to believe it. My Anne Scalasi would simply have called and said, "I know these guys who need a good PI." She's given me referrals before. Yet there was my guardian angel to consider. Only I couldn't find him when I left C. C.'s campaign headquarters, which made me nervous. Maybe they replaced him with a tail who actually knew what he was doing. No way. I drove clear to my office, twice around the Hubert H. Humphrey Metrodome, over to Como Park and then along the Mississippi River, first the Minneapolis side, then the St. Paul side. I was clean. That should have told me something. But it didn't.

SIX

I KNEW DENNIS Thoreau's neighborhood well. It wasn't far from the College of St. Thomas, where I spent several years deciding what to do with my life. That was before it became the University of St. Thomas and turned the surrounding residential area into a parking lot. School was in session, and I was forced to walk three blocks to Thoreau's house from the nearest open parking space.

The house was in the middle of the block. It was a small, weathered two-story in need of paint and surrounded by a neglected lawn. There was an unattached one-car garage in back facing a rutted dirt alley that must have been tough to negotiate in winter. I knocked on Thoreau's door and waited. I knocked again and waited some more. I walked around the house, looking through the windows. The front windows showed me nothing. However, through a side window I could see a man wearing a royal blue bathrobe lying on the carpet between the front door and the bottom of the staircase. I went back to the front door and worked the lock with a pick and wire I keep hidden in the lining of my sports jacket—it's illegal to carry burglary tools in Minnesota. It gave easily enough and I squeezed through the opening, trying not to disturb the body by bumping it with the door.

"Oh Christ!" I cried when the odor hit me, and I fought off a sudden urge to vomit. It was the kind of smell that you never forget, that you never confuse with anything other than what it is: the odor of decaying flesh, the smell of death. When I worked Homicide, I used to stick cigarette filters up my nostrils to mask the smell. Sometimes I would smoke a cigar; a lot of wagon men would smoke cigars. Unfortunately, I had long since given up smoking.

I found myself taking short, shallow breaths as I bent to the body, trying hard not to gag; beads of sweat formed on my forehead and my eyes began to water. He was nude except for the bathrobe. From C. C.'s description, I guessed it was Thoreau; his eyes were open, they were brown. There was a single bullet hole just above his right eyebrow but not much blood—a dark, dry ring encircled the hole; a dribble, also dry, followed the contour of Thoreau's nose to the floor. The back of his head was intact—no exit wound. He had been shot with a small caliber, a .22 maybe. I guessed by the odor he was at least three days dead.

Travel brochures littered the floor around his body, most of them for the Caribbean. One brochure, for Martinique, was wedged under his thigh. Was that where he planned to go with the money?

I did a quick three-sixty. The house was a shambles; it had been systematically destroyed, searched by someone who knew what he was doing. Chair cushions had been ripped open, carpet taken up, light fixtures removed; in the kitchen, food packages had been emptied onto the table and floor. I debated returning to my car for the rubber surgical gloves I keep—where else?—in my glove compartment. I decided against it and hunted slowly through the rubble for something that might have been overlooked, being careful not to touch anything that might hold a print. I found nothing. It was a very professional job and must have taken hours. I went upstairs and found more of the same—even the toilet tank had been torn away from the bathroom wall. In the bedroom, the king-sized mattress had been cut open, the box spring overturned. The contents of Thoreau's bureau had been strewn around the room.

It was while standing in the bedroom, sweating like a pig, that I heard it: the sound of a car door slamming. I went to the window, tripping on a tripod in my haste. Three squad cars bearing the distinctive blue stripe of the St. Paul Police Department had gathered in the middle of the street. One officer was standing next to his vehicle, looking at the house— I guessed one of Thoreau's neighbors must have seen me pick his lock and called it in. I cursed and moved away from the window. Again I tripped on the tripod. "Dammit," I swore, then thought better of it. The tripod was attached to a video camera; apparently it had been set at the foot of the bed. I checked the camera and was amazed to find it contained a tape. I yanked it out and glanced through the window again. The officers were approaching cautiously, hands on their holstered guns. I cursed some more. The last thing I needed was to be caught breaking and entering a house containing a murder victim with ten thousand dollars cash in my pocket— more than enough to buy a couple of guys dead.

The upstairs consisted of a bathroom and two bedrooms. The second bedroom, which had also been carefully explored, had a window that opened up over the backyard. It wasn't quite as high as my father's roof. I kicked out the screen, hoping it didn't make too much noise, and jumped. I hit the ground with both feet, jabbed myself in the eye with the tape, rolled, came up running. I made the alley without anyone shooting at me and did not stop until I hit the street. From there I walked as casually as possible toward the St. Thomas campus, trying hard not to stare at the blue Ford parked at the corner.

I found a restroom in a white brick building—Murray Hall, it was called—and inspected the damage to my eye. There was a slight swelling, hardly noticeable. Good. I didn't need any distinguishing marks. Next I went searching for the bookstore, which wasn't where I left it fifteen years earlier, asked directions and was pointed toward a building that hadn't existed when I was a student. It cost me seventy-nine dollars to disguise myself with a red backpack printed with the university's logo and a large, used textbook—*A History of Western Civilization.* I put the videotape and my jacket into the bag and slung it over my shoulder. I carried the textbook in my hand and slowly made my way to the campus grill where I sat at a corner table. I opened the book to Chapter Sixteen— "The Inquisition"—sipped a Dr. Pepper and waited for a K-9 unit to sniff me out.

College life swirled around me—it seemed more exciting than it really was. I know many people who would love to relive their school days. Not me. Except for the occasional course taught by the rare enthusiastic professor, I hated college. I spent nearly three years there working toward a business degree before deciding, out of sheer boredom, to transfer to a community college and try for a law-enforcement degree instead.

The grill filled and emptied at approximately fifty-minute intervals with young men and women—children, really, although I wouldn't have said so when I was their age—most of them taking life too seriously, not really appreciating how serious it can be.

As my heartbeat slowed to normal, I eavesdropped on four young women who encompassed the spectrum of natural hair color: black, blond, brown and red. They were sitting two tables away and talking about presenting a resolution to the All Student Council demanding the adoption of politically correct language on campus—"womyn" instead of "women," "freshperson" instead of "freshman," "teenage womyn" instead of "girl."

Their conversation annoyed me. None of their demands

addressed the real problems facing women in today's society, problems such as being paid only sixty-five cents for every dollar earned by a man, such as inadequate day care for children, such as sexual discrimination, harassment and abuse. None of them addressed the problem of a man with a neat little hole in his forehead not six blocks away. I pushed that last image out of my brain and concentrated on the women, wondering why they seemed so much more attractive than the women with whom I'd gone to college.

I gave it forty-five minutes; then I left the grill and made my way to the library, surprised and pleased by the number of students who actually sat reading within its silent walls. I found a spot near a window that looked out over Cleveland Avenue and watched for the cops. I gave it three hours and two chapters of the text. I could have read more but I was too busy glancing at the door and jumping at every noise. Finally, I took a deep breath, tossed the bag over my shoulder, tucked the book under my arm and strolled back to my car, walking several blocks out of my way to avoid going near Thorcau's house.

SEVEN

F OR A LONG TIME I could not drive the streets of St. Paul without a heaviness in my stomach. They all seemed to lead to landmarks of death. "Hey, that building over there, that's where we found Harley who had his penis cut off and stuffed into his mouth by his homosexual lover, and that park we just passed, Sally was found raped and murdered over there, right under the monkey bars . . ."

That changed during the years after I left the department; gradually time had removed the stink of death from my clothes, my hair, my nostrils, my brain. The faces of the killers, the dealers, the pimps, the pros, the gang-bangers and their victims, all those wonderful people who filled my life with such happy memories, faded like the World Series ticket stubs I thought might be a collector's item someday.

Then I killed four men and it all came back. The cops, the county attorney and a review board called it self-defense and I wasn't about to argue with them. But I haven't had more than a few consecutive nights of uninterrupted sleep since.

And I stopped carrying a gun, vowing that I would never kill another human being again.

"Goddamn it!" I screamed at the traffic on Rice Street. I did not want to deal with this. I was tired of taking dead people home with me. I preferred the simple life now, a life apart from the suffering of others. Chasing credit card thieves suited me fine. Sifting for secrets in someone's trash, conducting surveillance on suspected embezzlers, running skip traces with my computer—that's what I wanted to do.

Only, Death seems to follow me. And try as I might, I cannot shake him.

I parked directly in front of C. C. Monroe's campaign headquarters and walked inside, making as much noise as possible. Marion Senske didn't want anyone to know I was working for her? Well, screw that! Unfortunately, only one person seemed interested in my act—the receptionist. Everyone else was talking earnestly in small groups of three or four. The receptionist said Ms. Senske was expecting me, please have a seat; Representative Monroe and Ms. Senske were in conference and would see me presently.

I glanced toward the office in back. The door was slightly ajar and I could see a sliver of light.

The telephone rang and the young woman answered it, making notes on a pink message pad as she spoke. When she had finished with the first caller, the phone rang again and then a third time. She asked the second caller, "Could you hold, please?" and switched to the third line before the second caller could reply. I slipped away and headed toward the office. As I approached, I heard voices. They belonged to C. C. Monroe and Marion Senske. The two of them spoke as if no one in the world could hear them. I paused outside and listened.

"Look at your clothes! How dare you wear clothes like that?" Marion wanted to know.

"What's wrong with my outfit?"

"Nothing if you're a nightclub singer."

"The media love what I wear," C. C. said in her own defense.

"The media don't vote," Marion reminded her. "Dammit, Carol Catherine. We had this discussion last week after you frosted your hair . . ."

"And you made me change it back," C. C. whined. "I only wanted to see how it looked; I never had it done before."

Marion's voice dropped a few octaves. She spoke slowly. "We've discussed this a hundred times during the past six years, Carol Catherine, and you just don't seem to get it. It doesn't matter how long you've served in the House or how many elections you've won. There are people out there who won't vote for you simply because you're a woman. There are people who won't vote for you because you're young. There are people who won't vote for you because you're not married, because you don't have a family. And now here you are reinforcing their greatest fears, showing off your legs, showing off your chest, dressing like some chippy."

"What's a chippy?"

"Carol Catherine!" Marion was shouting now. "Look. We don't have time for this. We have to be at the studio in thirty minutes. That's barely enough time to take you home and change."

"I don't want to change," the younger woman whined some more.

"I don't give a shit what you want!" Marion screamed.

I decided I'd heard enough and walked into the room.

"Taylor," Marion said, obviously startled by my presence. C. C. didn't say anything. She turned to me and smiled, bringing a hand to her bare throat. She was wearing a black, one-button tuxedo jacket with a satin-trimmed collar that was fitted to show off her narrow waist; a short black skirt with a wide satin stripe; black nylons patterned with flowers; black heels and nothing else that I could see and believe me, I looked hard. Marion was right; it probably was inappropriate for a gubernatorial candidate. But it certainly won my vote.

"Did you get the tape?" Marion demanded to know after she caught her breath.

"We need to talk about that."

"Did you get the tape?" she repeated.

"Not so you'd notice."

"What does he want, more money?"

"It's a little more complicated than that."

"We haven't got time," Marion announced. "Meet us here after the debate."

"This won't wait," I said.

"It'll have to."

"I insist," I told Marion.

"No, *I* insist!" she shouted in reply. "I am in charge here, make no mistake!" And with that declaration, she pulled C. C. by the hand from the room like an unwilling child.

"Aww, Marion," C. C. whined.

"Let's go, dammit!" Marion barked. Three people—two men and the former female anchor—disengaged from their huddles and met her at the door. Marion shouted a few instructions to the receptionist and herded the gubernatorial candidate and her entourage outside to the black Buick Regal parked directly in front of the doors. Conan held the car doors open, then shut them all after everyone slid in. He rounded the car, squeezed behind the wheel and drove off while the receptionist and I watched.

"Ms. Senske said I was supposed to take care of you," the receptionist informed me.

In my younger days while chasing the women at St. Thomas, I probably would have made something of that remark. But I was well past that. I call it maturity. Others call it old age. "Let's get something to eat," I said.

She hesitated, then said, "I'm not allowed to leave the phones unattended."

"Isn't there someone who can relieve you?" She inspected me cautiously for a moment. I added, "There's a Vietnamese restaurant just down the street."

She didn't reply.

"It's a public place and I promise to keep my hands in my pockets."

She weighed the invitation a moment longer, then called, "Louise!" An older woman answered from across the room. "Could you catch the phones?" the receptionist asked. "I'm going to get something to eat."

"Of course, dear."

"I'll be back before the debate begins."

"No problem, dear," Louise said, but from her expression I guessed there must be at least one. She looked at me like she was sighting down the barrel of a rifle.

The receptionist fished a purse from a box under the cafeteria table and moved toward the door. She was about five-three and wore a white blouse with a lace collar and pocket, pleated trousers with a high waist and white sneakers. I didn't particularly care for the sneakers. I know professional women like to wear them on the job because they're infinitely more comfortable than traditional heels. Still, they look childish when matched with business clothes and women have enough problems in the workplace as it is.

"My name is Amy Lamb," she said.

"Hi, Amy," I replied, holding out my hand in the traditional fashion, proving there was no weapon in it. She gave it a brief squeeze.

"Do you carry a gun?" Amy Lamb asked between mouthfuls of chicken almond ding and fried rice.

"No."

"Really? I thought all private eyes carried guns."

"Some do. Usually they lock them away in the trunks of their cars."

"How much does a private eye make?" she asked, sipping her tea.

"Depends on how much you work. Some of the larger shops charge thirty-five dollars an hour. I get four hundred dollars a day but . . ."

"Four hundred? No shit?" she said and then clamped her hand hard over her mouth.

"I don't work every day," I finished.

She blushed a deep crimson. "I'm sorry."

"That's all right."

"I never cursed before I moved down here."

"I've heard worse."

"I'm from Starbuck. Starbuck, Minnesota. Ever hear of it?"

"Sure," I answered. I knew my state map. I could even recite the names of all eighty-seven counties in alphabetic order: Aitkin, Anoka, Becker, Beltrami . . .

"It's about two hours' driving time from here," Amy volunteered in case I was fooling. She spoke with the sing-song voice of adolescence, each sentence tailing up, ending with a question mark. She was much younger than I had originally guessed, younger perhaps than her professed chronological age of twenty. I found myself comparing her to the girl who'd sat in front of me in high school algebra, who'd scribbled her name, house number, street, town, county, state, country and then—to be exact—continent, hemisphere, planet, solar system, galaxy, and universe into her notebook, indicating exactly where she belonged in the scope of things. Try as I might, I could not picture Amy waging a social revolution with the women at St. Thomas, although it was probably for her that they fought.

"I really liked it," she said of her hometown.

"Why did you leave?" I asked.

"It was kinda small—not much opportunity, you know? And then, after I was graduated from school, well, my parents, they were concerned about me, wondering when I was gonna get married. We'd be at the dinner table and after Daddy said grace it would begin: 'When are you going to get married?' 'When are you going to settle down?' My parents were convinced that if I didn't get married soon all the nice boys would be taken and I'd be stuck with what was left. Y'see, in a small town like Starbuck, you turn eighteen you either go away to school or you get married, and I wasn't, you know, college material. But I wanted more than just getting married and spending every second Saturday at the Pope County Dairy Association dinner. So, what I did, I went to the community college in Morris and studied to be a legal secretary. I figured I could go to the Cities and get a job. Boy, that freaked 'em— my parents, I mean. My father would cut articles out of the *StarTribune,* articles about, you know, rape and murder and stuff. Remember when that serial killer was stalking those poor Indian women? My father cut out the articles and taped them to the refrigerator door. 'See what happens?' he'd say. But a woman, you know, you gotta be free, so after I got my certificate, I just hopped on that Greyhound. Mom cried, but Dad, Dad was cool; kinda surprised me. He slipped me a whole thousand dollars and said I was to call every other day or he'd come down and get me. I think he might have cried, too."

"Parents," I said, as if the word contained all the mysteries of the ages. "So what happens next?"

"I'm going to get a job with the state, once Representative Monroe is elected governor, I mean. When Ms. Senske hired me, she said do a good job and she and Representative Monroe would find a place for me after the election—me and Galen. Are you married?"

"No," I said, without elaborating. "Who's Galen?"

"I don't mean to pry or anything, but you seem so much more mature than most of the men I meet."

"You mean old," I corrected her.

"You're not so old," she said, flirting now.

"Trust me."

"I dated an older man before and it was no big deal," Amy assured me. "I find older men kinda attractive, you know?"

"Who's Galen?" I asked again.

"You don't like me," Amy pouted.

"Sure, I do," I told her honestly. "You're a beautiful, desirable young woman. Only I have a high school yearbook that's older than you. Besides," I said, leaning in close, whispering, "we're not allowed to get romantically involved with clients. The state could take my license."

"Really?" she whispered. "You mean like psychologists?"

I nodded and Amy glanced about the restaurant in case anyone was watching. She raised her hand shoulder high like she was swearing herself to secrecy, looked around some more and said, "Galen? Galen Pivec? You asked about him? He's with the State Capitol police. He provides security 'n' stuff for Representative Monroe in his free time; you know, crowd control, drives sometimes. You met him this afternoon."

"Conan?"

"Huh?"

"Never mind. Are you and Galen friends?"

"I guess. We talk a lot while he's waiting at the door—you know, waiting for Representative Monroe and Ms. Senske. But we don't date or anything," she added quickly, looking into my eyes, hoping I believed her.

I had a thought, but pushed it out of my mind, ashamed of myself.

"How do you get to be a private eye?" Amy asked.

"You have enough hours of experience, you can take out a license. If you don't, you can apprentice under someone else's license until you do."

"Did you apprentice?"

"I was a cop for ten years," I said and handed her my photostat just in case she thought I was making it all up.

She examined the photograph, looked at me, looked back at the photograph.

"Some people say I look like Alan Ladd," I said.

"Who's he?"

"An actor. He was pretty big in the forties and fifties."

"Louise would know him—if he was an actor in the fifties, I mean."

"Louise?" I asked.

"The woman who took over the phones? I used to live with her. She was the office administrator at the law firm where Marion—I mean Ms. Senske—used to work. I applied for this job as a legal secretary—that's what I am, really, a legal secretary, not a receptionist; I told you that, I think . . ."

I nodded, confirming that she had.

"Anyway, the day I arrived here, I got a copy of the newspaper, the classifieds, and started looking for a job. My first interview was with Louise and I guess she liked me right off, only she said she had to interview two or three more people before making a decision and I should leave my address and phone number and I told her I was staying at this motel near the bus station? Know what she did? She said, 'That's outrageous,' and she made me get my stuff and check out and she moved me into her place. She said it was only temporary and she made me pay room and board, you know, but I had my own bedroom and I could come and go as I pleased and it was pretty okay, until . . ." Amy Lamb's mood darkened, her voice along with it. "I just had to leave."

"I can understand that," I told her, thinking that I really did.

"Can you?"

"I think everybody should live alone for at least a year. That's how you find out who you are."

"Or aren't," Amy added.

I shrugged.

"Anyway, Ms. Senske asked Louise if she wanted to work on the campaign and Louise asked me and here we all are."

"Just one big, happy family."

"Oh, it is, it really is," Amy replied and ate another mouthful of fried rice. "It seems everyone is related to somebody, or a friend of somebody. Are you related to Representative Monroe?"

"No."

"What are you doing for her?"

"This and that."

"Is it confidential?"

"Yes."

"Oh," she said, disappointed.

"But maybe you can help me."

"Really? Can I?"

"Do you know a man named Dennis Thoreau? He was around the campaign the past couple of weeks."

"I know him," she said in a voice that made me think she didn't care much for him.

"And?"

"We went out once," Amy confessed. "He was the older man I told you about."

"What happened?"

Amy lowered her head and picked at her rice with chopsticks. Finally she said, "Let's just say he didn't treat me very well and let it go at that."

"Did he telephone Representative Monroe a couple times Saturday?"

"Not that I know of."

"Do all the calls go through you?"

"Yes, they do."

I had to think about that for a minute. "Did you ever meet Joseph Sherman?"

"Him," Amy answered without hesitation. "No, I never met him but he must have called a hundred times. He wasn't very nice, either. He used the 'F' word a lot. He kept calling and saying he wanted to speak to Miss Monroe but wouldn't tell me what it was about, so I wouldn't put him through; I just took his name and number. I'm very careful about that. You'd be surprised how many crank calls Representative Monroe gets."

"I can imagine. Did Sherman ever get through to C. C.?"

"Oh, yes. Representative Monroe was standing by the desk this one time when he called and she heard me talking to him and she took the phone."

"Do you remember what was said?"

"I don't know what he said. I couldn't hear and, you know, I was trying not to eavesdrop."

"What did C. C. say?"

"She said a lot of umm's and uh-huh's and I see's and stuff like that and then she said, 'Go ahead, call the police, call the newspapers, I don't care,' and then she gave me the phone and I hung up and I asked, you know, 'cuz I was concerned, I asked if there was a problem, and she said, 'It seems like every man in the world wants a piece of me,' and then she left."

"Was she upset?"

"Not really. She was smiling when she walked away."

"When did the conversation take place?"

"I don't know. Thursday, Friday . . . no, Thursday last week. Is that helpful?"

"Very," I said, not knowing if it was or not.

"If there is anything else I can do—" Amy offered, excited at the prospect.

I slipped a card out of my wallet and gave it to her. "You never know."

EIGHT

Bᴀᴄᴋ ᴀᴛ campaign headquarters, one of the cafeteria tables had been dragged from the wall to the middle of the room and a space had been cleared for a twenty-six-inch Magnavox. The TV was tuned to Channel 2 and already a dozen or more volunteers were gathered around it, although it was broadcasting the final minutes of a national news magazine—their heroine was still a quarter hour away. The other volunteers were working the phones, soliciting donations and reminding supporters to watch.

There was an energy coursing through the room that I could not define. Tension, anxiety, pure joy; all of the above. Everyone was smiling, everyone seemed to be feeding off everyone else's adrenaline. I had felt that energy only once before: while walking through the concourse at the Metrodome during the '87 World Series, before Kent Hrbek launched his grand salami into the right-field seats and every soul in Minnesota realized that this time—unlike four Super Bowls, two Stanley Cups and two presidential elections—*this* time we would not lose.

I sat with Amy Lamb on one of the cafeteria tables, watching the screen, our legs dangling over the edge, Amy gripping my arm. There was no romance in her touch. Still, I found myself wishing I had pumped more iron. Louise sat on the other side of me, keeping her hands to herself. I could not determine her age—anywhere from mid-thirties to late-fifties. Her brown hair was streaked with gray and pulled tight into a bun, her eyes were old and her face was lined. She might have been handsome once, but life had not been kind. She glanced at Amy's hands and then at me. Her expression was not kind, either.

The moderator, a local news anchor known more for her hairstyle than her competence, introduced the panel of questioners, local journalists all, none of whom was known to me. Then she introduced the candidates, eliciting deep-throated boos from the campaign volunteers for the governor and the mayor and a hearty cheer for C. C. One woman remarked that the governor's hair seemed to be getting darker the older he got, quipping that "fifteen years ago, it was gray." A young man noticed that both the governor and mayor were dressed nearly exactly the same; even their ties were identical. "They must shop the same place as my old man," he said. Louise noted how well dressed Representative Monroe was in a paisley two-piece dress that combined red, burgundy, purple and black against an olive background. A gold locket hung from a gold chain around her neck; her rich, butterscotch hair was swept back.

I laughed but no one else got the joke. And then all was quiet. At the Metrodome, we had never stopped screaming. Here, all voices were mute and the few that were compelled to comment were shushed into silence. The volume was cranked and the volunteers leaned forward.

The governor made his opening remarks, stressing lower taxes, lower taxes, lower taxes. Then the mayor's turn came and he themed jobs, jobs, jobs as the cornerstone of his campaign. Then it was C. C.'s turn, but she did not speak. Instead she stared, seemingly bewildered, moving her gaze from one candidate to the other until, prompted by the moderator, she said, "I can't believe what I just heard. Lower taxes? More jobs? Governor, you raised income taxes, property taxes and gasoline taxes twice each in the past twelve years. Mr. Mayor, the city of St. Paul has lost over twenty-one thousand jobs during your watch. Gentlemen, what *are* you talking about?"

The volunteers cheered. The studio audience cheered, despite warnings not to. I suspect my mom and dad in Fort Myers, Florida, would've cheered, too, had they seen the show. Carol Catherine Monroe had drawn first blood big time. The governor and mayor, visibly irritated, came after her with a vengeance. It was a mistake. C. C. parried each personal attack and thrust back with a carefully worded reply: "It is true, Governor, I only have a few years' experience but I have a balanced checkbook. You on the other hand have three decades of experience and the state is half a billion dollars in debt. How do you explain that?" and "Mr. Mayor, obviously I am a woman so it shouldn't be a surprise that I am interested in what you keep referring to as 'women's issues.' Do you have a problem with that? Do you think women's issues are unimportant?" And my favorite: "Gentlemen, why do you keep referring to my age and the fact I am single? Are you looking for a date?"

Representative Carol Catherine Monroe had caught her opponents off guard. Clearly, they had underestimated her. Still, they were seasoned politicians, and as the debate progressed they started getting in licks of their own.

The mayor accused C. C. of being merely a dupe of the "femi-liberals," and claimed she was "the puppet," and "Marion Senske, that well-known liberal anarchist, the puppet master." The governor joined the attack, suggesting that Marion had authored *all* the bills C. C. proposed in the House, none of which had passed. C. C. responded only by confessing that Marion was her friend and mentor, proclaiming gratefully that "while she never put words in my mouth, she has put ideas in my head."

With a quarter hour left in the debate, C. C.'s opponents

continued to hammer her relentlessly, first the governor, then the mayor, then the governor again, talking about what was needed at the capitol, or rather, what was *not* needed: a young, single, tax-and-spend liberal feminist known only for her good looks, who appealed solely to a left-wing constituency that consisted mostly of welfare queens, tree huggers and homosexuals. The moderator eventually interrupted the attack and gave C. C. time for a rebuttal. C. C. attempted to speak, but her words were incomprehensible. She stopped herself, pounded the podium, then tried again. "I thought we were here to discuss the issues," she muttered. And then she committed the one unpardonable sin of politics: She cried. Her chest heaved and shuddered and she began to weep plaintive, doleful tears. Her voice cracked and disintegrated. She lowered her head and closed her eyes.

"Being head of state is a difficult job," the governor declared after only a moment's pause. "It cannot be handled by one who lacks toughness."

"Crying over our problems is an indulgence we simply cannot afford," the mayor added.

Amy's grip went slack on my arm. Louise looked down. Many of the other volunteers looked away. "It's over," one of them muttered. Only C. C. didn't think so.

"An indulgence, Mr. Mayor?" she asked, her voice coming from deep inside her. "A lack of toughness, Governor?" She was angry, now. "To cry over people you care about? Is that what you think? Is that what you believe? Or is it just that you don't care enough to cry for anyone but yourselves?"

"What the hell?" one of the volunteers said.

"Yes, I'm crying," C. C. said, continuing her counterattack. "I'm crying for single mothers who are forced into poverty and for their children who go to bed hungry most nights. I'm crying for low-income families who can't afford a decent place to live. I'm crying for the elderly who are forced to eat dog food because of your policies, Governor. I'm crying for the dispossessed and the homeless who have no place to go but the cold, dirty, dangerous streets because you closed their shelters, Mr. Mayor. I'm crying for the people who can't get jobs, for the people who can't afford health care. I'm crying for the people who themselves cry each day because the government that is supposed to help them won't. Whom do you cry for? I mean, besides the PACs and special-interest groups that stuff your pockets with money?"

"My God . . ." Louise breathed.

"I care about the people of the state of Minnesota. All the people. Even those who don't have money to contribute to a campaign fund. Even those who can't or won't vote. I care about their problems and their fears and their tomorrows. You two . . . You care about getting elected. Nothing else."

It was a nice comeback and I wondered if Marion and C. C. had planned it all along. If they had, it was a singularly dangerous move and probably would not have succeeded if it weren't for what came next. In response, both the governor and the mayor claimed that they cried all the time, too; that they each out-cried the others. And they offered examples. The media played along, asking questions such as, "Governor, did you weep when you slashed the University of Minnesota's operating budget?" In reply came answers like, "I don't believe I wept, but I am sure I shed a tear or two." It was high comedy—or farce, if you prefer—and when the so-called debate mercifully ended, the volunteers were delighted.

"Is Carol Catherine Monroe tough enough to be governor?" an excited campaign worked shouted. "Ask the coroner after he examines the bodies."

But the workers did not get a chance to celebrate long. The telephones started ringing even before the program's closing credits had finished rolling. I had to turn the TV set off.

"I've taken in over seven thousand in the last half hour," I overheard one volunteer tell Louise as she moved from station to station.

"Representative Monroe really is going to be the first woman governor of the state of Minnesota," Amy told me yet again as she worked the switchboard.

"Maybe. Maybe not," I answered her but she was too busy to hear.

I closed the office door and leaned against it. "You'd better sit down," I told the two women.

Both ignored the advice.

"Did you get the tape?" Marion asked.

"Dennis Thoreau is dead," I answered.

"Wha . . ." C. C. staggered backward, found a chair in front of the desk and fell into it. Marion merely spread her legs farther apart and clasped her hands behind her back, parade rest.

The debate had ended one hundred minutes earlier. It had taken that long for the women to work the media and return to the triumphant applause of their campaign staff. Now Marion Senske was looking at me like I was a dead battery on a cold winter's night. She didn't need this, she really didn't.

"How?" Marion asked.

"What?" I answered.

"How was Thoreau killed?"

Interesting question. Most people ask "When?"

"He was shot in the face at close range," I replied.

"Oh God," C. C. whimpered

"When?" asked Marion.

"I'm guessing Saturday, sometime after C. C. spoke with him, but there's no way of knowing for sure until the ME determines the postmortem interval."

"ME?" C. C. asked weakly.

"The county medical examiner," I answered. "The cops would have called him long before now."

"You told the police?" Marion was outraged.

"No. They arrived when I was looking for the tape."

Marion grabbed my forearm with both hands and squeezed tight. "Did you get it?"

"No," I answered, pulling away. "I didn't have time. I doubt it was still there, anyway. Whoever killed Thoreau searched the house thoroughly. It was a very professional job."

"Oh God," Marion whimpered, groping for the chair behind C. C.'s desk. Her "Oh God" sounded just like C. C.'s.

"God had nothing to do with this," I said feeling vaguely superior. I could have told them about the tape I found, only I didn't know what I had yet. Probably a rerun of "Star Trek." Besides, they had lied about Sherman, and I did not know why. Instead, I took the envelope from my pocket, the one containing the ten thousand dollars, and tossed it on top of the desk. They both stared at it.

Finally, C. C. asked, "You don't think I did it, do you?"

There it was, the question I had been wrestling with since I found Dennis Thoreau, his mouth full of carpet.

"Do you think I did it?"

I looked into her aquamarine eyes, moist with tears; looked deep to see what truths were hidden there. I found only confusion, fear and . . . was it sorrow? If it was an act, it was a good one. Meryl Streep could take lessons from her.

"No," I replied.

"Thank you for trusting me," she said, and gave my hand a squeeze.

I could have let it go at that—probably should have—but I didn't like the way Marion was looking me up and down like she was deciding whether to choose me for her side in a game of dodgeball.

"It isn't a matter of trust," I said. "If you had killed him, you would probably have the videotape already. If you had the videotape, you wouldn't have hired me."

Besides, I didn't want her to be guilty. She was just too damned pretty to be guilty.

A light went on behind Marion's eyes. "You said the house

was searched. That means whoever killed Thoreau knew about the videotape."

"Yes," I said. "It's possible that Thoreau was killed for an unrelated reason—drugs perhaps. But I don't believe in coincidences."

"We no longer require your services, Mr. Taylor," Marion said abruptly.

"You don't think so?"

"No."

"Aren't you worried?"

"No."

"The man who was blackmailing you is murdered and the thing he was blackmailing you with is missing, but you're not worried. If it was me, I'd be scared to death. How come you're not scared to death, Marion?"

"In politics you learn to go with the flow," she answered and smiled.

"I'll remember you said that if I'm ever called to testify."

"Fuck you."

"Marion!" C. C. was shocked by Marion's language. I ignored it.

"You told me that three people knew about the tape. There's you and Carol Catherine," I said. "Who's the third?"

"Thank you for your time," Marion said.

"It's Anne Scalasi, isn't it? That's why you're so confident. You think she's protecting you."

"Your services are no longer required, Mr. Taylor," Marion repeated with greater emphasis. "We can manage from here."

I stood before the desk, my hands clenched. If she thought for one minute Anne Scalasi was protecting her, if she thought my best friend would cover up for murder . . . My God! She thinks Annie committed murder. For her. I was shaking my head from side to side when she said, "Good-bye, Mr. Taylor."

I was impressed by her coolness, her forced detachment. This was one situation that Marion had not planned, could not have foreseen, yet she would be damned if she was going to let it intrude on her grand design, interfere with the destiny she had ordained for herself and C. C. Monroe. Marion would do with this setback what I have always done with mine: She would deal with it. *Well,* I thought, *deal with this* . . . I took the four one-hundred-dollar bills from my pocket and fanned them on the desk in front of Marion. She looked at the bills and then at me.

"Nothing in writing, remember?" I said. "I never met you. So, I have no professional obligation to you."

It was an expensive gesture, I know, but I wanted her to be worried about something, if not Thoreau, then me. Well, maybe too expensive. I snatched one of the bills off the desktop and stuffed it into my jacket pocket. "I had some unexpected expenses," I announced.

I left the office.

"Good-bye, Holland," C. C. called after me. "I'm sorry things didn't work out."

NINE

$M_{Y\ HOUSE\ IS}$ a two-story Colonial built in 1926 by a well-to-do businessman who paid for its construction with silver dollars. In those days Roseville was all farm country. Now it's one of the oldest suburbs in the Twin Cities, a bedroom community feeding both Minneapolis and St. Paul, populated by row after row of houses whose most prominent feature seems to be an attached garage. I don't like the suburbs, probably because I've never felt comfortable there, and I don't understand how other people can feel comfortable there. There's no connection between the place and the residents, no sense of community. In the city you live on a street, you belong to a neighborhood. Schools, parks, the hamburger joint down the street, the bar up the block, the drugstore on the corner—they all become a part of you and you become a part of them, a fusion of identities. The suburbs? You can swap locations, mix and match the houses, change names and it wouldn't matter, no one would notice. In the Cities, you can be an Eastsider or a Highland Parker or a Nordeaster. But you can only live in Roseville.

I moved to Roseville at Laura's insistence. She had wanted a suburban neighborhood. Jennifer was still a gleam in our eyes back then. Even so, Laura wanted to live where she insisted the schools were better, the crime was less and the children were safer. So we bought the house, paying more for it than we could afford, even on two incomes. Now I own it outright, having used Laura's mortgage-insurance policy to pay it off—funny, we took out the policy on me to protect her; adding a rider for her was an afterthought. I've considered selling the house several times since Laura and Jennifer were killed, only I can't bring myself to put up a FOR SALE sign under the willow tree in the front yard where Jennifer played. Maybe it's because the house and what's in it is all I have left of them—that and some photographs I've already committed to memory.

I dropped the backpack on the kitchen table, opened it and retrieved the videotape, taking time first to read the note I found wedged in my front door. It was from Heather Schrotenboer. The note said she had come by about seven-thirty as planned and discovered I wasn't home. She guessed I was working and said she would swing by about ten-thirty. It was now 10:23.

I wanted to get to the videotape, but I also had to be ready for Heather. So I left the tape on the table and went upstairs to my bedroom. I unlocked the drawer built into the pedestal of my waterbed, selected a Beretta .380 from the guns I keep there and loaded it carefully. I slipped it into the back pocket of my jeans and went downstairs.

I grabbed a handful of chocolate-chip cookies and the videotape and went into what I used to call the family room when I still had a family. Ogilvy, my gray-and-white French lop-eared rabbit, was waiting for me. I opened his cage and he hopped out. I scratched his nose for a moment and then went to the TV and VCR, turning both on. I slipped the tape into the VCR, grabbed the remote and went to the couch. Ogilvy hopped onto my lap and I petted him some more. "Want to watch a movie?" I asked him. The rabbit did not reply. The TV was dialed to "Monday Night Football." The Bears were giving the Cowboys a game, trailing by three in the middle of the third quarter. I stayed with it for a minute, watching Steve Walsh, a local boy made good, complete his fifth consecutive pass for Chicago. I glanced at my watch: 10:35. I thought of Heather. If I worked this right, I should have time to catch the last quarter. Not that I'm a sports freak, mind you. I follow most games—football, basketball, hockey, golf, baseball—especially baseball, which we all know is the only sport God approves of. But I'm not a fanatic. I don't go around reciting obscure statistics like the record number of consecutive Gold Gloves won by former Minnesota Twins southpaw Jim "Kitty" Kaat (it's sixteen, by the way); it's just a pleasant way to pass the time.

I hit the play button on the remote . . .

I sat in the dark, munching chocolate-chip cookies, watching the images flicker across the screen. I've seen porno films before, mostly at bachelor parties, and I've viewed them with disinterest. Only I didn't know the stars of those films. This one I did. This one starred Carol Catherine Monroe.

"She might be our next governor," I told Ogilvy. He leaped off my lap and hopped to his cage, taking a hit of alfalfa.

C. C. was lying in bed, nude except for a gold chain and bad lighting, caressing her co-star whom she identified simply as, "Fuck me, Dennis; fuck me, Dennis." No inhibited language there. Dennis was an only slightly more lifelike version of the man I found earlier.

The camera zoomed in close on C. C.'s face, her head rolling back and forth, strawberry locks frosted with gold covering her eyes. It pulled back to reveal what "Fuck me, Dennis" was doing to her, then panned in slowly again as C. C. moaned, "Oh yes, oh yes, oh yes."

Oh, brother. I ate another cookie.

I was not impressed. The film did not fill me with excitement. It emptied me, left me feeling the way I did when I was a child hiding in the bushes, watching the older kids coupling on "Bare Ass," a white-sand beach along the Mississippi River. It was the same emptiness I felt several years later when my school friends and I lied our way into our first hard-core, quadruple X–rated film, paying five dollars to see just how unsexy sex can be.

There was no love, no affection, no tenderness. Thoreau attacked C. C. like she was a speed bag, giving her about as much consideration. I understood him. I've known plenty of men who treat women as prey. What I did not understand was why a woman would put up with it, how she could find pleasure with him, how she could respond as C. C. was responding—rolling her head and wetting her lips and moaning like an animal in heat. And then it hit me and I understood perfectly.

"It's acting," I said, waving my hand with a flourish at the TV screen. Acting, and nothing more.

Someone used the brass knocker several times more than necessary to summon me to my front door, apparently not trusting the doorbell. I hit the stop button on the remote and C. C.'s film debut was replaced by the football game. Chicago had taken a four-point lead. I turned down the volume and went to the door. Ogilvy followed me.

I peeped through the spy hole and saw Heather Schrotenboer standing under the porch light, flicking invisible lint off her chest. Heather was dressed to kill, wearing a deep red, closely fitted slipdress that ended just above her knees, with triple spaghetti shoulder straps and a neckline that plunged to her waist. She also wore gold earrings and a gold bracelet but no necklace, although I kept searching for one anyway.

I opened the door. "Hi, kid," I said, turning my back to her, leading her into the living room. Did I say she looked like a high school girl? Not in my high school. I flashed on C. C. and Thoreau thrashing about the bed, warning myself to be smart.

"Nice dress," I told her.

"Oh, this old thing," she replied, grinning.

"You coming from somewhere?"

"No," she said. "I just felt like dressing for the occasion. What I was wearing the last time we met, I'm sure you thought I was a boy."

"No," I admitted. "I never thought that."

"Do you think I'm attractive?"

"Oh yeah," I said slowly under my breath.

"Hmm? What?"

"Yes," I answered. "I think you're attractive."

She smiled. "I think you're attractive, too," she said.

"It must be the light."

She floated—C'mon, Taylor, get a grip!—She *walked* to me and ran her fingers under my collar. She spoke into my neck; her breath was sweet and warm. "Why did the police arrest you?" she asked.

"They thought I killed a guy."

She didn't even flinch. "Did you?" she asked, practically begging to become a co-conspirator.

"How could I? I was with you."

"It must be exciting."

"What?"

"Killing a man."

"Huh?"

She wrapped her arms around my neck and kissed me hungrily, making soft animal-like moans as she ground her lips against mine. I was tempted—oh Lord, I was tempted—only that wasn't why I invited her to my house. I pulled her arms down and pushed her away. She looked at me, more amused than surprised. Until she saw the gun I was pointing at her heart. She backed away slowly, her eyes never leaving the barrel. I waited three steps, four. On the fifth I squeezed off three rounds, angling the gun toward the carpet, careful not to splatter her dress and all that bare flesh with powder. She fell back into and then out of a stuffed chair, landing on the hardwood floor, the hem of her short skirt hiked to midthigh. She stared at me, terror stricken, her mouth hanging open.

Ogilvy was also frightened and he squeezed into a corner. I scooped him up with one hand and hugged him to my chest. "That's okay, bunny, you don't have to be afraid," I said, trying to soothe him. I moved to Heather's side, sat on the floor next to her. I held up the gun, giving her a good look at it. "Blanks," I said.

"Are you crazy?" Heather shrieked.

"No, but you must be, cheating at cards with professionals. In the old days they would have tossed your body out of a speeding car. In these more enlightened times, they'd probably be satisfied with breaking your fingers."

"I . . . I don't know what you're talking about."

"Let me explain. After a hand, when the cards are being thrown in for a new deal, a body might hold on to one or two to use later, concealing them in her armpits or under her knees. This is called 'holding out.' By the way, anyone ever tell you that you have delightful knees? Hmm? Oh, another thing: the next deal is yours, you study all the cards that were discarded during the previous hand. You see five that you like. So you pick up the cards one hand at a time, and as you do so, you put the card you want on the bottom of each group of five cards. Then you put all five hands together on the top of the deck, engage in some flummery while shuffling and then deal them out, with cards five, ten, fifteen, twenty and twenty-five coming to you. This is called 'picking up.' Picking up and holding out are considered cheating."

Heather denied nothing. She merely asked, "What are you going to do?"

"Me?" I pressed the muzzle of the gun against her chest

and slowly let it slip down between her breasts, using the neckline of her dress to hold it up, stretching the material into a tight V. She was trembling. "You did me a favor, so I'm going to do you one. I'll get the people you cheated off your case, but it's going to cost you."

"You . . . you want me. Don't you? Don't you want me?" Heather stammered. She reached up and with both hands caressed the muzzle of the Beretta still pressed between her breasts. She arched her back, her head resting against the chair and closed her eyes, moaning slightly. I flashed on C. C. again. Only, unlike C. C., Heather wasn't acting. She was having a wonderful time.

"Swell," I muttered. She was an adrenaline junkie. She wanted to be frightened, it was how she got off; this was probably the most fun she had ever had. Swell, just swell, goddamn it. Didn't she get it? Didn't she understand? I wondered if I could get a few photos of Dennis Thoreau, a nice round hole in his forehead, show them to her. Ahh, man, what was I doing?

To Heather's obvious disappointment I stood up, still holding Ogilvy in one hand, and returned the Beretta to my pocket.

"I want seven thousand, two hundred and fifty-five dollars; that's the money you took off my client last week and the money you took off me Saturday."

"Nothing else?" she asked, surprised.

"You have until Friday," I said. "After that it's out of my hands. Do you understand?"

She nodded that she did and I helped her to her feet. She immediately began smoothing her body-conscious dress into place.

"And if you can't play a legit game, don't play at all," I added.

Heather smiled—an amazing thing. "Will you take a check?"

"Friday," I said. "In cash. And if you don't return it, it won't be me who will come looking for you." With that I pushed her toward the front door.

She stopped at the door, turning toward me, her hands behind her back, posing like one of the models in a Victoria's Secret catalog. That smile, where had I seen it before? Oh yes, I remembered. A doctor, an oncologist who murdered his mistress and got away with it for fifty-seven days before Annie and I busted his ass. He thought he was invincible, thought he could do anything. He smiled like that. Right up until the judge dropped the gavel on him and the county cops led him away.

"Aren't you going to offer me a drink?"

I opened the door and pushed Heather through it, clicking off the porch light before she reached her car.

"You know something, Ogilvy," I said, scratching the rabbit behind his ears, "the way some people behave, you wonder if they've lost their will to live."

I didn't bother to watch any more of the videotape. I hit the rewind button and waited, catching the final two minutes of the game as Emmitt Smith trampled the Bears' rush defense, pushing over for the winning TD from six yards out. After the machine had done its work, I took the videotape and slid it into an empty box. I labeled the box *STAR TREK V—THE FINAL FRONTIER* and put it on the shelf with my collection—I have about forty tapes. Where's the best place to hide something? In plain sight.

I suddenly felt a desperate need to take a shower. I put it off, sitting down with a yellow legal pad instead, making detailed notes on everything I heard, saw or read, replaying the day slowly in my memory. Later, I would transcribe the notes onto my PC; I had a hunch this case was not going away.

Having the tape raised a lot of interesting questions, not the least of which was: What am I going to do with it? I did not want it; I hadn't known it was the videotape C. C. and Marion sought when I removed it from Thoreau's house. Yet I was not surprised to learn it was. After all, someone had gone to a great deal of trouble to make sure I found it.

Anne Scalasi's name came to mind.

Another question beckoned when I stood naked in front of my mirror, wondering if I looked older today than yesterday: Did I have the only copy?

And still another arose when I was finally standing under the shower, letting the hot water run down my back.

Who operated the camera?

TEN

I WOKE EARLY without much enthusiasm for the sunshine that streamed through my bedroom windows. I'd had a difficult night of it, tossing and turning, dozing more than sleeping. But not because of Dennis Thoreau. Unlike the other dead men who invaded my sleep, Thoreau did not belong to me. None of it belonged to me. I had wandered into it, like a neighbor who inadvertently intrudes on a domestic dispute. It wasn't my problem and if I was polite I'd say, "Excuse me," and get the hell out of there; give the tape to Anne Scalasi—anonymously, of course, since removing evidence from a crime scene is a felony in this state—and walk away, letting Annie figure it out. Only now I was curious. The questions I had formed last night were still nagging me. Besides, good manners never were one of my virtues. And I did not like being trifled with.

But was I willing to take on the expense of continuing the investigation, of dragging Thoreau's name through my databases without a client? No, not really, I decided, regretting my expensive gesture of the night before. Yet, as the nuns at St. Mark's Elementary School were fond of telling me, the Good Lord always provides a way.

In this case He provided it in the form of a telephone call

from Carol Catherine Monroe. She was desperate for my help. Or so she claimed. I replaced the receiver and rolled out of bed, pleased to have a reason to get up in the morning, and padded downstairs.

I did not recognize Conan at first. He was standing next to the information desk in his State Capitol Security Force uniform, the uniform tailored to fit his well-muscled body.

But he recognized me. He moved quickly, taking several long steps, positioning himself between me and the elevators.

"Something, yes?" I asked.

His eyes narrowed, his lips curled into an ugly snarl; I expected him to growl or at least bark. He did neither. Instead, he stepped away without a word, returning to the desk. If he was trying to get my attention, he did a helluva job. I backed into the elevator, watching him until the doors swished shut.

The State Capitol Office Building has eight floors, two below ground, six above. The floors are color coordinated; don't ask me why. I took the ancient elevator to Blue. The doors opened onto a reception area. The legislative session had ended the first Monday following the third Saturday in May as prescribed by our state constitution and no one was on duty at the desk, which is probably why C. C. had asked me to meet her there instead of at campaign headquarters. I walked down a long corridor dotted with a half dozen unoccupied desks and a dozen office doors. The doors were all closed and presumably locked, except one on the left, toward the end of the corridor.

C. C. Monroe was not in her office when I arrived at 9:30. She'd had a breakfast fund-raiser scheduled and Marion Senske had told her it was best she keep to her routine. That meant I was forced to sit with Marion and wait. I didn't mind waiting and Marion's attitude toward me had shifted. Yesterday she wanted me out of her life. Today she wanted me on her side.

"You must think I'm an awful bitch," she volunteered.

"Not at all, I think you're very good at it."

"Practice, practice," she said and smiled—sort of.

"I'm surprised you allowed C. C. to call me," I told her. "Wasn't your friend at the St. Paul Police Department available?"

Marion ignored my question. She slipped a wad of bills out of the desk drawer and handed them to me. "These belong to you," she said. I stuffed them into my jacket pocket without counting them.

Marion was nervous. She tapped her foot relentlessly and the tapping started to work on my nerves. I looked for a distraction. I asked how the campaign was progressing.

"Good," she replied. "We took in nearly a hundred and seventy-five thousand dollars last night alone. That gives us two million. We're putting it into TV and radio spots that will saturate the market during the final two weeks before the election."

"That's a lot of money, two million dollars," I told her.

She disagreed. "The opposition has more."

"Tell me something. Carol Catherine's performance last night, her angry tears? Did you script that?"

"Goddamn it, where is she?" Marion asked, standing up, glancing at her watch, then the clock on the wall. "She's never been on time a day in her life. I keep telling her . . ." Marion stopped and stared out the window. "You make do with what you have," she sighed.

"I'll take that as a yes." When Marion did not respond, I asked, "Does C. C. ever do anything without your help?"

"Occasionally, I'll let her sign her name to something."

C. C. stepped through her office door on Marion's words. "Are you talking about me?" she asked.

"Where the hell have you been?" Marion wanted to know.

C. C. ignored her, shutting and locking the door after first poking her head out into the corridor and looking both ways.

She was obviously scared silly and kept pulling at her hair. Fifteen minutes before she'd called me, she said, a man had called her, a man who identified himself only with his demand: ten thousand dollars in tens and twenties.

"What exactly did he say?" I asked when C. C. was sure we were not being spied on.

She answered in a conspiratorial voice just above a whisper. "He said, 'I know what you did and so will everyone else unless you pay me ten thousand dollars.' He said, 'Bring the money to Loni's Coffee House on Cleveland Avenue across from the university's St. Paul campus at noon today.' He said, 'Come alone.'"

"He said 'I' and 'me'? Are you sure?"

"Yes."

"He didn't say 'us,' he didn't say 'we'?"

"No."

"Did you recognize the voice? Ever hear it before?"

"I don't think so. It didn't sound muffled or anything."

"What else did he say?"

"He said not to call the police."

"Yes, well, he would, wouldn't he? Did you receive the call at campaign headquarters?"

"No," C. C. said. "He called me at home; he had my unlisted number."

I acknowledged that fact in my notebook. It may or may not be significant. Give me a half hour, I could get her unlisted telephone number, too.

"Do you think he has the videotape?" Marion asked.

"No," I said, and then almost explained how I knew. Dumb, real dumb. Fortunately I checked myself. "Maybe," I added. "I don't know. He didn't mention it, did he? He merely assumed Carol Catherine knew what she was buying. It could be a completely different matter."

It could be Joseph Sherman.

I turned toward C. C. She had spoken to Sherman and then

denied it. A couple of days later, he was wanted for murder.

C. C., her eyes unblinking, said, "What?"

"I was just wondering if there was something you haven't told us."

"No, I don't think so."

"Perhaps Dennis Thoreau had a partner," Marion suggested.

"Perhaps," I agreed. I hadn't forgotten about the camera operator.

"Perhaps Thoreau and his partner had a falling out," Marion continued. "Perhaps the partner thought Thoreau wasn't going to share the blackmail money. So, the partner kills Thoreau and takes matters into his own hands—the amount the caller is asking for is the same amount Thoreau wanted."

I liked it. I turned on C. C.

"Tell me about the movie," I asked her. "Who else was there?"

"What do you mean?"

"When you filmed it, who else was involved?"

"No one!" C. C. exclaimed, utterly astonished that I would ask such a thing.

"No one was operating the camera?"

"Certainly not! What kind of person do you think I am?"

I let her question slide and continued asking my own. "Did a friend of Thoreau's . . ."

"I never met any of Dennis's friends," C. C. insisted.

"Did Thoreau have your unlisted telephone number?"

"Yes," she said in a small voice.

"A partner!" Marion cried out in triumph and slapped the desktop; it must be wonderful to be right all the time.

"Who was Thoreau's partner?" I asked C. C.

"I don't know."

Liar, liar, pants on fire.

"What should we do?" Marion asked.

"You could always call your friends in the police department," I suggested again.

Marion didn't reply. She pursed her lips and tapped her toe and rubbed her hands together. Pontius Pilate came to mind.

"You already called your friend, didn't you?"

"She asked me if I wanted to press charges. When I declined she said there was nothing she could do. That's what she said the first time." Marion shook her head. "I asked you a question. What should *we* do?"

"I think we should meet this alleged blackmailer, don't you? Find out what he has for sale."

"And if he's selling the tape?"

"If he knows about the tape, then he's probably also a killer and we should turn him in."

Marion Senske tapped her toe some more and thought it over. "Do you know what the newspapers . . ."

"This has nothing to do with the newspapers," I interrupted her. "This has nothing to do with politics. This is about doing what's right."

"I agree," C. C. chimed in almost cheerfully. "We have to do what's right."

"Shut up, Carol Catherine," Marion told her.

C. C. bowed her head and kept quiet, a dutiful child.

"You're not a police officer anymore," Marion reminded me. "You're not obligated to enforce the law, you're obligated to protect your client. Carol Catherine Monroe is your client."

"I think we had this conversation once before," I said. I was fast losing interest in C. C.'s problems and part of me wanted to forget the whole sorry business and move on. The other part? It's like watching a bad movie; you hang in there only because you want to see how it ends.

"So, what are we going to do?" C. C. asked.

"Meet your friend for lunch," I answered.

"I'll get the money," Marion volunteered.

"Wait a minute," C. C. said. "I don't want to go . . . I mean, can't . . . People will recognize me."

C. C. was wearing a burgundy turtleneck sweater and a

long, full skirt of the same color; both matched her fingernail polish. They also made her hair seem brighter, richer and hard to miss.

I glanced at my watch. "We have plenty of time," I said. "I'll take you home and you can change. Jeans, sweatshirt; we'll put your hair under a hat. You'll look like a college kid."

"I . . . Can't you go for me?" she asked Marion.

"I think the blackmailer would see that she isn't you," I told C. C.

"Besides, I have a meeting with the media people," Marion reminded her. "And I have to rearrange your schedule. The Minnesota Farm Bureau is expecting you in Duluth; I have no idea what I'm going to tell them." Marion consulted her watch, made a few silent calculations and sighed. "We really haven't got time for this."

"Nobody cares about me," C. C. said weakly, staring down at her folded hands.

Marion smoothed C. C.'s hair with a gentle hand. "It will be all right, Carol Catherine. We'll deal with this and in three weeks we'll be governor."

C. C. looked up at the older woman and they both smiled brightly. For a moment they forgot about Thoreau, forgot about the blackmailer.

Governor. The word hung in the air like a gas, like helium—something they'd been breathing for so long that it made them light-headed, made them dizzy. They weren't thinking straight.

ELEVEN

MARION OPENED the desk drawer and slipped out an envelope containing ten thousand dollars, the same envelope she had given me yesterday. This time she gave it to C. C. She took it like it weighed half a ton.

"I just had a terrible thought," Marion said, turning toward me. "What if there is more than one copy of the videotape?"

"What if . . ." I repeated. "Let's worry about the original first."

C. C. put the envelope into her purse, hung the purse over her shoulder, slipped a charcoal coat over her arm and stepped into the corridor, which was now occupied by a handful of secretaries stationed at the desks outside the offices. C. C. acted like she was walking her last mile, ignoring the greetings that followed her to the elevator.

We entered the elevator and sent it to the ground floor. When the doors slid open, she took my arm and we proceeded across the lobby. Conan noted our passing with an expression of grave disapproval. No doubt he thought she could do better.

We found her car on the second floor of the capitol parking ramp, a two-door Nissan Sentra. *A politician who's not concerned about buying American, now there's a switch,* I thought. I held the driver's door open for her, told her she would drive to my car, I would then follow her home. Only she did not get in. She turned her back to the car, turned to look at me, the door between us, her fingers brushing mine where they rested on top of the door frame. She was close enough to kiss. I stepped back, putting distance between us. She frowned.

"All this is happening because I wanted a job with the PCA," she said.

"You should have sent a résumé like everyone else."

We found my Monza and I followed her out of St. Paul. C. C. lived in the suburbs, in the north end of her district not too far from the freeway. Her house was in the middle of a long block, on the same side of the street as the mailboxes. It was a small split-level, yellow with blue trim and shutters. The attached garage had a thirty-foot-long asphalt driveway leading to it. She signaled and pulled into the driveway. I parked on the street. She was unlocking the front door when I reached her.

"Don't mind the mess," she said, probably out of habit because the place was immaculate. It reminded me of a showroom in a furniture store.

"I bought it two years ago. I'll have to sell it when I become governor and move into the mansion. Would you care for a drink?" C. C. asked as we stepped into the living room. "I have some beer."

"No, thank you."

"We have time."

"No, thank you."

She hesitated, then came to me, moving close. The perfume was lilac, her breath peppermint.

"You better change your clothes," I told her.

I made myself comfortable in an overstuffed chair. I'm a patient man. I could have sat there all day, sat there until the snow came and went, sat there until the Minnesota Vikings actually won a Super Bowl or until hell froze over, whichever came first. I found myself smiling. This is what I do for a living and despite C. C.'s lies, I was having a good time.

C. C. surprised me by acting just as relaxed when she returned to the living room wearing sneakers, faded blue jeans and a white sweatshirt with UNIVERSITY OF MINNESOTA written in maroon and gold across the chest. Her hair was pulled back and tucked under the collar of a well-worn bomber jacket. I could see her in the University of St. Thomas grill discussing sex discrimination with the other underclassmen, no problem— although I doubted she would take the discussion seriously. She sat in a chair across from me, her legs folded under her, and pulled a pack of Virginia Slims from her pocket. She lit one, blew a cloud of smoke into the air above her head and then waved it away with her hand. She took another puff and coughed slightly. She was not a smoker, just an errant child breaking the rules, daring someone to catch her. I was fascinated. Carol Catherine Monroe was the least preoccupied person I had ever met.

I surprised myself by asking a stupid question: "Has anyone ever told you you should be a model?"

"When I was young," she answered. "People told me I should model the way they tell boys who are tall that they should play basketball." She took another drag of the cigarette. "You think I'm beautiful. That's okay, everyone does. Especially women, women more than men. When I was a kid, all my friends were guys. They weren't boyfriends, they were pals; I played hoops with them and baseball and even hockey sometimes. They let me play because I was a good athlete. Only the other girls didn't see it that way. They saw the way I looked and convinced themselves I was out to steal their boyfriends. I wasn't and I said so. It didn't make any difference. I would get off the school bus and it would start—girls hollering names at me, girls I didn't even know. I had my hair pulled out, I was hit in the face, I had green food coloring thrown in my hair, I was beat up . . . I had to change high schools three times."

She took another pull from the cigarette, filling her lungs with smoke, exhaling slowly. "It's not easy being me. If I wasn't such a strong person I would have had a nervous breakdown."

Jeezus, now she had me feeling sorry for her and I didn't want to feel sorry for her, so I said, "I believe sooner or later we all get exactly what we deserve."

She choked on the cigarette smoke. "You think I deserve this? I thought you were on my side."

"To the extent that I think you are innocent of murder I am on your side. As for the rest of it . . . You're a careless woman, Carol Catherine. Bad things happen to people who are careless."

C. C. crushed her cigarette to death in an ashtray I thought was a candy dish. "You think I'm a slut."

"I didn't say . . ."

"You think I'm a slut because of what I did with Dennis Thoreau. You think I'm a whore. Well, I'm not," she said, her voice rising with indignation. "What do you know? You think a woman who's young and attractive, who looks sexy"—she emphasized the word—"she's always trying to turn herself on. Right? Well, I'm not. Yeah, I get a lot of offers; you know the kind I mean. You wouldn't believe the offers I get. They make me sick. I dated Dennis because he was kind to me and considerate, because he made me laugh. Okay, maybe it was a stupid thing to do, making that tape. And maybe Dennis wasn't as nice a guy as I thought he was. But I'm just like everybody else. I don't always do what's in my best interest."

She leaned back in her chair, waiting to see how I would take it, waiting to see if her explanation satisfied me, softened me, perhaps. She reminded me of Amy Lamb, a woman nearly fifteen years her junior and equally mature. I flashed to a newspaper headline—GOVERNOR MONROE—and shuddered.

"I don't know what you can help and what you can't," I told her firmly. "I only know this: There are some mistakes that are never forgiven, for which there is no redemption, no absolution. Only penance. So, choose your sins carefully. They'll be with you always."

"Who cares?" she said.

At 11:45 I was sitting at a small table beneath a white canvas with a splash of black paint reaching diagonally from one corner to the other. The typed card attached to the frame read: PATH TO INFINITY, $135.00. I ignored the painting, pretending to be engrossed in a copy of *The Cities Reporter* as I watched the door, a café mocha growing cold in front of me. I reached under my blue sports coat and touched the spot where my Beretta would have been if I was still carrying. I took my hand away with only a little uneasiness.

There were six other customers in LONI'S COFFEEHOUSE ESPRESSO CAPPUCCINO MOCHA WATCH FOR LIVE MUSIC AND READINGS. Two couples sitting boy-girl-boy-girl surrounded a small table in the center of the room and conspired quietly; a young woman sat alone near the far wall, nursing a lime Torani and reading a John Sandford thriller; a professor graded blue books at the table next to mine. The professor gave me a running commentary under his breath as he attacked the papers with his red pen. It went like this: "*G-R-E-E-C-E,* not *G-R-E-A-S-E,* holy mackerel . . . *I* before *E* except after *C,* my God, can't any of these kids spell? . . . You're beautiful, honey, but unfortunately you're also as dumb as a brick . . . I'd flunk you out, my friend, but I'm afraid you'll take my class again . . . I'll be damned, someone actually read the material . . ." Meanwhile, the lunch hour crowd swelled, mostly students from the campus across the street. They were loud and undisciplined and dressed as poorly as they could afford and I wished I was one of them; they behaved like they didn't have a care in the world.

At exactly noon by the large electric clock above the stainless-steel espresso machine, C. C. entered, clutching her purse to her chest like it was a life preserver. She found an empty table toward the back and sat facing the counter. When Loni asked her pleasure, C. C. stared at her so intently that the woman took two steps backward; she served C. C.'s cappuccino at arm's length. A few of the college kids gave C. C. a don't-I-know-you? glance but no one approached her.

By 1:30 the coffeehouse was nearly deserted again, except for me, C. C. and the young woman drinking the Torani, who glanced at the clock, muttered, "Uh-oh," quickly gathered her belongings and left in a rush. That Sandford, he's a spellbinder.

At 1:45 I rapped my knuckles on the counter, startling C. C. "You win some, you lose some and some get rained out," I told her.

"What does that mean?"

"It's an old baseball maxim. It means there's no game today."

"Why not?"

"You tell me."

"I don't understand."

Careful, Taylor, I told myself. Don't give yourself away.

I smiled at the woman and told her to go back to the capitol, told her to put the money in a safe place, told her to contact me if the blackmailer called again. A short time later, sitting in my car, watching C. C.'s Nissan disappear down Cleveland Avenue, I asked myself a question aloud that I had been asking silently several times while downing Loni's café mochas one after another: "Who was operating the camera, C. C.?"

TWELVE

IT WAS PUSHING three in the afternoon when I unlocked my office door, copies of the *StarTribune* and *Pioneer Press* tucked under my arm. The red light on my answering machine was blinking furiously; the numerical display said I had five messages. They could wait, I decided. I couldn't. I made a beeline for the building's facilities—after two and a half hours in a coffeeshop my back teeth were floating. I took the newspapers with me.

The local news section of each publication was devoted almost entirely to articles on the debate—the references to C. C.'s performance were nearly as complimentary as the photograph the *Trib* ran under the headline: TEARFUL MONROE SCORES BIG. She also had a photograph in the metro section of the *Pioneer Press,* although much smaller and not quite as flattering. It ran next to a story about a high school senior who was suing his school for violating his rights by refusing to allow him to wear to class a T-shirt advertising the products of a national beer company. School officials claimed the T-shirt breached its policies against promoting drugs, tobacco and alcohol. The student's parents said they would support their child, "no matter what it takes." The Minnesota chapter of the ACLU said it also would support the student, noting that the school's position "is a blatant First Amendment violation."

On the other side of the page was a much smaller story reporting that the SAT and ACT scores of Minnesota high school seniors were falling like stones with experts blaming a lack of discipline at home and the "unwillingness of most students to make the sacrifices necessary to maintain a higher level of learning." No parents were quoted supporting their children in their ignorance; the ACLU did not comment.

The stories on the deaths of John Brown and Dennis Thoreau were difficult to find, tucked as they were in the back pages. According to the article about Brown, the cops were looking for Joseph Sherman, an ex-convict who had allegedly accompanied Brown when he left the halfway house. The article on Thoreau suggested that his slaying might have been drug related, that whoever killed him might have searched his residence for drugs.

After I returned to my office, I poured myself a Summit Ale from the stock I keep in my small refrigerator. I took a long pull from the brown bottle and sat behind my desk in an old swivel chair Laura's father had given me. We still talk now and again, Laura's father and I. During the services for his daughter and grandchild he did not shed so much as a single tear, telling the mourners, "It was God's will." I decided he was one callous sonuvabitch and wanted nothing more to do with him until about a year later when his wife informed me that he'd quit the church. Apparently, he had as much trouble accepting God's will as I did.

I took another drink of the dark liquid and thus fortified, dialed Anne Scalasi's extension at the St. Paul cop shop—I figured she had a lot of explaining to do. The phone rang four times before I heard the telltale "click" that meant the call was being transferred to another extension. It rang twice more and was answered by a voice that quickly mumbled, "Homicide, McGaney."

"McGaney, this is Taylor. I'm looking for Lieutenant Scalasi."

"Taylor, I was just thinking of you."

"Why's that?"

"I just received a phone call from your friend Heather Schrotenboer."

"Really?"

"She wanted to confess."

"Confess to what?"

"Confess that she wasn't with you Saturday night, that you forced her to provide you with an alibi."

"You're kidding."

"You guys have a lovers' quarrel?"

"Something like that."

"Tsk, tsk."

"So, why haven't you arrested me?"

"I know you didn't do it."

"Then why did you arrest me the first time?"

"Your good friend Lieutenant Scalasi is not available at this time, would you care to leave a message?"

"Yes, but I don't think you'd deliver it."

"Temper, temp . . ."

I hung up the phone before he got to the second syllable. "Annie, Annie," I mumbled. "What the hell . . ."

I swiveled around and looked at that part of downtown Minneapolis I could see through my window. It wasn't too late, I told myself. I could still walk away from this. I pulled the roll of bills Marion Senske had given me from my pocket. Nine Ben Franklins. Two days' work plus expenses. I tucked them back in my pocket. Screw it, I decided. Life's too short for this crap—clients who lie to me, who sing me sad songs to keep my loyalty . . . Screw it. I'm outta here. Then I remembered the answering machine. I hit the replay bar; the tape rewound and delivered the five messages:

"Mr. Taylor? This is Amy Lamb. Ahh, it's ahh, eight-forty-five. I need to talk to you. It's really important. But I, I

can't . . . I'm going home. I can't . . . Call me at this number."

She recited her home phone number. She sounded extremely anxious.

"Ahh, this is Amy again, Amy Lamb. I'm at home now. Please call me. Please, Mr. Taylor."

"This is Scalasi. What? You don't keep office hours anymore?"

"It's twelve-fifteen. Mr. Taylor, you have to call me. I know who killed both John Brown and Dennis Thoreau."

"This is Heather Schrotenboer. Could we get together and . . ."

I practically broke my hand snatching up the telephone and pounding out Amy's number, not even listening to the last message. The phone rang four times and was answered by a machine—everybody has a machine these days. The voice it used was Amy's, clear and confident.

"Call me," I told the machine. "Call me right now."

I hung up the phone and stared at it. It didn't ring. It didn't ring for nearly fifteen minutes, so I dialed Amy's number again and was greeted by the machine again. I stared at the phone some more.

I called C. C.'s campaign headquarters.

"I'm sorry, Miss Lamb has gone for the day," Louise told me. "She had a very painful headache. You get a lot of those in the course of a political campaign. This is my seventh."

"Seventh headache or seventh campaign?"

"I don't under . . ."

"I need Amy's home address."

Louise hesitated before telling me, "I'm afraid we don't give out that information."

"This is very important."

"I'm sorry . . ."

I hung up, waited two beats, picked up the receiver and punched directory assistance.

"What city, please?"

"I don't know, it could be St. Paul or Minneapolis. I need the number for Amy Lamb. It would be a new listing."

I heard the keys of a terminal before directory assistance told me, "There is no listing for Lamb, Amy. However, there are three listings for Lamb, first initial 'A.' Two in Minneapolis and one in St. Paul."

"Give me all three."

"I'm sorry, sir, our policy is to give out a maximum of two numbers."

"Give me the Minneapolis listings."

Neither of them matched Amy's number. I repunched 411, reaching a different operator, and asked for Lamb, first initial A in St. Paul. The number on the recording she played for me matched.

I called again, this time punching O. I told the operator that Amy's phone was not being answered. "Perhaps I have the wrong number. Is that Amy Lamb on Lexington Avenue?"

"No, sir. The number you dialed is on Fratzke Avenue."

"Thank you."

I called right back, getting a male operator this time.

"Is that Amy Lamb at two-four-five-seven Fratzke?"

"No, sir. Nine-eight-eight."

Nine-eight-eight Fratzke Avenue was one half of a small, well-kept duplex shaded by a maple tree on one side and a majestic pine on the other. It sat back from the street on a small hill. Six steps reached up from the boulevard to a long, narrow, concrete path that divided the front yard neatly in two, stopping at a tiny porch with two front doors. I was pounding frantically on Amy's door, wondering if I should pick the lock, when I heard a voice behind me. It belonged to a woman no longer young, with thinning silver hair and stooped shoulders.

"You want somethin'?"

"I'm trying to locate Amy Lamb."

"If she ain't answerin', she ain't at home."

"My name is Holland Taylor. Amy called me from her place of business . . ."

"She works for that slut, C. C. Monroe," the woman informed me. She tried to spit but couldn't work up enough phlegm.

"I know," I said, choosing not to debate C. C.'s questionable morals just then. "Amy said she was going home, she said she was very ill. I called several times and there was no answer. I'm worried about her . . ."

"She was here when I left."

"When was that?"

"About noon, after my soap."

"What time did you get back?"

"I done my shopping; I was back by oh, 1:30."

I glanced at my watch. It was 4:15.

"Was she here when you returned?"

"I don't spy on my tenants," the old woman told me abruptly.

"Of course not. But perhaps you heard her moving about, heard her television."

"No, usually I do," the woman answered quietly, genuinely puzzled.

"Do you have a key to Miss Lamb's . . . ?"

"'Course I have a key," the woman said impatiently. "I own the place, don't I?"

"Would you . . . ?"

"I ain't lettin' you in there alone."

"Come with me. I just want to make sure she's all right, I won't touch anything."

"Damn straight you won't touch anything," she said. She went into her apartment after first ordering me to "Wait there." She took her own sweet time about it. Finally she reappeared, said, "C'mon then," and unlocked Amy's door. I pushed past her into the living room.

The old woman screamed with more energy than I thought

she could possibly muster. She screamed as I led her out of Amy's house and into her own. She screamed as I sat her down on a threadbare sofa and she screamed as I dialed 911 on her black rotary telephone. I was tempted to slap her across the face, but that only works in the movies.

I left the duplex and moved the length of the sidewalk, sitting on the steps overlooking the boulevard. She didn't stop screaming until well after the police arrived. I didn't blame her.

THIRTEEN

OFFICER JAMES CURTIS of the St. Paul Police Department's Northwest Team, riding alone without sirens or lights, screeched his unit to a stop directly in front of me. It took him about fifteen steps to move from the driver's door to where I sat. The effort left him breathless.

" 'S been a long time, Taylor," he said between short-winded puffs. His right hand rested on the butt of his holstered Glock 17.

"Too long," I assured him.

"You call it in?"

I nodded.

Curtis glanced backward at his unit, gave it some thought, then returned to it, opening the rear passenger door.

"You mind?"

I shook my head no and left my perch. When I reached the open door Curtis said, "Do me a favor."

I didn't have to ask what the favor was. I assumed the position and he searched me thoroughly without comment. After he finished I slid into the car and he locked me in. Without a backward glance, Curtis went to the house, hesitating on the porch, deciding between doors. He picked the one the screaming woman was behind. A few minutes later the woman was quiet and Curtis had returned to the porch. He took a deep breath and went inside Amy's apartment. He was pale when he came out thirty seconds later, pale except for his eyes. They were red with anger and sorrow. He returned to the squad and radioed Homicide for assistance. Except he didn't use the appropriate code number. Amy Lamb wasn't a number to him. When he finished he flung the hand mike away and sat there rubbing his eyes.

"I hate this job," he said.

An elderly man with silver hair, who probably thought he had seen it all, stood in the center of his yard two houses down and pretended to rake leaves while he watched the small army of officers, technicians, wagon men and medical examiners that descended on 988 Fratzke Avenue. He reminded me of my father, who hadn't raked a leaf since his eldest son turned nine years old, but would get angry just the same when my brothers and I frolicked in the piles we made and scattered the leaves across the lawn. The old man seemed particularly interested in a slender woman with short-cropped hair who was directing the activities.

Anne Scalasi loved this shit; the almost gleeful way she described the habits and behavioral characteristics of killers, you'd think she was talking about former boyfriends.

Anne used to be an elementary school teacher. For giggles, she'd joined a Ride-A-Long and gone patrolling with Anoka County deputies. She was hooked the moment she first heard the siren from inside the car; hooked like a largemouth on a Bass-oreno. She immediately quit her day job and became a nighttime dispatcher in a suburban police department. During the day she went to school, first junior college, then the academy—she was top of her class at both.

And she married a cop.

Eventually, Anne became the suburban department's first

female officer and still later, its first female detective. She soon caught the attention of the state attorney general's office, which hired her as an investigator, only they didn't give her much to do. She decided her employment was merely an affirmative action ploy and accepted a position with the Minnesota Bureau of Criminal Apprehension.

The BCA liked her so much they sent her to the FBI's National Center for the Analysis of Violent Crime in Quantico, Virginia, where she was specially trained to investigate mass murders and serial rape killings. Once again she scored first in her class and the FBI wanted to keep her. Instead, she returned to the BCA under the stipulation that the bureau would loan her to any local department that might require her expertise. The BCA agreed, then refused to allow her to work any case where it did not declare jurisdiction. So she joined the St. Paul Police Department, which was happy to accept her terms.

Now she commanded the unit, replacing the man who had hired her, taking the job many people thought I would eventually hold.

Anne ignored my presence while she examined the scene and interviewed the old woman. Finally, at her bidding, Curtis led me to where she was standing with McGaney and Casper. Casper was speaking earnestly, trying to impress the boss, using his hands and saying, "The most brutal murders are domestics, okay? When you get five, six gunshots like we have here, you're talking husband-wife, girlfriend-boyfriend, boyfriend-boyfriend, am I right?"

Anne said, "Probably."

Casper grinned at McGaney like he thought he deserved some ice cream and cake. McGaney rolled his eyes and shook his head.

Anne smiled at me when I approached. She had a smile that could melt snow; certainly it melted the resolve of many a stubborn suspect—it was her most endearing feature and I felt like slapping it off her face.

"I've seen highway workers move faster than you guys," I told them.

"We didn't keep you waiting, did we, Taylor?" McGaney asked.

"Screw you."

"Touchy," Casper said, then added, "I heard the shrink kicked you off the couch."

It occurred to me how much Casper's personality would benefit from a few well-placed blows to the face; make him a better human being. I formed a fist, prepared to drive my top two knuckles through Casper's fat, flat nose, but Anne pulled my arm down.

"What's with you?" she wanted to know.

I pulled away. "Whaddya think?"

"You're taking this way too seriously," McGaney warned.

"Think so?" I asked him. Yet I knew he was right. I used to be able to do it, look at death without letting my feelings get in the way—a policeman detached, making bad jokes to relieve the horror. Somewhere along the way I lost the knack. Still, I should have known better. As a homicide cop I was nearly perfect. I was better than Anne Scalasi. Better than anyone. For as long as I'd been able to do it.

"What are you doing here?" Anne demanded.

I answered her with short, curt sentences. "Amy Lamb called me. She left a message on my machine. She said she knew who killed both John Brown *and* Dennis Thoreau."

Casper's jaw dropped, actually dropped; McGaney's pen hung suspended in midair above the notebook; Anne's smile took on an ugly symmetry, frozen as it was on her face. She stared at me, as did the others. The traffic moved past us on Fratzke, sounding like surf in the distance. No one spoke, not until McGaney mumbled, "What do you know about Dennis Thoreau?"

"Only what I read in the newspapers."

"A neighbor reported seeing a man picking Thoreau's lock,"

Casper reported. "How 'bout that, Taylor? You wouldn't pick a lock illegally, would you?"

"Not if I thought someone was watching."

I looked at Anne Scalasi, our eyes fixed in a kind of death struggle: The first one to blink loses. Without prompting I announced, "I met Amy Lamb yesterday while investigating John Brown's murder. You remember John Brown?"

Anne did not respond, did not turn from my gaze.

"This morning she called me," I repeated. "She left a message on my machine. She said she knew who killed both Brown and Dennis Thoreau. I have the cassette if you want to hear it."

She didn't say if she did or didn't.

"I tried to reach her by telephone. I called her several times. There was no answer. I left a message on her machine. You probably heard it. I drove over. You questioned the old woman. You know the rest."

McGaney transcribed my remarks into a small notebook. "Where did she work?" he asked as he wrote.

"She answered the phones at C. C. Monroe's campaign headquarters."

Anne Scalasi looked away. Her gaze fell on the front door of the duplex, on the wagon men leaning against a trundle waiting for forensics to finish so they could wheel Amy down to the ambulance. She muttered something I couldn't make out, took my arm and led me toward the street. I had never seen her this agitated. Apparently, neither had McGaney and Casper. After taking a half dozen steps, Anne turned back to them.

"Find out how well the landlady knew the victim. Find out if she spent much time in the victim's house. Find out if she can tell us if anything is missing—VCR, TV, whatever. Especially look for personal objects that might be missing."

McGaney said, "Don't worry, Lieutenant. We're on top of it."

"I want a hard search, six-block radius. The shooter might have ditched the gun. Find it. And do a license plate check on every vehicle within the radius. Ask the neighbors if they've seen any unfamiliar vehicles parked nearby."

"Yes, ma'am," Casper said.

"There's an incredible amount of blood," Annie continued. "Make sure the techs check the bathroom and kitchen sinks, determine if the killer cleaned up before leaving the scene."

"We're on top of it, Lieutenant," McGaney repeated, miffed that Anne would treat him like a rookie; everything she requested was SOP.

"Get Mankamyer to work his magic," Anne added. "Find out if the bullets that killed Amy were fired from the same gun that killed Brown and Thoreau."

"Lieutenant . . ."

"Just do it, goddamn it!"

"Yes, Lieutenant."

Anne went to the driver's side of Curtis's car, opened the door.

"Lieutenant?" Curtis said, standing beside his squad.

Anne stopped, fixed the patrolman with her death-ray vision.

"Nothing," Curtis said.

I took the passenger seat, barely shutting the door before the car was in gear and Anne pulled away from the curb. She flipped a U-turn, drove two blocks and parked on the opposite side of the street. A van plastered with the call letters of a local TV station sped past us. "Vultures," she muttered, letting the engine idle for a moment before shutting it down, all the time gripping the steering wheel like it was the throat of her worst enemy.

Anne doesn't tan and she wears little makeup. Even so, her face appeared more pale than usual and her brown hair looked like it hadn't seen a stylist in quite a while. She released the wheel and leaned back against the seat, closing her eyes.

"Tired?" I asked.

She nodded. "Haven't gotten much sleep lately. Trouble at home."

"Really? I thought it might be a guilty conscience keeping you awake."

Anne did not respond, her eyes still closed.

"You and the old man going to be all right?" I asked, genuinely concerned now. Anne and I had never spoken about her husband, yet he was a part of nearly every conversation we'd had. We were partners for over four years, Anne Scalasi and I. We'd faced death together, standing back to back. Most people don't know what that means, the emotional bond it forges between a man and a woman. Still, we never did anything about it, even after Laura was killed and the sexual tension between us became almost unbearable. We stopped seeing each other regularly after I pulled the pin four years ago, yet the feelings, they were still there, just beneath the surface. I felt them as I sat next to her in the car, wondering how to phrase the question I needed to ask. She beat me to it.

"I didn't kill Dennis Thoreau."

"Okay," I said.

"I didn't," she repeated more emphatically.

"I believe you," I said.

"Only people without imagination kill. I have plenty of imagination. I want to get rid of someone, I'd find a few bindles of coke that he took out of his pocket and threw away when he saw me coming, at least ten ounces; he'd go away for a long time."

"That's one way," I agreed.

We sat silently for a few moments before Anne asked, "What would you do if I had killed him?"

"I'd give you up."

"Just like that?"

"It's against the law to aid and assist a felon. It's called 'accessory after the . . .' "

"I know what it's called," Anne said, frowning, her eyes still closed.

"What about Amy Lamb?"

That jolted her eyes open. "You think I'm responsible for that?"

"Yes."

"You sonuvabitch!"

"Fine, I'm a sonuvabitch. Now tell me what's going on. From the beginning."

"Don't talk to me in that tone . . ."

"You don't like it? Tell you what, Annie. I'll call Internal Affairs and the city attorney; we can all sit down together and have a pleasant chat. How 'bout that? Would you like that better?"

That slowed her down. She leaned forward and grasped the steering wheel at the ten and two positions. "How much do you know?" she asked quietly.

"I don't know anything. I'm only guessing."

"Go 'head and guess."

"You're protecting C. C. Monroe, gubernatorial candidate."

"Bullshit!"

I continued. "Marion Senske called her friend in the St. Paul Police Department and said, 'Please, please make the big, bad man go away.' You agreed."

"Bullshit!"

"Fine," I said. "What's your story?"

Anne sighed, then said, "Marion called me. Said Thoreau was blackmailing C. C. Asked me to put a stop to it. Quietly. I told her I couldn't do anything unless she signed a complaint."

"And?"

"And then I went over there."

"What were you thinking?"

"Marion's done a lot for women in this state," Anne answered in a weak and totally uncharacteristic voice. "She was very supportive when I helped found the Women Police Officers Association."

"Sisters united," I said.

"Something like that."

"So you went over there and discovered Thoreau's body."

"Yes. My first thought was that Marion had decided to take matters into her own hands. So, I searched the house. The tape was gone. That clinched it for me."

"Sure it was gone? How hard did you look?"

"You were there. Did you see anything I missed?"

"Was I there?"

"Cut it out, Taylor," she said, frowning.

"No, I didn't see anything you missed."

"Marion looks real good for it. She or C. C. Or both. Probably both."

"So, why don't you bust 'em?"

Anne didn't answer the question, so I did.

"Because Internal Affairs will want to know how you came to discover the body. They'll want to know how you came to learn about the videotape. They'll want to know why you didn't call it in immediately. And if you tell them, you're gone. The highest-ranking female police officer in the history of the department bounced for malfeasance, for crissake. On the other hand, if you don't come clean, somebody will get away with murder."

"No!" Anne screamed. "How dare you say that to me. You know me better than that."

"I'm not sure I know you at all."

"If C. C. Monroe is guilty I'll drive her to Shakopee myself. Count on it! But there can't be any doubt, reasonable or otherwise. Not this time. Before I accuse C. C. Monroe I have to have it locked seven ways to hell and back. I have to give her to the grand jury on a platter with an apple in her mouth—to the grand jury *and* the media. You can see that, can't you? If I told the truth about how I came to find Thoreau's body, how I came to accuse C. C., I'd be sacrificing my career for nothing. I don't have any evidence. And you know C. C. and Marion will deny everything. They'll claim it was politics. They'll claim I was doing it for the mayor. What's going to happen to the credibility of the police department if we're accused of investigating a gubernatorial candidate for political reasons? What's going to happen to *my* credibility?"

"Has it occurred to you that C. C. and Marion might be depending on that—you protecting them in order to protect yourself and the department?"

"No, no," Anne pleaded. "Not me, not the department. The case. I'm trying to protect the case. Can you imagine what a defense attorney would do . . ."

"The case, the department, you . . . What difference does it make? C. C. and Marion still get what they want."

"No, they won't. Taylor, what do you think this is all about? Why do you think I got you involved?"

"Why don't you tell me?"

"Okay, check my reasoning. Someone killed John Brown and we determined almost immediately that it was probably Joseph Sherman. Sherman killed Terrance Friedlander, who was running against C. C. Monroe. I know how you work. I know the first thing you would do is run to your computer . . ."

And then I understood. The realization hit me like a truck.

"You set me up!" I cried. "You bitch, you set me up! I was supposed to get caught in that house; that's why you had me followed and then pulled the tail when you knew where I was going, so you could catch me in the house."

"I needed something to justify an investigation."

"Fuck your investigation. You used me. We're supposed to be friends, Annie."

"I had to . . ."

"Jeezus, you were going to bust me, right? Bust me with a dead man at my feet and ten Gs in my pocket. To save my ass, I'd have to confess to why I was there and who hired me and then you could go after C. C. without having to admit your involvement."

"That's about right," Anne agreed.

"What about me?"

"You would have walked."

"Without my license? B and E is a felony. The Department of Public Safety can take my license for a felony."

"Oh, quit whining. I would have protected your license."

"Yeah, sure, after I spilled my guts about C. C. Monroe. Wouldn't that be good for business? Everyone loves a PI with a big mouth; I can see the clients lining up already. Goddamn it, you set me up, you bitch."

"Still, you have to admire the logic of it all. I just knew Marion would think I sent you to help her. She's so arrogant."

"She's arrogant? You bitch."

"Will you stop calling me that."

"Why? Isn't it politically correct?"

"I needed help. Your connection to Brown made you the logical choice."

"Then you should have asked me."

Anne turned her head away. "I figured if we worked it right, you'd never have to know what I did. Look, I didn't want you to think I was that stupid. I didn't want you to think less of me. Okay, maybe I'm being selfish. But you and I, there's something between us. Something strong. No, don't shake your head. I know you have my photograph on your desk."

"Well, you are my friend," I said.

"And I need that friendship now more than ever." Then with a voice that came from deep inside and got stronger with every word, Anne said, "But I think C. C. Monroe and Marion Senske are guilty of murder. If that's true, they're going down for it and I don't care what it costs. I don't care if it costs your friendship or my career. Nobody gets away with murder in this town. Nobody."

"Oh, Annie . . ."

"I need your help, Holland. There it is. I need your help."

I didn't know whether to wrap my arms around her or punch her in the mouth. I did neither. Maybe I did love her; her photograph was on my desk, after all. Maybe she loved me. Maybe if she wasn't married with three kids, maybe . . . But this thing with C. C. had nothing to do with that. This had to do with Anne Scalasi smashing the law, her career, her integrity all to hell—and then tricking me into cleaning up the mess—so she could remain a role model for women everywhere. Even now she was lying. She found the videotape, she must have. She put the tape in the camera for me to find, so I would have it in my possession when the cops busted Thoreau's house, so she would have an irrefutable excuse to go after C. C. That's the only way it made sense.

Still, I might have forgiven her. Except for Amy Lamb, 988 Fratzke Avenue, St. Paul, Ramsey County, Minnesota, USA . . .

"Bullshit," I said, using one of the lady's favorite curses. "You want my help? I get four hundred dollars a day plus expenses."

"Taylor . . ." My name died in her throat.

"Let's get something settled right now," I told her. "I don't give a damn about C. C. Monroe or Marion Senske or Dennis Thoreau or John Brown and right now you're not very high on my list, either. What I do care about is that little girl in there. She's dead because you didn't do your job when you had the chance. Now, I'll tell you what I'm going to do. I'm going to find her killer and stuff him in a sack and drop him off the Lake Street Bridge. You want to help, that's fine. Otherwise, stay the hell out of my way."

"You're not the law, anymore," Anne reminded me.

"Neither are you, Annie."

I opened the passenger door and slid out. The squad was already pulling away from the curb when I slammed it shut.

FOURTEEN

I HAD MANAGED only six blocks from Amy's duplex before raw sorrow closed my throat, making it nearly impossible to breathe. I pulled the Monza to the shoulder of the street and stopped. I thought of Amy's parents, afraid something like this might happen to their lovely daughter; I thought of her father taping the news of her death to the refrigerator door. I wanted to cry but did not. I had things to do and it was time I got to them.

I have always been able to recognize my own emotions and compensate for them. Love, fear, joy, pity: those were easy. Despair? Despair was the hardest of all. It took me a long time to turn it into something else. I turned it into anger, helping it along by cursing the cars that weaved around me, saluting the drivers with my middle finger when they leaned on their horns. Anger is good. You can do things with anger. You can function. Only you must be careful because anger can quickly turn to hate and hate colors everything: the way you walk, the way you talk, what you see and what you don't. Hate makes you do things that are not in your best interest. Hate makes you kill.

Louise was sitting behind the reception desk at C. C. Monroe's campaign headquarters, paging through the latest edition of

Time magazine, her eyeglasses attached to a gold chain and hanging around her throat like a necklace. She looked up when I entered, set the glasses on her nose and smiled. Apparently she hadn't heard the bad news. Well, she wasn't going to hear it from me.

I asked her if she remembered me. She said she did. "Did you ever reach Amy?" she asked.

"No," I said. I told her I was worried. "When did she leave?"

"About eight forty-five. I guess she wasn't feeling well."

"Yet, she came in."

"Amy is pretty dedicated. She arrived early, maybe a quarter to, and read the papers. It's the first thing we do, see what they're saying about Representative Monroe."

"Then what happened?"

Louise seemed mystified by the question. "Nothing happened," she said. "Why should something happen?"

"You said she wasn't feeling well."

"About, I don't know, quarter after, she said she was feeling poorly and she was going to take a walk, get some fresh air. She asked me to cover the phones for her. She was quite pale."

"Where did she go?"

"I don't know, toward the capitol. Why?"

"Then what happened?"

Louise shrugged in reply. "She came back, made a phone call; she still looked pale and shaky and I said she should go home if she was feeling poorly. She said she would."

"That was about eight forty-five?"

"Yes."

"Does Amy have a car? Did she drive?"

"No, she takes the bus."

"Maybe a boyfriend picked her up," I asked hopefully.

"She doesn't have a boyfriend," Louise replied quickly. "At least that's what she said."

"Another friend, someone who might have given her a ride home?"

Louise shrugged again. "I don't think she knows too many people here, she's from outstate. Anyway, she didn't wait for a ride. She just left."

I returned to my car. Sitting behind the steering wheel, I made out a quick timetable, noting the associated events surrounding Amy's death:

7:45 — Amy arrives at campaign headquarters, reads newspapers.
8:10 — Amy takes walk.
8:45 — Amy returns, calls me at office.
8:45 — C. C. calls me at home.
8:50 — Amy takes bus to duplex.
9:30 — I arrive at State Capitol.
9:45 — Amy calls me at office.
11:45 — I arrive at coffeehouse.
12:00 — C. C. arrives at coffeehouse.
12:00 — Landlord leaves duplex.
12:15 — Amy calls me at office.
1:30 — Landlord returns to duplex.
2:30 — C. C. and I leave coffeehouse.
3:00 — I reach office, listen to messages.
4:15 — I reach duplex.

The most important times were these:

12:15 — Amy calls me at office.
1:30 — Landlord returns to duplex.

Seventy-five minutes. More than enough time to die.

And where was I while Amy was being killed? I was sitting in a second-rate coffeehouse baby-sitting C. C. Monroe, supplying her with an alibi, waiting for a blackmailer that as far as I could prove didn't even exist.

I returned to the campaign offices. Louise was still sitting behind the desk.

"Who else knew Amy was going home early?"

"What?"

"Who else knew when Amy left?"

Louise seemed confused. "I don't know, anybody who worked here, I guess. It wasn't a secret. Why are you asking me this? What's going on? Is Amy all right?"

"Did anybody ask for her specifically?"

"No. Yes, well, she did get a phone call right after she left."

"From whom?"

"I don't know, I didn't recognize the voice. The caller asked for Amy. I told her she just went home. She thanked me and hung up. What's the problem?"

"She?"

"Yes, a woman."

Anne Scalasi and McGaney were entering campaign head-quarters as I was exiting; I held the door open for them. I didn't smile in recognition. They didn't either.

"Taylor, you mess up this investigation I'll have your ass," Anne told me.

I ignored her.

I parked in a slot reserved for the representative from the district where I live and walked quickly from the ramp to the State Office Building. It was late in the day and most of the people who worked there were either gone or on their way out. I punched the blue elevator button and rode up to C. C.'s floor. A woman was standing at a desk near C. C.'s office, pulling a plastic hood over a word processor. I walked past her to C. C.'s door. It was locked.

"She's not here," the woman said to my back. "No one's here."

"You know where she is?"

"Duluth. She's campaigning in Duluth."

"All day?"

"She had a late start, didn't leave until about three."

"Marion Senske?"

"Is with her," the woman answered. "You with the press?"

"Does it show?"

The woman looked me over, moving her eyes from my Nikes to my jeans to my sports jacket and white shirt. "Who else can get away with dressing so casually?"

I walked with her to the elevator.

"What do you do here?"

"I'm a secretary. There are about a dozen of us. We handle five, six reps each."

"You screen her visitors?"

"C. C.'s? Sure."

"Did she have any today?"

"No. She didn't have any appointments scheduled because she wasn't supposed to be here."

"Maybe a young woman without an appointment, Amy Lamb, five-three, light brown hair?"

"I really couldn't say. I only work half days when the legislature isn't in session; I came in at noon. Representative Monroe wasn't here when I arrived. And when she did come in, she only stayed a few minutes."

The elevator doors slid open before we reached them and a member of the State Capitol Security Force stepped out.

"Evening, John," the woman said.

"Ellen," he said in reply, nodding to her and then to me. He walked past us down the corridor, shaking the knob on each office door as he went.

"What do you think of Representative Monroe?" I asked the secretary when we were in the elevator going down.

"You gonna quote me?"

"Nope."

"Promise?"

"Promise."

"I think she's a lightweight. If it wasn't for Marion Senske, she'd be selling cosmetics door-to-door."

"C. C. Monroe and Marion Senske killed both John Brown and Dennis Thoreau," I said aloud as I drove I-94, taking the bridge across the Mississippi, heading back to Minneapolis. "They did it to silence them so C. C. could win the election. Amy Lamb figured it out when she read the newspaper articles about them. She confronted C. C. and Marion, but they blew her off. Amy decided to call me; she called the number on my card, my office number. C. C. and Marion beat her to me, calling me at home. They invented the blackmailer to keep me occupied and to provide C. C. with an ironclad alibi. Meanwhile, they sent someone to kill Amy.

"No, stop it! Stop it!"

Don't fall into that trap, I told myself.

I've seen it happen before; I nearly did it myself a couple of times when I was with Homicide. You want so desperately to be right that you make up the answer first, then arrange the facts to fit. Only, in the end, the answer you invent won't make you any happier than not knowing at all. The trick is to keep everything in its true size, to not lose perspective. Failure of perspective is what nails you. Keep the crime separate from your life, don't allow what's going on around you to affect your judgment, don't impose anything on the victim or the suspect that comes from somewhere else—keep it clean.

"Suck it up and do it right," I told the reflection in my rearview mirror. "Just this one last time, do it right."

FIFTEEN

DETECTIVE WORK isn't mathematics—known variables adding up to a logical conclusion. It's random, like a maze that more often leads to a dead end than to cheese. I'm the rat, scurrying along, running into walls, following my nose until I either find the meal or starve to death.

As soon as I reached my office, I removed the tape from my answering machine and replaced it with a fresh cassette. I sealed the cassette in an envelope, wrapped a thick rubber band around it and put it in my safe.

I fired up my PC and transcribed all my notes onto the hard drive, organizing them as best I could. When I finished I backed away from the machine. *Think about it,* I told myself. If I'd been at home I'd have gone out to the driveway and shot baskets. Instead I found a jazz station on the radio and sang along with Diane Schuur and Harry Connick Jr., cleaning as I sang, dusting all my nooks and crannies. I was particularly careful while dusting my hockey stick, the one Wayne Gretzky broke against the North Stars way back when he played for Edmonton. And the "homer hanky" I waved when the Minnesota Twins won the 1987 and 1991 World Series. And the framed photograph of me and Kirby Puckett—Kirby is the one in the Twins uniform; I'm the one with the stupid grin.

I remembered a few more details, formed a few more thoughts while I dusted, and keyed them into the system. I went to my windows, watched the lights of the city and shoppers strolling the Nicollet Mall.

The Nicollet Mall is our answer to New York's Fifth Avenue except there is no automobile traffic. Only buses. People meander the winding streets, crossing with impunity, queuing up at the shops and restaurants, listening to the street musicians who play for the change the people toss into their open instrument cases. Periodically the cops will drive the musicians out, but they always return. One musician, a tall black man with tired eyes whom I call "the Saxman," always plays the same corner, the one where Mary Tyler Moore tossed her hat in the air at the beginning of her TV program. I once heard Sonny Rollins in concert and I swear this guy could give him a run. Maybe once, twice a week I'll drop a few bills into his red felt case and listen to him play. He'll see me and nod. I nod back. We never speak to each other. What's there to say? "Man, why are you playing saxophone on a street corner?" "Man, why are you listening?"

The best time to be on the mall is at noon when thousands of young women scramble over the street, trying to get their shopping done before the lunch hour expires. Especially in the spring, when they shed their bulky winter garments and flit from shop to shop like butterflies in search of a place to land. The most attractive young women in America come from Minnesota's small towns, filling the Twin Cities' office towers with their freshness and exuberance, with their wholesome and wholly unaffected beauty. You can lean on the lamppost at Seventh and Nicollet and watch them—watch them while the Saxman plays soft and low, watch them as they move through their lives completely unaware of life's cruelties and dangers. They fill the air with their sweetness; you can breathe it in and hold it like the bouquet of a fine red wine. Sometimes it's enough to make you cry. And when the Saxman is really on, you watch the young women in their spring dresses and you pray that it will always be this way, that you'll never find one of them lying spread-eagled on the hood of a car in a dark parking ramp somewhere, her body ripped, her beauty wasted. Like I have.

I thought of Amy Lamb and went back to my cleaning.

I was sitting at the PC, preparing a list of names and on-line directories to drag them through, when my telephone rang. The voice that answered my hello surprised me. It belonged to Cynthia Grey.

"I need to speak with you," she said.

"Go 'head."

"In person."

"I'm busy."

"It's important."

What was important to her wasn't necessarily important to me, I decided. But I was just about finished in my office and the prospect of going home alone, of facing another lonely night, this one filled with images of Amy Lamb . . . I asked Cynthia where I should meet her and she directed me to a dive on Franklin near the freeway in Minneapolis.

"For someone who doesn't drink, Counselor, you seem to spend a lot of time in bars."

SIXTEEN

L E CHATEAU was a blue-collar strip joint located in a neighborhood where men slept in the open using newspapers for blankets and their hands for pillows. Rectangular, with a flat roof and no windows, it bore not even a faint resemblance to a French castle; the only daylight that ever made its way inside seeped through the spy hole in the thick metal door. Above the door a neon sign flashed LIVE NUDES LIVE. Inside another sign read TABLE DANCES $15. DON'T BE OVERCHARGED. It was suspended from the ceiling by a thin chain. Beneath it a bored, overweight bouncer collected the cover.

"I'm looking for a . . ."

He glanced up wearily at my words.

"Never mind."

Men were gathered in groups around six-chair tables, others sat alone, still others crowded the brass rail fixed to the stage, dollar bills set in front of them. Most were peering through cigarette smoke at the anatomically correct Barbie doll who swung from the pole in the center of the stage, nude except for pearls, stiletto heels and a toothy grin. Some were watching the highlights of last night's football game on ESPN, their heads twisted toward the TV above the bar.

There was no sound except for the music the woman danced to. The men watched the show without comment, without smiling, without any overt sign of admiration or appreciation or arousal. Five men dressed in suits sat in a booth just to the right of the stage, two white guys and three Japanese. They could have been playing draw poker for what their faces gave away; they looked like they'd been sitting there for five hours. The audience did not even applaud when pearls finished her act and was replaced at the pole by a large brunette.

"Herrrrrre's Joannie," an unseen announcer intoned over the scratchy speaker system. No one seemed to care.

I found Cynthia Grey sitting alone in a booth watching Joannie, not really seeing her. She smiled at me when I caught her attention.

"Mr. Taylor," she said.

"It doesn't bother you," I asked, "being alone in a strip joint with a bunch of overwrought men?"

She shook her head almost absentmindedly. "The only women in here who count are naked. A woman in street clothes might as well be invisible."

"You sound like you've spent a lot of time in places like this," I told her. She flashed me a look; was it anger? No. Exasperation. She turned back to the stage and I waved down a waitress, a tall young woman with blond hair and a mid-western smile—she looked like she had just finished feeding the chickens and was about to bake some bread. "Boy, is she out of place," I said after she left with my order.

"She goes on in thirty minutes," Cynthia assured me without expression.

I admit to looking at the waitress much differently when she returned with my Pig's Eye beer.

"My kind of joint," I told Cynthia. "Warm. Cozy."

Cynthia did not respond, focusing instead on Joannie, who had begun drawing circles on the floor with her vagina.

"Why do they do it?" I wondered out loud.

"For the money, Mr. Taylor. Why else? They do it for the money."

"It couldn't possibly be worth it. I mean, how much can you make swinging from a pole, doing lap dances for fifteen bucks a throw?"

"Enough to pay your way through law school," Cynthia said, then swung around, facing me.

"You interest me, Counselor," I told her.

The waitress returned and I ordered another round; Cynthia was drinking ginger ale.

"Try not to judge people without getting to know them first," Cynthia told me. "The woman who's dancing now . . ."

I turned to look at Joannie.

"Her husband deserted her after their third child was born, left her penniless; said he couldn't take the pressure of being a parent anymore."

"What's she doing here?"

"Surviving."

The waitress hurried back with our drinks and asked if I wanted to run a tab. I told her no and took a five from my pocket. "Keep it," I told her when she reached for my dollar-five change, and she actually smiled. (And you thought Cary Grant was slick.) When the waitress left, Cynthia moved to my side of the booth. (Cary Grant *and* David Niven.) She wrapped her hands around my arm and looked into my eyes.

"Like I said, you interest me, Counselor."

Right on cue a plump man with short, graying hair slid into the booth across from us. Cynthia gripped my arm tighter.

"I'm Joseph Sherman," the man said.

My first impulse was to wrestle him to the ground and start beating him about the head and shoulders. Instead I took a sip of my beer; not too much, I wanted the bottle full in case I decided to hit him with it.

"Harboring fugitives, Counselor?"

"It wouldn't be the first time," she told me.

I chuckled and said, mostly to myself, "I guess she's right."

"Who?" Cynthia asked.

"This morning a woman told me that we don't always do what's in our best interests. I guess she's right."

I looked across the booth. Sherman was nervous, measuring every shadow, recording every ambient sound, swiveling his head back and forth to make sure nothing could sneak up on him, his right hand in the pocket of a brand-spanking-new silk sports jacket. He also wore tailored wool slacks, black dress shoes and a white cotton shirt that still held the original wrinkles. The guy'd just got out of the joint and he was better dressed than I was.

"They say you killed John Brown," I told him.

"He didn't do it," Cynthia answered, tightening her grip on my arm.

"Sure of that, are you?"

"He called me early this afternoon. He remembered my name; John Brown gave it to him. He explained what happened and I believe him. I knew we needed help and I thought of you."

"How nice." It suddenly occurred to me how tired I was. I felt a yawn coming on and let it go, yawning in Joseph Sherman's face. He didn't react the way I thought he would. Instead of becoming angry, his face cracked like he was about to cry.

"What do you want me to do?" I asked him.

"Miss Grey said you would help me. Miss Grey said . . . she said you could fix things."

I looked at Cynthia. "She said that?"

"Will you listen to him? Will you do that much?"

I turned back to Sherman. "Take your hand out of your pocket!" I shouted at him and like a startled child, he did. His hand was empty.

"Can I get you something?" the waitress asked, summoned by my voice.

"No," I told her. "Sorry." She smiled again but not as brightly and moved away.

"All right, I'm listening," I said in what my daughter used to call my "indoor voice."

"I didn't do Brownie," Sherman said. "I couldn't kill him, as God is my judge, I couldn't kill anybody. He was dead when I got back . . ."

"Tell it from the beginning," I said.

"You're not going to believe this . . ."

"Probably not," I agreed. I looked at Cynthia, glanced at her hands, then back at her face again. She relaxed her grip.

"It really began six years ago," Sherman said. "They say I hit a guy with my car, a politician named Friedlander."

"I know all about Terrance Friedlander," I told him.

"You do?" asked Cynthia, somewhat skeptically.

"I'm a trained detective," I told her.

"I was framed," Sherman continued, talking quickly and without confidence. "They say I got drunk and hit Friedlander with my car, only it wasn't me."

"I'm supposed to believe this?" I asked him. "Man, you pleaded guilty, remember?"

"My lawyer said to. He said they had me by the short hairs. He said if I didn't make a deal they'd put me away for manslaughter, maybe. I was a drunk. I was an alcoholic. All this started comin' down on me like heavy rain. I didn't know what to do. I didn't have any friends and I didn't have any money. What would you do?"

I ignored the question.

"Anyway, up in the Heights after I dried out, I got to thinking about it. Okay, maybe I'm not so bright, it took me a while, but I got to thinking. They said when they found my car it smelled of whiskey. I was a vodka man; that's all I drank, vodka. Vodka is odorless. Okay, so now I start thinking some more. I ask myself, Who benefits most? Friedlander buys the farm, who gets the most out of it? Not me, man."

"Who?" I asked.

"C. C. Monroe," Cynthia answered.

Loud laughter came from a table in the center of the room where four young men looking like a college chess team were hooting over the silicone-augmented physique of still another dancer. It was matched by laughter of a different kind from two men who were leaning on the bar and chiding a third man who kept insisting that the Vikings needed a new quarterback, one who wasn't black. One of his companions reminded him that Warren Moon won a division championship, which was a damn sight more than Gannon or Salisbury ever did. Still, the man was not to be pacified. He reminded his friends that the Vikes had a black coach, the Gophers had a black athletic director and a black basketball coach; that the city of Minneapolis had a black mayor—a woman to boot. "Is a white quarterback too much to ask? I need somebody to root for!"

Who said we have poor race relations in Minnesota?

"Well?" Cynthia prodded.

"I like Moon," I said.

"Wha . . . what are you talking about?"

"What are you talking about?"

"C. C. Monroe is a murderer."

"Who says?"

"I say," said Sherman.

"Uh-huh."

"I know what you're thinkin'. You think I'm a an ex-con, okay? You ain't gonna believe me. Ain't no one gonna believe me because I'm an ex-con. I'm nothin', that's what you're thinkin'."

The look in his eyes encouraged me to lean back in the booth and take hold of the Pig's Eye bottle by the neck. I wondered what he'd been like before Oak Park Heights, before prison started working on him. Was he an amiable drunk or mean? Was he a clear and present danger or just a poor schlepper trying to get by? I wondered what he was like then because I knew what he was like now. Now he was a hardened criminal. Prison does that. We take the men and women who have the most difficulty functioning in society, the poorest, the least educated, the most socially maladjusted, and we lock them up in cages for years as if that's supposed to rehabilitate them. It doesn't. But it does change them, yes sir. It turns them into the most dangerous human beings on earth. And after we feel they've been changed enough, we abruptly release them, kick them back into the mainstream and tell them, "Be good."

Joseph Sherman would be going back to prison. If not today then tomorrow; if not for John Brown, then for something else. He was just marking time outside and we both knew it. Joseph Sherman was born for the prison yard; he became its child the day the iron door first clanged shut behind him.

Suddenly I felt sympathy for him. And embarrassment for myself. He was right, I had dismissed him simply because he was an ex-con. I released my grip on the bottle. "I'm listening," I told him.

Sherman smiled a slow, knowing smile; maybe he thought he had won something. "I know I don't have no proof," he said. "So, what I did was, when I got out, I called Monroe."

"Why?"

"Blackmail."

"No."

"Yes. I figure this: I tell her I'm gonna call the cops, I'm gonna spill it that she killed Friedlander unless she pays me not to. She pays me, that's my evidence. I take the money to the cops, they gotta reopen the investigation."

"You're not exactly a rocket scientist are you, Sherman?"

Cynthia was outraged by my remark. "Taylor!" she cried loudly.

Sherman was just as angry. "It worked, didn't it, smart mouth?" he said. "It worked twice."

"Did it?"

"This is what happened," Sherman continued. "What I did, I kept calling Monroe's campaign headquarters, kept calling for weeks until I finally got past this snotty receptionist. I tell Monroe what's what, but she plays it real cool, see. She says go ahead, call the cops, call the media, she doesn't care. Only the next day a man calls me; says he's calling on 'the representative's behalf.' That's what he says. I say, ten thousand dollars. He says to meet him in the parking lot for the payoff at midnight Saturday. I bring Brownie 'cuz I figure I need a witness and 'cuz, well, you know, it was a little scary. So we leave the house and we stop and have a few beers and then we go to the lot—it was off West Seventh Street—and we wait. After a while, 'cuz of them beers, I gotta piss, so I went to the gas station. When I got back, it's like a quarter past twelve, and Brownie is leaning against the door; I figured he's passed out. Only when I shake him, God, the blood . . . I got scared and ran. What would you have done?"

"I would have waited for the cops."

"They would have thrown me in jail."

"What the hell do you think they're going to do now?"

"You're not helping," Cynthia told me.

"Was anyone else in the lot?" I asked Sherman. "Any other vehicles?"

"I don't remember any."

"Witnesses? Someone who might have heard something, seen something?"

"There was this woman," he answered, excited.

"What woman?"

"When I found Brownie, I saw her walking."

"Away?"

"No. Toward us, toward the truck."

"What did she look like?"

"I don't really know, 'cuz I was, I was scared, you know? I remember she was tall. Five-ten, six feet, that's tall for a woman. Only I didn't get a good look, what with Brownie, and I started running."

"You carrying?" I asked him.

Sherman looked at Cynthia.

"I asked you a question," I said loudly, startling him again.

Sherman nodded.

"Nine-millimeter?"

"A Taurus," Sherman said.

Low-end semiautomatic, manufactured in Brazil, holds fifteen rounds, retails for about four hundred bucks. "Where did you get it?" I asked.

"I know a guy."

"How much?"

"Six fifty."

"You were ripped off."

Sherman shrugged.

"You buy it before or after Brown was killed?"

"After," he said. "After, I swear."

"John Brown was killed with a nine."

Sherman shook his head.

"Let's go back to the frame. Why pick on you?"

"I don't know."

"Did you know C. C. Monroe?"

"No."

"Marion Senske?"

"No. I don't think so. In those days, I wasn't exactly keeping up with, you know, current events, okay? But I don't know those people. None of 'em."

"How did they get your car?"

"Must've stole it."

"How did they get your keys?"

"I don't know. Maybe I left 'em in the ignition. I was doin' stuff like that back then, you know, 'cuz of the vodka."

I turned to Cynthia. "You said he contacted you early this afternoon. When this afternoon?"

Cynthia looked at Sherman. "About one, one-thirty?"
Sherman nodded.

I turned back to Sherman. "Where did you call from?"

"What?"

"Where did you call from?"

"What difference does it make? A pay phone. A pay phone off Como and Raymond. In St. Paul. Near the U."

Plenty of time, I decided. Kill Amy, clean up, drive five, six miles. No problem. "Do you have a car?" I asked him.

"No, the cops got my vehicle. I've been using the bus, taxis."

"Spending all that telemarketing money," I volunteered. He couldn't have managed it with the bus, but a taxi? Taxis were easy to check; Annie was probably already on it.

I tensed. Part of me was yelling, *Take him, take him!* Another part was saying, *Wait, wait.* Wait for what? Maybe he's innocent. So what? Take him and let Anne Scalasi sort it out. What about Cynthia? What about her? She could get in trouble. And this guy could be a murderer. *Think it through,* I urged myself. He has a gun, a Taurus, puts a hole in you the size of a softball. I flashed on Amy, the holes in her. *Think it through.* There's a table between us and you're sitting down and Cynthia is holding your arm. Not good. See how it plays.

"Why did you wait until this afternoon to call the counselor?" I asked.

"'Cuz that's when I knew for sure."

"Knew what?"

"Knew about her. I told you it worked twice. The first time I called, she sent someone to kill me, only they made a mistake and got Brownie instead. This time she was there, man. She was there."

"You're talking about C. C., aren't you?"

"Yeah. I call her this morning. I tell her I know everything. I tell her to meet me at this coffeehouse near the U. Sure as shit, she shows up."

He leaned back, proud of himself.

"Did you approach her," I asked, knowing the answer.

"No. No way, not after what happened the first time."

"I see," I said, not sure if I did or not, taking a second to think it over.

More people had crowded into Le Chateau, jockeying for a place at the bar or the rail. Over the sound system, Queen intoned "We Are the Champions," the nude dancer catching every dramatic movement. The college kids had given up their hollering and were now sitting motionless, just as bored as everyone else; the football fans at the bar stared quietly at their beers, nothing more to say to each other.

"You want my advice?" I asked Sherman.

"Yeah."

"Give yourself up."

"Some advice."

"And give me the piece," I told him. I wanted the gun, I wanted it bad. I held out my hand and willed him to slip it into my palm. He didn't.

"I have to think."

"Listen to me," I said. "Are you listening? A young woman was killed today; she was killed shortly before you called Cynthia."

"What's that got to do with me?"

"This morning she left me a message saying she knew who murdered *both* Brown and a second man. Her name was Amy Lamb; she was C. C. Monroe's receptionist, the one you couldn't get past. The second man was Dennis Thoreau. He was C. C. Monroe's ex-boyfriend."

"Dennis Thoreau?"

"If you're not careful, I mean real careful, the cops are going to blame you for everything. You have to give yourself up."

Stupid, stupid, stupid. I should never have told him about Thoreau and Amy. I knew it was stupid the minute I did it. Five minutes ago Sherman was a frightened, beaten man.

Now he was desperate. Stupid, Taylor. Stupid.

"I ain't gonna give myself up. I ain't goin' back to prison," he said loud enough for several heads to turn.

"What's going on?" one of the heads wanted to know.

"Counselor, talk to your client," I told Cynthia.

"I ain't goin' back, Miss Grey," Sherman told her.

"I think Taylor is right . . ."

"No."

"I can help you if you give yourself up. There's nothing I can do while you're running."

Sherman shook his head violently. "No!" he shouted and sprang to his feet, a bird flushed out of the corn, trying to outfly the shotguns. I reached for his arm; I have no idea what I expected to accomplish. He pushed my hand away and slipped the Taurus out of his pocket and pointed it at me. It had a satin nickel finish and a Brazilian walnut grip. I stared at it for what seemed like a long time.

Sherman tried to run for the door. Cynthia intercepted him. No one else said a word, no one else moved.

Cynthia ignored the gun and held Sherman's arms, talking to him softly. He maneuvered around her in a kind of bucolic dance, then slipped past the bouncer and out the metal door. Cynthia, looking defeated, returned to the booth and sat across from me. I finished the Pig's Eye. It was tepid.

"Now what?" I asked her.

"He said he'd meet me tomorrow morning. Nine o'clock. I'll take him in."

"If he shows."

"Yeah, if he shows."

"Don't waste your time, Counselor," I warned her. "This guy has a one-way ticket back to prison and if you're not careful you could end up sharing his cell."

"He came to me for help. What would you do?" she asked quietly.

"Mind my own business."

"This is my business."

"Have it your own way." I stood up. "C'mon, I'll walk you to your car."

I offered her my hand. She took it and I helped her to her feet.

"There are a couple of things you should know, Counselor," I told her once she was standing next to me.

"What?"

"I'm going to find out who killed Amy Lamb. If it's Sherman, I'm going to hand him to the county attorney with a ribbon tied around his ass."

"And I'll defend him," Cynthia vowed. "What else?"

"You seem to care about people, especially people who need caring for. It's a quality I appreciate."

"It's nothing special."

"Yes, it is."

It was nearly midnight and cold. Not cold enough for your breath to steam, but cold enough to remind you that it was mid-October in Minnesota; baseball season was suddenly a long time ago.

Cynthia's car was parked on the wrong side of Franklin Avenue near the bridge. We were strolling past an ancient gas station, boarded up and long forgotten, when I heard the soft shuffle of feet behind us. Up ahead was an alley. There was no traffic.

"You should have found a safer place to park," I said.

"What?"

I pushed Cynthia flat against the wall and turned, keeping her behind me. The footsteps belonged to a large black teenager, maybe sixteen, who wore an Oakland Raiders football jacket. The jacket was old and creased. The switchblade in his hand was shiny and new. Another black teenager stepped out of the alley. He wore the same colors.

"Hey, motherfucker, up with it!" the first mugger shouted. The second mugger smiled.

"Guys, I'm in a real bad mood," I warned them, thinking about the Beretta that was doing me a helluva lot of good in the drawer of my waterbed. The first mugger moved in close, too close for his own good, and started to Hollywood me, brushing the blade of his knife along my cheek, telling me I was a smart motherfucker, telling me what he was going to do to my woman after he took care of me because I was such a smart motherfucker.

"Is that how you talk to Sally Washington?" Cynthia asked in a loud voice. "What would she say if she heard you talking like that, if she knew what you were doing?"

I knew Sally Washington; I'd met her once. She was much loved in the poorer quarters—an activist who disregarded politics, who was more interested in actually helping people; a midwestern Mother Teresa. Apparently the muggers knew her, too.

The second mugger took a step backward. "You know Sally?" he asked tentatively.

"I know Sally. I work with Sally. I work with her at the children's clinic; I helped her get the funding."

"You don't know Sally," the first mugger insisted.

"Yeah? Let's go over to the clinic and ask her. Right now. You can explain what you're doing, pulling knives on people . . ."

"The clinic isn't open," the first mugger said.

"The clinic is always open," Cynthia told him.

"That's right," the second mugger said. "C'mon, man, let's go."

"No, wait," Cynthia said. She fished in her oversized purse and took out her wallet. From the wallet she extracted a fistful of bills and held them out to the second mugger. "Here. You need money that bad, here, take mine."

"No, man," the kid said, refusing the cash. "You a friend of Sally's. We can't take your money."

"Why not? You think Sally will be impressed that you only

rob people who aren't her friends? Here, take my money."

"We don't mean nothin'," the first mugger said.

"You don't mean nothin'? What's that? You need money, you need a job, I can help you. You want to steal, you want to hurt people, here, take my money. Hurt me."

The first mugger lowered the blade, the tip now pointing at Cynthia's knee. I didn't wait to see if he was moved by what she was telling him. I grabbed his knife hand with my left and with my right I delivered a four-knuckle strike to his throat and then drove a blade kick straight down on his kneecap. The gentleman who taught me that particular kick had made me practice until I could snap a broom handle with one thrust. Believe me, a knee is considerably less resilient than a broom handle. As the first mugger went down, I pivoted toward his buddy. He tried to throw a punch at my face. I ducked and threw a ridge hand to his solar plexus. He staggered. I stepped behind him and followed up with a claw hand to his throat, flipping him backward onto the concrete. Time to leave.

I grabbed Cynthia's arms and tried to pull her away. She resisted.

"What are you doing?" she wanted to know.

"What's it look like?"

"Those poor kids. . ." Cynthia broke free and turned back toward the muggers. The second one was standing, helping the first to his feet. "Wait, wait!" Cynthia called to them as they staggered down the sidewalk and past the gas station. "I'm sorry!"

"Counselor . . ." I said, shaking my head.

"Why did you do that? You didn't have to hurt them . . ."

"They might have *killed* us."

"They were going away; they were going to leave us alone."

"Did you want to bet your life on it?"

"This is BS. You're just trying to prove what a macho guy you are. Well, I'm not impressed."

Perfect. Just perfect. The perfect end to a perfect day. So

much for helping distressed damsels in the nineties.

"I said you cared about people, Counselor. Now I think maybe you care too much. It's affecting your judgment; it's making you vulnerable."

"Who asked you?"

I followed her to the car, listening to her knocks. "Mean, ruthless, cruel and uncaring," she called me. Yes, well, perhaps. Still, a man's gotta do what a man's gotta do. That's trite, I know. But it's my only excuse.

"You're nothing but a damn cop." Cynthia spat and slammed her car door shut. I walked back to my own car feeling let down, a frosty breeze causing me to shiver, wondering why I should care what a do-good nut case like Cynthia Grey thought of me.

SEVENTEEN

I DON'T KNOW what temperature the Mr. Coffee brews at, but I decided it was much too high when the first sip burned the inside of my lip. It was only 7:15 in the morning yet I had been awake for hours—hadn't really gone to sleep, what with images of Amy Lamb's blood-splattered body filling my head. I had returned to my office early enough to be the first car in my parking lot and spent the dawn retrieving the cassette tape from my safe and typing notes into my hard drive.

I was standing near the Mr. Coffee when the knock came. It was a light knock, almost as if my visitor was afraid I would answer. I swung the door open slowly. Before me stood a woman cradling an open purse in her arms.

"Hello, Louise," I said. "May I help you?"

"Are we alone, Mr. Taylor?" she asked.

I answered yes.

That's all she wanted to know. She reached into her purse and pulled out a small semiautomatic handgun. I didn't wait to determine make or model. I threw the coffee at her and jerked the gun from her hand while she screamed in pain and terror. She dropped the purse, both hands going to her face. My instinct was to punch her. Instead, I pushed her hard into the chair in front of my desk. She nearly tipped it over. I unloaded the gun, a .25 Ruger. All God's children have guns these days, praise the NRA.

Louise was in pretty rough shape, doubled over in the chair, trying in vain to rub the scald from the hot coffee away. I slipped the gun into my pocket and bent to recover my mug and her purse. Both were sitting in a puddle, about a half-cup's worth of Cameron's Colombian Supremo that had missed her face. *I'll have to mop that up later,* I decided as I wiped the mug dry and refilled it; the purse could dry itself. I sat behind my desk in front of the woman, who was just beginning to regain her senses.

"I could call the cops and have you arrested for attempted murder or I can shoot you and call it self-defense," I told her. "Which do you prefer?" From her expression I could tell neither suggestion appealed to her. "What are you doing here?"

She didn't answer so I dumped the contents of her purse on my desk. I rummaged through it, finding a thick paperback entitled *Discovering Your Homosexuality: The Joy and the Pain.* She gasped when I picked it up and began to thumb through it, stopping at a page with a corner folded down. The chapter headline read "Are You Gay?"

"I am not queer," she insisted.

What, did my lips move? "I believe the proper term is 'gay.'"

"I know what the proper term is. I'm not . . . gay!"

"I really don't care." I tossed the book on the pile and said, "Listen, I've been treating all this somewhat lightheartedly, mostly because you're the injured party here. But if you don't start talking to me real fast . . ." I picked up my coffee mug. "Things could get a mite nasty." I took a sip and set the mug back on the desk. The subtlety was not wasted on her. Only, rather than answering my question she asked one of her own.

"Why didn't you tell me about Amy?" she sobbed.

I lied. "I wanted what information you could give me before your grief confused the facts. I wanted it clean," I said.

"Why didn't you tell me?" she sobbed louder.

And then the truth. "I didn't want to be the one to break it to you." It was selfish, I know. I wanted to avoid Louise's pain and anguish; like a ballplayer who turns his back on a fallen teammate, I just didn't want to see it. Sometimes I'm a helluva guy.

"I loved her!" she wailed.

"I understand," I said, glancing down at the paperback.

"No you don't!" she screamed. "I mean I loved her. No, that's not what I mean. I mean . . . Oh God!"

I watched the woman sob into her hands and I might have felt sorry for her, I might have hugged her shoulders and said, "There, there," except for the gun in my pocket. And except for the words floating back to me, Detective Casper's words: "When you get five, six gunshots like we have here, you're talking husband-wife, girlfriend-boyfriend, boyfriend-boyfriend, am I right?" Yeah, he was. The most brutal homicides take place in the closest relationships, and for pure savagery no one can beat homosexuals. With homosexuals you get true crimes of passion—not passion over which TV program to watch or who gets the drumstick or who owes who money—I mean passion as in if-I-can't-have-you-no-one-can-have-you passion. The real McCoy.

"You and Amy were lovers?" I asked.

The woman shook her head no. Then she shouted, "No!"

Now I really was confused.

"We were roommates," the woman said between sobs.

"Amy told me."

"Did she tell you why she left?"

"No," I admitted and Louise sobbed even deeper and harder. I took a sip of coffee.

"We were roommates for five months," Louise said. "Friends."

"Just friends?"

Louise nodded. "She used to walk barefoot in the house. I must have told her a hundred times to wear shoes. I told her

159

that the oil from the bottom of her feet stains the carpet. She thought I was being silly. That's the word she used, silly. And after a while, I began to walk barefoot in the house, too. Oh, Mr. Taylor, she brightened my life so much; she meant everything to me. I don't mean mother-daughter, I mean . . . I'm not queer—gay, I mean. I'm not. I've never been with a woman. Never wanted to be. Never even thought about it. Only, one night, we were drinking wine and listening to CDs. It was a kind of game. We would listen to my music and then we would listen to hers and pretty soon I would be putting on Madonna and she would be listening to Judy Garland, and one night, a Tuesday night, we were drinking wine and listening to music—we were on the couch together and listening to music—and I kissed her. I kissed her on the mouth. It was spontaneous, a spontaneous thing. I wasn't thinking at all and she was more surprised than anything and I was surprised and I said I was sorry, I said I didn't know why I did that, I said . . . That beautiful, sweet child, the look in her eyes . . . What did I do, Mr. Taylor? What did I do?"

Good question, Louise. What did you do? I finished the coffee and poured another cup while she wept.

"She went to her room and she wouldn't come out and when she did come out she said she was going to find a place of her own; she said there were no hard feelings and we could still be friends and she was grateful to me for everything I did for her but she had to get a place of her own. And, and she said not to worry. She said she wouldn't tell anyone. That's what she said." Louise was becoming angry now, her voice rising along with her indignation. "That's what she said to me. Like I had something to hide. I'm not gay, I'm not, I'm not . . ."

And she probably wasn't, I decided. You get lonely, you reach out for someone. Sometimes you reach out for the wrong person. Happens all the time. I knew guys who did hard time, they never thought of themselves as gay, would have busted up anyone who accused them. But once they were inside, alone

. . . Ahh, hell, let it go, I told myself. *You're way over your head.* I took a sip of coffee. When I finished I asked, "What are you doing here, Louise?"

"I saw the way you looked at her when you two went to dinner, the way she looked when she came back. She was a little girl, damn you!"

"Young, not little."

"You bastard!" she screamed and then started weeping again. It was getting old, all these tears.

"Quit crying and tell me what you're doing here!" I yelled. Amazingly, she stopped. Just like that.

"I wanted to punish you."

"For what?"

She didn't say.

"Do you think I slept with her?"

Still nothing.

"Did you think I killed her?"

"If it wasn't for me she wouldn't have been living alone. If I hadn't . . . If I hadn't . . . She would have trusted me to take care of her, to protect her."

"That's not what I asked you."

Louise shook her head and buried her face in her hands yet again. But at least she didn't cry.

I didn't know quite what to do. She could easily have killed Amy, yet somehow I didn't think so. The St. Paul cops were gathering physical evidence at Amy's home. If any of it supported a female killer I'd give them Louise's name and gun. As for now . . .

"Go away," I told her.

"What?"

I waved at my office door. "Just go away."

She stood reluctantly, opened her coffee-stained purse and filled it with her personal belongings scattered on my desktop. She moved in slow motion, watching me, her mouth working like she wanted to say something but couldn't get the words out. Finally, she shuffled toward my office door and grasped the knob with both hands, the purse tucked under her arm. "I loved her, I really loved her," she said to the door. And then, "I'm not gay." The door didn't reply, so I did.

"No, just lonely," I said.

Louise opened the door and looked back at me. "Can I have my gun?" she asked.

"No."

C. C. Monroe was dressed in black: black fitted turtleneck with long sleeves tucked inside black gloves, a long black skirt and high black boots. A black scarf was knotted around her throat. Nothing was exposed except her incredible face, framed in butterscotch.

She was standing under the arch just outside the front door of the St. Paul Police Department, describing beautiful, young Amy Lamb with glowing adjectives while raging in general against the increase in violence directed toward women in general and condemning in particular a male-dominated society where women are thought to be less than human. It was a striking performance, made more so by the tears that welled up in her eyes and fell, seemingly on cue, whenever she delivered those brief phrases most conducive to a TV news sound bite.

Standing behind C. C. and not looking pleased about it was Anne Scalasi. Compared to C. C.'s eloquent outrage, Anne's quiet descriptions of the department's investigation—and lack of results—sounded lame and evasive.

Marion Senske was unobtrusive in the background, her eyes moving over the crowd, not looking for anything specific, just seeing.

The cadre of reporters surrounding C. C. and Anne certainly had no interest in me; did not see me hand Martin McGaney an envelope with a rubber band wrapped around it; did not hear me ask McGaney if he had anything on Sherman yet. McGaney, who was preoccupied with his superior's performance, merely shook his head. I glanced at my watch. It was 9:30. I wondered if Cynthia Grey was hiding Sherman somewhere, waiting for the circus to pull up stakes and move on.

I wanted to speak with C. C., with both her and Marion, but didn't like my chances, especially with the media looking on. I decided to try another time and was leaving the press conference when I heard a voice hail me. The voice belonged to Kerry Beamon, a crime reporter for the *StarTribune*. Beamon was tall and gangly with a long, shaggy beard and a bald spot on the back of his head, like a monk. He wore wire-rimmed glasses on the point of his nose and was dressed like he had just finished cleaning the garage.

"Long time no see," Beamon told me.

"Too long," I said, instead of "not long enough." The man was a pompous bore, but you don't get information by being sarcastic or patronizing, I don't care what Robert B. Parker writes. And I'll say one thing about Kerry Beamon—there was very little that was news to him.

"What are you doing here?" Beamon asked.

"I came by to visit Anne Scalasi," I answered. "But I see she's busy. How come you're not up there? You're the crime reporter."

"Yeah, but this isn't about crime. This is about politics. My paper has a couple of political writers on it."

"Uh-huh."

"So," Beamon said, smelling scandal the way a shark smells blood, "you're here to visit Scalasi."

"That's right."

"You guys are pretty tight."

"I suppose."

"Been partners for what?"

"A long time."

"Until you retired."

"That's right."

"You, ahh, you two have something going on the side?" he asked, winking at me like we shared a secret.

"Get a life, Beamon."

"No offense, no offense."

"She's a happily married woman."

"That's not what I hear."

"What do you hear?"

"I hear she and the old man are on the outs. I hear he's pissed because she made chief of Homicide and he's still driving a unit in the Midway."

"I don't believe it."

"Well, that's what I hear."

"You're a rumor monger, Beamon."

"It's only a rumor when you whisper it. When you say it out loud it becomes news. Speaking of which . . ."

Beamon pointed out a good-looking Geraldo Rivera type standing among the reporters, a notebook in his hand, casually asking C. C. if she wasn't just a little embarrassed for using the murder of an acquaintance to make the political statement that she was tough on crime.

"I am tough on crime," C. C. Monroe answered. "And yes, I am holding this press conference because I knew and cared about Amy Lamb. That's the point. We all know women who have been victims of violent crime. Something is seriously wrong with a society in which we all know women who have been assaulted and abused and harassed and raped. A society like that has to be changed. Don't you agree?"

The reporter didn't answer. Instead he busied himself by writing in his notebook, pretending not to see the contemptuous grins of his fellow journalists.

"Good for her," Beamon said.

"Do you support C. C.?" I asked him.

"Naw, I support no one. But that cheesy little shit, I'd love to crush his balls."

"Who is he?"

"Hersey Sheehan."

"He's the guy from the *Reporter*," I told Beamon. "The guy who got the goods on the governor and the mayor."

"Sleazy bastard, he's making us all look bad, all this sensational shit. The public is pissed something fierce and are they blaming the governor or the mayor? Hell, no. They're blaming the media. Course, circulation is up."

"How does he do it?"

"How do any of us do it?" Beamon replied. "Sources."

"Who?"

"I don't know. But I'd love to have 'em."

"Guess," I told Beamon.

"No idea. Little asshole is keeping 'em real tight."

"C. C. Monroe?" I suggested.

"Naw, I don't think so."

"She's the only one who hasn't been burned," I reminded him.

"True, but the sharks are circling."

"Why?"

"Like you said, she's the only one left. You want a guess, I think the mayor fed the governor to Sheehan and later the governor gave him the mayor outta revenge."

"Why Sheehan?"

"He's out of the mainstream; he doesn't give a shit where his stories come from."

"Wouldn't a legitimate newspaper print the story? Wouldn't you?"

"Sure. But we would also say where it came from. You don't go off the record with something like this."

"And now you say he's after Monroe?"

"We all are."

"Is anything there?" I asked.

"What is Monroe? Thirty-two? Thirty-three? You can't be thirty-three these days without having some kind of past, without doing something stupid—smoking dope in the girls' lockers, something."

"Is that news? Do you print something like that?"

"We do now."

EIGHTEEN

I WATCHED AS Hersey Sheehan studied his reflection in the store window. Something in what he saw must have pleased him because he kept looking for it in every flat, glossy surface he passed. This narcissism made Sheehan a difficult subject of surveillance; he was forever slowing down, speeding up and stopping to admire himself or any attractive young woman who happened by. Once I was forced to walk past him, careful not to look him directly in the eyes, when he turned around and briefly followed a woman he'd found particularly fetching.

I had tailed Sheehan's vehicle from the St. Paul Police Department's parking lot into downtown Minneapolis, coasting up to a meter across from the redbrick building near the old train depot that housed the presses of *The Cities Reporter*. Sheehan parked in the Employees Only lot next door, but instead of going into the building, he skipped down Washington Avenue, then up Marquette, stopping at a fast-food joint for a cheeseburger and fries. I passed. The only thing fast food had going for it in the past was that it was both fast and cheap and these days it is neither.

My reasons for following Sheehan were vague at best. On the one hand, Sheehan's tireless search for smearable dirt could have led him to Amy Lamb, Dennis Thoreau and John

Brown, whom he'd mistaken for Joseph Sherman—although why he might want to kill any of them was a mystery to me. On the other hand, if C. C. Monroe and Marion Senske actually were responsible for the deaths, it was doubtful they did the job themselves. More likely they hired someone to do their killing, someone who might have already been in their employ investigating the opposition candidates and passing secrets under the table to Sheehan.

Yes, I admit it was weak. But as it clearly states in Chapter Four of the *Universal Private Eye Instruction Manual, Third Edition,* and I quote: "When in doubt, follow someone."

I shadowed Sheehan back to *The Cities Reporter* and waited. To pass the time, I listened to a jazz station on a portable AM/FM radio I keep in the glove compartment—never use the car radio when the car isn't running because it drains the battery, especially in cold weather. (And never leave the car running because a car idling for hours at a time is bound to attract attention.) I unrolled my windows to avoid steaming them up. It probably wasn't necessary. It was cool but not uncomfortable. A van is better, of course. You can stand and stretch in a van. You can fit it with curtains so no one can watch you watching them. You can load it up with a refrigerator, a chemical toilet, a comfy chair, air conditioners, heaters, cameras, binoculars, telescopes, radios and cellular telephones. I really ought to get one one of these days.

I had no idea what time it was and fought the impulse to look at my watch. Time has no meaning when you're on surveillance except to mark the arrivals and departures of your subject; you're not going anywhere, there's nothing you need to do. In fact, there's nothing you *can* do while on a stakeout except watch. If you have a partner, you can talk. Considering some of the long, rambling conversations Anne Scalasi and I have had, you'd wonder why we weren't working for one of those Washington think tanks; why we weren't regulars on "MacNeil/Lehrer." When you're alone you listen to music if possible and try to stay alert. You think—you can't help but think—about a hundred different subjects. Only you must keep your mind from wandering too far. I once saw a suspect walk directly past a daydreaming investigator—the investigator didn't even see him.

Between pumping quarters in the parking meter and to keep my mind off Amy Lamb, I drew a portrait parlé of Sheehan, a word picture that described him to the smallest detail:

NAME: Sheehan, Hersey
AGE: 25–30
SEX: Male
HEIGHT Five-ten with shoes on
WEIGHT: 180 with clothes on
BUILD: Medium
POSTURE: Stiff [he reminded me of Jack Webb]
COMPLEXION: Tanned [in Minnesota in mid-October? He
    probably has his own tanning booth]
COLOR: White
EYES: Brown, squinting, long lashes
HAIR: Brown, short in front, long in back, slight wave,
    part on the left side
MUSTACHE: Brown, thick
EYEBROWS: Thick, arched
EARS: Yes
NOSE: Large, narrow, straight
FOREHEAD: High
FACE: Narrow
LIPS: Pinched
NECK: Short
CHIN: Pointed
CHEEKS: Full
CHEEKBONES: High
TEETH: Big, white
SHOULDERS: Broad

WAIST: Thin
STOMACH: Flat
FEET: Big
LEGS: Long
HANDS: Big, well kept
FINGERS: Long
WALK: See posture
DRESS: Expensive [I didn't know what his salary was but
    I knew where it went]
MARKS AND SCARS: Only his girlfriend knows for sure
SPEECH: Strong [from what I heard at the press conference,
    he could give Sam Donaldson elocution lessons]
HABITS: Women?

Eleven quarters later, Sheehan left the redbrick building and walked to his car. Nuts, I missed on his height (it was closer to six feet) and his hair (the part was on the right side). His chin seemed a little weak, too. Oh well. Practice makes perfect.

Tailing a car by yourself in heavy city traffic is arduous at best. Fortunately, Sheehan didn't stay in the city. He grabbed the I-35 on-ramp and drove south, past the city limits, past the suburbs into farm country. I drifted along behind him, five hundred yards back and in the other lane. It was a pleasant enough drive: gently rolling hills, stands of trees, farms, cows, horses. I remembered counting farm animals when I was a kid driving with my parents, inflating my totals to better my brother's count. I wasn't too worried about being spotted as long as we stayed on the interstate. A lot of cars travel the entire distance between towns and cities; it's not unusual to see the same vehicle behind you for a hundred miles—which was just about the distance we'd traveled, taking the Albert Lea exit about fifteen miles north of the Iowa border. Sheehan pulled into the parking lot of a Holiday Inn just off the main drag. I drove past, flipped a U and parked at the truck stop across the street. A sign outside the motel read WELCOME GOVERNOR.

I gave Sheehan a good head start and then crossed the street. The weather had turned colder, but I didn't mind. I prefer fall to summer. I burn in the summer. I cover my body with all kinds of toxic chemicals, yet it makes no difference. I burn. Then I peel. Then I burn again.

I walked through the lobby like I had a room with a view of the pool, following three men and a woman, all in shiny suits. They led me to a hospitality room where a dozen or more reporters had gathered around an empty podium and about four, five dozen supporters had gathered around them. A man looked me over when I entered the room and I flashed him my best don't-worry-about-me-I'm-no-threat-no-sirree smile. After that I went unnoticed, hovering near a table loaded with beer, wine, soft drinks and assorted munchies on the far side of the room. I filled my pockets with pretzels—I hadn't eaten all day.

Just before six, making sure he would make the local TV newscasts, the governor appeared to a smattering of applause. He shook hands with a few followers, greeted a few more and smiled as he went behind the microphones mounted on the podium. Despite the smile he looked like a man who was being marched before a firing squad. And, mama, did the reporters let him have it: What about this? What about that? How damaging was the debate? Have you reconsidered withdrawing from the election? Has the attorney general filed charges? Volley after volley. Through it all the man kept smiling, actually joked with the reporters, who joked back. John Dillinger and Melvin Purvis had a similar relationship.

Hersey Sheehan did not ask a single question, caustic or otherwise. Instead, he stood near the front of the pack of reporters, notebook in his pocket, arms folded across his chest, being seen and not heard. He seemed to enjoy the governor's attempts to avoid looking at him.

171

The press conference broke up after about an hour and the governor consented to interviews by each of the TV crews in turn. Sheehan moved to the exit but was detained by a small knot of the governor's supporters. I threaded past him and loitered in the corridor. Loud voices filtered out of the room. I could only make out two words: Fuck you. They came from Sheehan as he tramped past me, through the lobby and out the door. He was smiling.

Sheehan wasted no time getting back on I-35, this time heading north. I listened to the Timberwolves on the radio as we drove. By the time we reached Owatonna, they had built a thirteen-point lead over the Magic in Orlando. By the Northfield exit, the lead was stretched to twenty-one. But by Lakeville, the Magic, led by Shaquille O'Neal, were trailing by only seven points. The game was tied when we reached the Cities.

I was disturbed when Sheehan pulled into the parking lot across from my office building. *Real good, Taylor. You've been burned,* I told myself. Only I wasn't. Sheehan walked past my building to a tavern in the middle of the next block that I hadn't been inside since the UNDER NEW OWNERSHIP sign had gone up. Well, there was no time like the present. I went inside.

Jeezus, what had happened to the place? I wondered. Instead of a quiet, intimate saloon with a TV set above the bar, it had been transformed into a haven for yuppie sports fans. The booths had been replaced by dozens of small, two- and four-person tables, some of them pushed together into larger groups. Sports paraphernalia filled the walls. Big- screen televisions were everywhere, all tuned to the Timberwolves game. As for the waitresses, gone were the comfortable knit shirts and jeans, replaced by tank tops and hot-orange microskirts; the waitresses dipped when they served drinks to avoid giving the boys behind them a show. And the prices! I'm sorry, I think four fifty for a tap beer is excessive. I ordered a Summit Pale Ale and nursed it as I searched the place for Sheehan from my perch on a leather stool near the door. I found him in the back, near the restrooms, sitting at a small table. He was talking to a black man whose face I could not see. As much as it pained me, I signaled the bartender for another, then went to the restroom, purposely looking away from Sheehan as I passed. After I finished my business I grabbed a quick look at the black man as I casually sauntered back to my stool. Only I didn't feel casual. I felt like diving under a table.

Freddie was a grave robber; he'd dig up anything for a buck. And he was mean. Pit bull mean. He was very loose with his hands and he took pleasure in carrying his gun so everyone could see it.

I always figured his churlishness was the result of the merciless teasing he had suffered as a child. Seems his Ma saw Sidney Poitier in *Lilies of the Field* in '63 and wanted her boy to grow up just like him. She even gave him the actor's name: Sidney Poitier Fredricks. She dragged Freddie to dance classes and acting classes and forbade him to play football because she didn't want his face damaged. Whenever Freddie would get in a fight, which was often, Ma would check his baby face, pleading with him to be a good boy, trying to make him understand that his face was his fortune. Finally, Freddie won a small part in a community theater production of *Raisin in the Sun*, he even earned a good review, three lines in the community weekly. Ma was so happy, she finally allowed Freddie to go out for the high school team, persuaded, no doubt, by Freddie's list of black actors who had gained success on the football field: Woody Strode, Bernie Casey, Jim Brown, Lou Gossett Jr. (as far as Freddie knew Gossett had never played ball, but he had won an Oscar for *An Officer and a Gentleman* and Freddie figured every little bit helped).

173

Things went well, too. He made second-string All State his junior year. Then a linebacker blindsided him, busting his jaw, cracking two teeth and twisting his lip into a perpetual snarl. Ma was devastated. Freddie insisted he could still act, but Ma said never; the way Freddie looked now he could only get parts playing drug dealers and pimps and there was enough niggers doing that crap already—that's what she said. So Freddie took a scholarship to play Division III football. By his sophomore year, he was declared academically ineligible and had dropped out of college to join the Air Force. He became an AP stationed at Clark Air Force Base in the Philippines. For two years his job was to protect the hurricane-wire fence that enclosed the entire base. He would zoom around in a Jeep, his faithful German shepherd at his side. One day he caught three thieves climbing the wire; over their shoulders were sacks of warm beer heisted from the NCO club. Freddie shot them down. Then he turned the dog loose. To pacify an outraged Filipino government, Freddie was quickly court-martialed, found guilty, sentenced to life and shackled to a seat on the next flight home.

By the time he reached San Francisco, the guilty verdict had been overturned. Freddie was granted an early, honorable discharge and the AP lieutenant accompanying him had sprung for a case of Freddie's favorite beverage, Colt .45 Malt Liquor. Rumor had it the Air Force even fiddled with his service record, giving him enough investigative hours to qualify for a PI license. He would later boast, "Cappin' those three slopes was the best career move I ever made."

In short, Freddie was an embarrassment to our profession and the fact that Hersey Sheehan was conversing so pleasantly with him convinced me Kerry Beamon was correct: Sheehan was a sleaze. Call it guilt by association.

I drained the beer and ordered a third without thinking about it. I was out of pretzels, so I asked the bartender for a menu. Six-fifty for buffalo wings? With prices like these, the menu should be leather bound and come with a gold tassel. I slid it away.

"Unbelievable," the guy next to me said.

"What?"

"The prices," he answered, nodding toward the menu.

"I've seen worse," I told him.

The guy was dressed in a dirty white T-shirt, jeans torn at the knees and Topsiders. I estimated his beard at three days. He took a long pull on a Marlboro and told me how he'd just been laid off by his advertising agency because some asshole in another department lost a big account and his entire group got the bounce even though they didn't work on the account while the asshole was still with the agency—all before he exhaled.

"Politics, it's all politics," he said. "Nobody cares about the people who do the work. Do you know how many awards I've won for these guys?"

I excused myself and got the hell out of there.

I hid in the shadows of an alley across the street from the tavern and waited for Sheehan. It was a mistake. My first clue was when the muzzle of a handgun was rammed into my spine. The second was when Freddie said, "How you doin', Holly?"

I hated that name. "I've been better, Sidney," I said, trying to sound nonchalant. "How 'bout you?"

"Can't complain," he replied, jabbing me a little harder. "You tailin' me?"

"No."

"Then you're tailin' my man; I take the back door and circle around to learn why."

"Ahh. So, how did the Wolves do?"

"Shaq beat 'em at the buzzer."

"Give it to him, the guy's a player."

"So, why you tailin' my man?"

"I didn't know he was your man."

"You seen us talkin'."

"I figured he was writing a story on race relations."

"There's somethin' you should know, Taylor."

"What's that, Freddie?"

"I never liked you."

Freddie grabbed the collars of my jacket and shirt, jolted me deeper into the alley, swung me around and bounced me off the building. I pulled free and went into a cat stance, ninety percent of my weight on the back foot, my front foot high on the ball, both shoulders facing front, my hands in a guard position—an excellent posture for close encounters. Freddie pointed his gun at my face and thumbed back the hammer.

"Don't even think of tryin' that gook shit with me, man. I'll kill ya."

I dropped my hands to my side and straightened up.

"Put your hands in your pants pockets," Freddie said. His eyes were confident, invulnerable. I did what he told me.

"Now kneel."

I knelt.

Freddie stepped away from me, deactivated the gun and exhaled.

"You looked taller in them pictures in the newspapers," he told me. "You don't look so fuckin' tall now. You kinda look puny to me."

"I've lost weight. Hospital food does that to you."

"How long were you in there?"

"Couple of weeks."

"Got a lot of ink for that one."

"I'm a hero, the papers said so."

"Fuck them papers, you always in the fuckin' papers."

"Only twice."

"That's twice more than me."

"What are you talking about? Didn't the *Sun* call you the

next James Earl Jones a while back?"

Freddie grabbed a fistful of my hair and pulled. He waved his gun in front of my face like he was going to hit me with it. I got a good look. It was a Colt Commander. A nine.

"Don't be doggin' me, man," he warned.

"Are you threatening me?" I asked, real calm.

He grinned and shook his head, utterly amazed. Of course I'm threatening you, his eyes told me. Whaddya think? C'mon, get with the program.

"I kick your ass anytime I want," he announced, releasing my hair. "What you gonna do? Run to the cops? Run to your fancy-ass friends? What that guy pay you for stoppin' that takeover thing?"

"Twenty-five thousand."

"Fuck that!"

"God's truth, Freddie. He wanted to give me the hand of his eldest daughter in marriage, too, but . . ."

Freddie pushed the Colt back into my face.

"You best watch your mouth, Taylor. You think you're tough shit gettin' in the papers, but I don't see no reporters now."

He had a point.

"All that press," he said, contemptuously. "You ain't nothin'. I'm better 'n you. Better 'n you any day."

"That just might be," I told him. "You got the governor. I couldn't have done that."

"Yeah, man. That's right, I got the governor. And I didn't use no damn computer, neither."

"That was something, getting the goods on a governor. How did you do that, man?"

Freddie grinned.

"Tell me about it."

"No big thing," he said, a picture of modesty. "Simple surveillance is all, just like when I was with the APs. You think this guy is like the president? You think he's got security, Secret Service guys followin' him around and shit? Man, you could pop a governor a hundred times a day. And that car he drives—big fuckin' black Buick—it's like dog shit on snow, you know what I'm saying? So, I sit on 'im a while, see what the man does when he ain't kissin' no babies. You know the governor's mansion on Summit Avenue in St. Paul, it has the long driveway up front? What most people don't know, it's got a rear entrance, too. One night that big black Buick pulls out of the alley and the man's drivin', just him and no one else, and I follow him—how tough can it be?—and the dumb fuck leads me to this house in Edina and before he even gits to the door, a woman opens it. A white woman, not bad, neither. She's wearin' this, whaddya call it, this chemise thing and nothing else and she comes out and she slips him the tongue right there in the front yard for everyone to see like they was fuckin' bulletproof or somethin'. They go in and I sneak up to get the address, you know? And I peek under the window shade and they're doin' it right there on the living room floor, no shit. So I git my camera. I use a Pentax—I don't need no fancy-ass Nikon or shit, just a simple Pentax—and I figure to get some shots through the shade, maybe sell 'em off to *Playboy,* you know, do a spread: Governors of the Midwest. Only, shit, man, the guy's leavin' already. He's humped the bitch for only like fifteen minutes and he's all done, so the best I can do is snap a few shots of him comin' through the door.

"Now I see what I need to see, I don't need to see no more, so I motor outta there. Next day, what I do, I call the Hennepin County tax people and I asks, who owns the property at the address and they give me a name of this woman. So I think about it and I figure, hey, maybe this woman works for the government so I look her up in the state of Minnesota telephone directory, you know, the government directory. Only she wasn't in there. So I check this directory for lobbyists, the *Member Directory of the Minnesota Governmental Relations Council,* they call it. There she be, Council of General Contractors; nice photograph, too."

"Beautiful, man. Just beautiful," I said, feeding Freddie's ego. He was positively beaming and I wanted him to tell me more before he caught on to what I was doing.

"How'd you do the mayor?" I asked.

"He was easy, too," Freddie said. "What I did, I got this guy what works for a credit union; I slip him a workin' bee and he gives me the mayor's personal bank account. Turns out the asshole's been payin' six bills a month to this bitch, been doin' it for years. I get her address out of the book and I go over there, pretend I'm doin' a Gallup, and guess what? The bitch, she ain't got no old man but she's got this five-year-old kid. So I go to the birth records and take a look at the kid's birth certificate. Know what it says? 'Father unknown.' Fuck. Now, I'm pissed at this guy. You got a kid you gotta take care of 'im, man, you don't ignore 'im, pretend he don't exist. That bites, man. Anyway, I figure I need somethin' more so I go back to my guy at the credit union and I give 'im another fifty-dollar bill and he works on the woman, gets her employment history. You ready for this? The bitch worked in the mayor's office until she got pregnant; then she leaves and gets this cake job workin' for the Family Planning Department over to the City Health Center. Unreal."

"What's this crap about tax returns, then?"

"I don't know, man, that's Sheehan's shit. I don't know why . . ." And then he stopped, his eyes widening.

I pressed him. "Does Sheehan know that C. C. Monroe is paying for it?"

"I don't know any C. C. Monroe," Freddie said defensively.

"Marion Senske, then."

Freddie didn't answer.

"Marion and I have a business arrangement, too," I assured him. "She pays in cash, hundred-dollar bills. Nothing on paper. I don't know her, she don't know me. How about you?"

Freddie didn't speak, but I could hear his breath coming harder and faster.

"She hired me two days ago," I told him.

"You jerkin' me, man. She don't need no fuckin' newspaper private eye. She got me, she don't need you."

"This doesn't have anything to do with your job, Freddie."

"Fuckin' bitch, she don't need you."

"Listen, Freddie," I told him. But he had heard enough. He swung the Colt in a high arc and laid the barrel against the side of my head. The blow seemed worthy of quiet contemplation; I found myself conducting a clinical review of the damage it caused as I sank slowly into darkness, completely detached, like a rookie cop listening to a lecture on forensic medicine.

NINETEEN

I OPENED MY EYES and waited for them to adjust, seeing first the reflections, then the shadows of the night. I lay on the trash-strewn asphalt for a while longer, waiting for someone to render aid and comfort. No one did, so I pushed myself vertical and staggered out of the alley. Using the buildings for support, I slowly made my way to my office, shivering uncontrollably with every step. When did it get so damn cold? Several couples passed me. "Drunk," a young woman hissed. I wish. I nearly threw up during the elevator ride to my floor, but my stomach had settled somewhat by the time I reached the restroom at the end of my corridor.

My hair was wet and the collars of my shirt and jacket were stained with blood, but there wasn't much of it and that made me angry. A man who's been pistol-whipped, who feels the way I felt, there should be more blood. I considered a trip to the emergency room of the Hennepin County Medical Center and rejected the idea, deciding I wasn't badly hurt and remembering the last time I was in a hospital under the care of doctors and nurses who seemed to have had more important things to do. The longer I stayed, the more contemptuous of them I became. I did not thank any of them when I was discharged. That's what I buy insurance for.

I sat in my swivel chair and tried to chase away my headache with Tylenol and Summit Ale. Nice try. I leaned back, closed my eyes. *What do I do next?* I wondered. Going home seemed like a good idea. That's when I heard shuffled footfalls followed by the distinctive "click" of my office doorknob turning. I lunged across the room and grabbed Wayne Gretzky's broken hockey stick, brandishing the jagged end at the door as it swung open.

Cynthia Grey did not speak a word, just stared at me with a quizzical expression on her face.

"I was practicing my slapshot," I told her and set the stick back against the wall.

"I've been trying to reach you all day," she said.

"Why?" I asked, returning to my chair.

"Joseph Sherman is missing. He was supposed to meet me this morning; we were going to the police together. He never showed."

"Did you check the bus depot? The airport?"

"It's not funny, Taylor. You frightened him last night with talk of those other murders."

"I meant to frighten you."

Cynthia sighed. "I want you to help me find him before the police do."

"Not high on my list of priorities right now," I confessed.

"I don't understand your . . . What happened to your head?"

"Nothing."

"Nothing!" she exclaimed, not believing me. She moved to my side and took hold of my head, brushing my hair aside to examine the wound.

"Aay, that hurts," I told her.

"Do you have any antiseptic?"

"I always carry some in case of emergency."

"I have some," Cynthia said, opening her purse and taking out a small bottle of iodine.

"I don't believe it," I told her.

She brushed some on the wound and again I cried out, "Aay!"

"I don't think it's deep enough for stitches," she informed me. "How did this happen?"

"A guy pistol-whipped me."

"Who?"

"A jealous rival."

"You're a violent man," Cynthia said.

"No, I'm not," I protested. "I'm just having a bad week. Besides, in this business we're not always 'touched by the better angels of our nature.'"

Cynthia smiled. "Shakespeare?"

"Abraham Lincoln."

"You read."

"No, I picked it up from a documentary on PBS."

"You interest me, Detective."

"Why, because I watch TV?"

"I don't know why. Since we met Monday morning you haven't done a single thing that I approve of."

We regarded each other for a pregnant moment. She wasn't exactly my cup of tea, either. Hell, I didn't even drink tea. Still, there was something about her. I found myself wishing she were a little prettier—her hair more lustrous, her eyes brighter, her chin smaller, her lips fuller, her waist thinner . . .

"Well," she said.

"Well," I repeated.

"I'll drive you home," she suggested.

"I can drive myself," I told her and to prove it, I stood up too quickly, lurched forward, caromed off my desk, fell against the wall and let her catch me by the arm. "Just a little dizzy," I said. "I'm all right."

"I'll take you home."

"No, thank you."

"Yes."

"No."

"Humor me."

"Fine," I agreed, just as long as we understood who was doing whom the favor.

Ogilvy came bounding into the room when I switched on the living room light, his big ears a-flapping. Cynthia jumped; she probably thought he was a rat.

"My God, it's a bunny!" she exclaimed.

"It's a rabbit," I corrected her as she knelt and reached out her hand for Ogilvy to sniff like he was a dog.

"Hello, bunnyyyyy."

"Watch it," I said. "He's a killer."

"He's so cute," Cynthia said, disregarding my warning.

Ogilvy sniffed her hand thoroughly. Nope, no carrots there. He hopped a few steps away and turned to look at her. I think he liked what he saw because he hopped right back for some more fur smoothing. I didn't blame him. After some thought I concluded that there was nothing wrong with Cynthia's hair, eyes, chin, lips, waist . . .

"He's darling," Cynthia said. "What's his name?"

"Ogilvy."

"That's soooo cute!" she squealed.

"I didn't name him."

"Who did?"

"The little girl who lives next door, Tammy. She appeared on my doorstep one day after my wife and daughter were killed. She was holding a cardboard box. Inside the box was Ogilvy, along with a pamphlet describing his care and feeding. She gave me the rabbit because she didn't want me to be too lonely. Then she ran off before I could say anything."

Cynthia watched me when I told her the story, her eyes bright.

"Kids," I said, shrugging.

She looked away.

"Here . . ." I stepped around her and went to the kitchen to retrieve a carrot. Yes, rabbits really do love carrots although mine prefers popcorn. I gave the carrot to Cynthia, who held it out to Ogilvy.

"Here you go, bunny. Here fella," she said. Ogilvy commenced eating the vegetable out of Cynthia's hand.

"Where do you keep him?" she asked.

"I have a kennel in the other room. He usually sleeps there."

"But you give him the run of the place?"

"Believe it or not, a rabbit is easier to house train than a dog or cat; it took me one day, literally. The only problem is you have to coat the cords on your lamps and such; rabbits love to chew on electrical cords. Would you care for some wine?"

"I don't drink," Cynthia reminded me.

"Orange juice? Root beer?"

"Juice would be nice."

Ogilvy had finished his carrot, so Cynthia rose to follow me into the kitchen. Ogilvy butted her ankle with his head.

"Huh?"

"He wants you to keep petting him," I told her. "Just rub his nose. He likes that." Cynthia obliged and Ogilvy started grinding his teeth. She jumped back. "It's okay. That means he's happy."

"Obviously a male," Cynthia allowed.

I opened a carton of juice and poured two glasses; remarkably, my headache had disappeared. When I bent to hand Cynthia one of the glasses, she pulled me down and kissed me. It was a soft kiss, but it sucked the air out of my lungs.

"Why did you do that?"

"Why not?"

I sat in a chair and considered my reply.

"Have you been lonely, since your wife died?" she asked me, like we were friends. She was still petting Ogilvy.

"A little, for a while. Now . . . I like living alone. Come and go as you please, no one to answer to. How about you?"

"I live alone, too."

"Great, isn't it?"

"Wouldn't have it any other way," she said.

I drank my juice, drank it like it was Gatorade and I had just finished a marathon. Then, to change the subject, I asked her if she wanted a tour of my house.

We started on the ground floor. I showed her the fireplace, the beamed ceilings, the hardwood floors, the arched door-way leading to the dining room, the two corner china cabinets, the French doors leading to a three-season porch, the completely modern kitchen, the wood-paneled family room where I kept Ogilvy's kennel, all the while regretting how little of the house I actually used.

"This is amazing," Cynthia said.

"The house?"

"No, how neat it is. I thought men were sloppy."

"I like to clean when I'm bored."

"You must be bored a lot."

"Ha, ha, ha."

I took her upstairs and showed her my bedroom. We did not linger there. I showed her my library. I have about three thousand titles, everything from Richard Adams to Virginia Woolf.

"You do read," Cynthia announced, surprised. "Why didn't you want me to know you read?"

I had to shrug at that.

"Have you read all these books?" she asked, waving at them with both hands.

"Of course not. Why would anyone want a library filled only with books they've already read?"

The tour ended at the guest room, where I stored all of Laura's antique dolls. Cynthia admired them silently, want-ing to touch them, to fondle them, but holding back. One doll in particular held her attention: the queen of Laura's collec-tion, a Simon-Halbig worth eight thousand dollars that Laura had discovered at an estate sale and bought for three hundred and fifty—an acquisition that still astounds the members of her doll club.

Laura had loved collecting, loved investigating antiques shops armed with her reference catalogues, magnifying glass and flashlight, loved haggling with the owners. She was a dandy negotiator, always played by the rules; the proprietors of the antiques stores in the Minneapolis warehouse district and along Grand Avenue in St. Paul seemed to genuinely enjoy doing business with her. About a half dozen of them sent cards after she was killed and only one was tasteless enough to suggest liquidating her collection. If I ever decide to do that, he's the last person I am going to call.

"Tell me about her, your wife," Cynthia said.

"I can't."

"Too painful?"

"No, I just don't have the words."

Cynthia shook her head sadly. "I've never loved anyone that much."

"It's either that or a poor vocabulary," I joked. Cynthia seemed shocked by my callousness. "I don't want to talk about Laura," I added. "I don't want to get all gloomy and depressed. I've had enough of that."

"When she died?"

"When she was *killed*," I corrected her.

"Is that why you quit the police? Because she was killed?"

"Something like that." I didn't want to tell that story, either; how I fell apart after Laura and Jennifer were taken from me. People would talk to me and I couldn't make out what they were saying; my brain translated their words into gibberish. I went to a grocery store and in the middle of the condiment aisle I lost it; all those brand names, the different colored packages, they overwhelmed me—I couldn't even remember my own name much less what I wanted to buy. I couldn't cope so I crawled into a bottle, which only added to my problems. It took three, four months before the shock wore off and by then I wasn't the same person. I had changed. My values had changed. I was a helluva cop; the Ranking Officers' Association had once named me Officer of the Year. Before Laura and Jennifer were killed, I loved what I was doing. Afterward I couldn't tell you what I was doing it for.

Yet I worked at it harder than ever. I went in early, came home late, never took days off. And when I wasn't working, I was hitting the bars with my fellow officers, chasing CBs with water until I was numb. I told myself it was the stress. I was drinking because that day I'd busted a twelve-year-old for beating an elderly woman to death for the change in her purse. But it wasn't stress. I was drinking because when I wasn't working, I had nothing else to do.

Then George Meade blew his brains out. I had broken in with Meade. He was a twenty-year man when I rode with him and all he did was complain about the job. When he hit thirty years the department threw him out; gave him a gold watch and one helluva party. I was never so drunk in my life. Six months later he swallowed his service revolver because the job was all he'd had, too.

The idea that I would end up like Meade terrified me. So, I drank even more heavily. Finally I was stopped one night by a Roseville cop who didn't like the way I was driving Highway 280, using two lanes. I was wearing my drinking jacket— my police windbreaker—and we cops, we stick together, so he didn't bother with a breath analyzer even though we both knew I was way over the limit. Instead, he followed me home and poured me into bed. I had become a drunk, just like the sonuvabitch who killed Laura and Jenny. The next day I resigned. I vowed to quit drinking and to find something I could care about besides my job. I beat the booze. But the job . . . I guess I had been a cop too long.

"Why did you become a private investigator?" Cynthia asked.

"It's something to care about."

"I can relate to that."

"Can you?"

"Yes," she told me. "I never knew . . ." she hesitated in mid-sentence, regarding me from across the room, then continued.

"I never knew my father, and my mother dumped me on my grandparents and took off when I was six. When I was twelve my grandparents died. I spent the next four years being shuttled from one foster home to another until I ran away and started living on my own and dancing . . ."

"At places like Le Chateau?" I interrupted.

"And doing other things," she added without elaboration. "I had no self-esteem, no self-worth; I hated myself. So I popped a fistful of pills. That didn't work, so I tried again by swallowing furniture polish. That didn't kill me, either; it only sent me to the hospital. I told them I was suicidal, I told them I needed help. But I had no medical insurance, so instead of treating me, they put me in a ward with these people who had profound emotional and mental problems, some of them untreatable. That was an education, I'm here to tell you. I learned my troubles were nothing. After I was discharged from the hospital I promised I'd never feel sorry for myself again and mostly I haven't. I managed to earn a high school general equivalence diploma, worked my way through the U, finished tenth in my class at law school and here I am."

"Here you are, 'lifting your lamp beside the golden door,'" I -oted. "'Give me your tired, your poor, your huddled masses yearning to breathe free, the wretched refuse of your teeming shore, send these, the homeless, tempest-tost to me.'"

"It's something to care about," she said, not offended at all.

I led her down the staircase and into the living room where Ogilvy was waiting for us. We stood about two feet apart and appraised each other for what seemed like a long time.

Finally, Cynthia said, "I should leave."

"Should you?"

"I don't know. Should I?"

I touched her cheek. Her eyes were wide and moist. My hand trembled just so. I leaned toward her . . . and the sound of a gunshot followed by splintering glass filled the room. I pulled Cynthia to the floor and rolled to the light switch. Damn. Every light in the house was on. "Stay down!" I warned her and crawled to the front door on hands and knees. I instinctively reached for the gun on my hip that was not there—if this kept up I was going to start carrying it again.

The large oak door stood ajar but the screen door was shut. I hit it hard with my shoulder, happy I hadn't thought to put the storms up yet, and dove off the stoop onto the wet grass, rolling until I was in the shadow of the giant willow. I waited. No more shots. No noise at all. I have good night vision and it wasn't long before my eyes adjusted to the lack of illumination. Fear pumped adrenaline through me, masking the achiness in my head and limbs; my mind reached a rare kind of clarity—I was cured, praise the Lord. I sprinted to the lilac bushes. I crashed through the hedge and rolled onto the boulevard. No sign of our nocturnal assailant. I circled the house. Still nothing. Eventually I made my way back to the willow. I squatted under it, daring something to move. Nothing did. My mind covered a dozen scenarios as I waited. Freddie, Sherman, C. C., Marion, Louise, Sheehan, even Heather Schrotenboer: Everything fit and nothing fit. As I squatted in the darkness, the throbbing returned to my head and then sought out previously unaffected parts of my body—the base of my neck, the small of my back, the inside of my knees. The pain rekindled a recent memory of a hospital room, the gagging odor of antiseptic, the harsh whisper of Anne Scalasi warning me not to die if I knew what was good for me.

I went back inside. Cynthia was sitting on the floor, her back to the wall, Ogilvy in her lap. She was trembling as she gently stroked the rabbit's fur. I put my arms around her, held her, told her it was all right, told her that whoever fired the shot was long gone. She didn't seem to need much comfort, but I held her anyway.

"Do you know who it was? Did they shoot to kill or to frighten us? Will they try again?" she asked. Decent questions all. Too bad I couldn't give her decent answers. And then she surprised me. She smiled. She smiled and nodded toward the small hole head-high in the stucco wall.

"This is some kind of technique you've developed, Taylor. Scare a girl to death and then take her to bed."

It had been a long time for both of us and it was awkward, like we were kids experimenting in the back seat of a Dodge. The zipper of her skirt stuck, I pulled her hair, we kept getting tangled in the sheets; it wasn't at all like the movies, like Richard Gere and Julia Roberts. I preferred it that way, however. Unrehearsed. I think she liked it, too. But I did not ask, "Was it good for you?" I didn't want to be one of those people.

Cynthia fell asleep holding my hand, her leg casually draped over mine. When she rolled away something made her reach out to touch me, to make sure, even in deep sleep, that I was still there.

I waited until she was snoring, a soft purr like a kitten's, before I rolled silently out of bed, grabbed a robe and tiptoed out of the room. I made my way downstairs and turned on a small lamp in the living room. I found a penknife in the junk drawer in the kitchen and used it to carefully pry the bullet out of the wall, taking my time, making sure I didn't damage it. The bullet was big with plenty of heft. Sure looked like a .9mm to me.

TWENTY

"Hey."

"What?" I answered the voice that was shaking me out of deep slumber.

"I have to go. Hey."

"Hey, yourself," I mumbled. The sun was thinking about rising and gray light illuminated the room. It nearly matched the gray of the sweatshirt Cynthia was wearing—my sweatshirt—with COLLEGE OF ST. THOMAS printed across the chest in purple letters. I had to admit, it looked a helluva lot better on her than it ever did on me.

"I have to go. Do you need a ride to your car?"

"Yeah."

"Will you hurry?"

"Yeah. Ten minutes. What's the rush?"

"I need to go home and change," Cynthia said.

"Why don't you wear what you had on yesterday?"

"People will talk."

"What will they say?"

"They'll say I have a fella."

"Do you have a fella?"

"I don't know. Do I?"

"Do you want to talk about it?"

Cynthia glanced at her watch. "Will it take long? I have to go to my office and then I have to get over to Federal Bankruptcy Court."

Despite her brusque manner, I had a sense that Cynthia was searching for some kind of assurance. So was I.

"I was happy you were here last night," I told her. "I'm happy you're here now. I'll be unhappy when you leave. But I'll understand if you don't come back."

"Do you want me to come back?"

"Yes, I do."

She thought about it and said, "I don't go to bed with men. I mean, I have, you know . . . I told you something about my . . . misspent youth. But I never cared before, really cared, not   just pretended to care to make it seem all right. It was always somebody, never someone."

"Until now?"

She thought about it again. "Until now," she said and then she leaned over and kissed me. I took her in my arms and pulled her down onto the bed. I held her and kissed her and held her some more.

"Call your office. Tell them you'll be late."

"I can't," she said, her voice heavy with regret.

"Cindy, Cindy, Cindy . . ." I repeated.

"I'll meet you for lunch if you promise me something."

"Anything."

"Don't ever call me Cindy."

Detective Martin McGaney was drinking coffee from a blue and gold mug with the inscription THOU SHALT NOT KILL, THE LORD SAITH. AND WE WORK FOR HIM. Everyone who works Homicide in St. Paul gets an identical mug. Mine is tucked away on the top shelf of the cabinet above my kitchen sink.

"I was wondering when we would hear from you," McGaney told me as I stood in front of his desk. He looked tired. So did Anne Scalasi, who'd just happened to discover a crucial piece of paper McGaney needed when she saw me enter the squad room. I wasn't surprised by their fatigue. The first few days of a murder investigation are critical; you work it into the ground. And these guys had three murders.

"Ask the citizen what he wants," Anne told McGaney.

"What do you want, Citizen?"

"Nothing much, just dropped by to watch my tax dollars at work."

"Tell the citizen to go away," Anne said.

"Go away, Citizen."

"After all the trouble I went to find the perfect gift?" I set the spent bullet on the ink blotter in front of McGaney. "Simple, understated. I was going to wrap it, but . . ."

"What is it?" Anne asked. This time she was addressing me.

"I'll bet you fifty bucks that's a nine-millimeter slug," I told her.

Anne rolled the bullet in her fingers, then felt the weight in the palm of her hand. She flipped it to McGaney.

"I'll bet you another fifty bucks it matches the slugs taken from Thoreau, Brown and Amy Lamb."

"Where did you get it?" Anne asked.

"I dug it out of my living room wall. It was deposited there late last night by someone who took a sudden dislike to me."

"As opposed to those of us who have learned to dislike you over time," Anne said. "I don't suppose you can identify the shooter."

"Person or persons unknown."

"That's informative."

"I don't suppose you've found Joseph Sherman yet," I asked.

"We expect to make an arrest at any time," McGaney assured me.

"Why would Sherman want to shoot you?" Anne asked.

"It's a long story."

"I have time."

"Yeah, but I don't."

"Officer McGaney, inform the citizen that he is obstructing justice."

"Officer McGaney, inform the lieutenant that I am not the only one."

"Tell him that when this is over I'm going to kick his ass."

"Was that kick or kiss?" I asked.

Anne Scalasi was angry. "Don't push me too far, Taylor," she hissed.

"I'll tell you what I know when I know it," I hissed back, then thought better of it and, determined to keep it light, said, "There's no pleasing some people. Give a woman a bullet and she doesn't even say thank you."

"It's a thankless job," Anne told me.

"Isn't this sweet," McGaney remarked. "I'm touched, I really am. Two old friends getting together, it brings a tear to my eye. Let's all hug each other."

"Shut up, Martin," Anne said. And then she added one word. "Mankamyer." She was behind her desk before McGaney could get to his feet.

"You two remind me of an old married couple," McGaney told me as I followed him out of the squad room.

"Sure," I agreed. "An old married couple on the verge of a divorce."

"There's a lot of that going around," McGaney said.

"Are Anne and her husband really getting a divorce?" I asked; I'd been wanting to ask someone.

"Looks that way," McGaney said, confirming my fears.

"Damn."

"Yeah," McGaney said. "You know, my wife and I are celebrating our second anniversary next week. Considering what this business does to marriages . . . You were married."

"I was."

"Did you have troubles?"

"No."

"How did you manage to keep it going?"

"I didn't," I said honestly. "She did."

"Hey, you guys," Casper called to us as we stepped into the corridor. "You gotta talk to this woman, I mean . . . She says she knows who killed Thoreau, but man, is she weird."

McGaney rubbed his face. "Has she confessed to anything before?"

"She isn't confessing, she's accusing."

"Get the lieutenant," McGaney said.

"Hell no, not me. You talk to her first."

McGaney sighed and walked into the interrogation room, the same interrogation room where they had interviewed me. I followed.

The woman was about twenty-three with the kind of wholesome beauty that was spoiled by makeup. Her dress was simple and white, her eyes were dark and brooding, her hair was black and brushed the top of the shoulders. She spoke quickly, like someone had a stopwatch on her.

"I'm Brenda Clark," she said, extending her hand to McGaney. "The Lord has sent me."

McGaney smiled broadly. "That's nice," he said. "I'm Detective McGaney. This is Holland Taylor. He's a . . . an investigator."

The woman crossed her ankles. They were nice ankles.

"Detective Casper said you can help us identify Mr. Thoreau's killer?"

The woman pivoted in her chair and smiled at Casper, who smiled back. "It was the Reverend Leonard Hoppe."

"*Reverend* Hoppe?" McGaney repeated.

" 'For we are not contending against flesh and blood, but against the principalities, against the powers, against the world rulers of this present darkness, against the spiritual hosts of wickedness in the heavenly places.'"

"Say what?"

"Sixth Ephesians," I told McGaney.

The woman smiled brightly at me. "You know the Word of the Lord?"

"I can also recite the entire roster of the 1987 Minnesota Twins."

"Shut up, Taylor," McGaney told me.

"Ms. Clark . . ." he said.

"Miss Clark," she corrected him.

"*Miss* Clark. How do you know . . ."

"The Lord told me."

"He did?"

"Not directly, of course."

"No, I don't imagine . . ."

"His messenger came to me. I was reading the morning newspaper," she said, turning toward me. "So much pain and suffering. I began to pray. I asked the Lord, What can I do to help turn the tide against the Prince of Evil who has caused so much suffering? Suddenly, a dark-skinned, handsome man came into my kitchen; that's where I was, in my kitchen," she added, speaking casually, as if that sort of thing happened to her all the time. "I knew right away I was in the presence of a great spiritual power, an angel. He didn't speak. Instead, he pointed at the newspaper and the pages started to turn, one by one, until finally they stopped and then the paper just burned away except for this."

She pulled a clipping from her purse and gave it to McGaney, who showed it to me. It was an article from the *St. Paul Pioneer Press*. The headline read St. Paul Man Slain in His Home. The edges of the clipping were singed.

"I asked the angel, 'What does this mean?' and he said, 'He who has sinned against God and man speaketh the Word of the Lord. He is possessed of the demon and must be saved or destroyed, for his flock must be protected from the Evil One.'

Just then I heard Reverend Hoppe's voice loud and clear on the radio and I knew it was he who was possessed by the demon and then the angel's face began to shine as if there was a powerful light behind his eyes and then the angel was gone . . . It was a very interesting experience."

"I bet."

"Who is Reverend Hoppe?"

"He's a radio evangelist on WKKK radio," Casper said.

"Unfortunate choice of call letters," I suggested.

"It is because preachers have tried to spread the Word of the Lord through television and radio that the demons have attacked," Brenda Clark said. "The airwaves are the realm of the spirit world, it is where the demons reside, and when the preachers took to the airwaves, well, the demons didn't like it and they came out against them." She turned to me again. "That is what happened to Jim Bakker and Jimmy Swaggart."

"I knew it," I said. "I just knew it."

"Did you confront the reverend, Miss Clark?" McGaney asked.

"I attempted to. After the angel came, I drove to the radio station with the clipping and I saw him in the parking lot. But he was not alone. He was with . . ." She shook her head in disbelief. "He was with Vivian Olson, kissing Vivian Olson, caressing her."

"I'm sure he meant it in the most paternal way," Casper volunteered.

The woman turned and looked at him but did not speak.

"Vivian Olson?" McGaney asked.

"She's the assistant station manager; an evil, evil woman," Brenda Clark said. "A plaything of the devil, Satan's strumpet. I realized when I saw them together that Reverend Hoppe could not be saved, that he must be destroyed." She turned to me again. "Lay down with dogs and rise up with fleas," she said.

Casper chuckled and Brenda Clark, McGaney and I all turned toward him in unison, staring at him like he was

Lucifer himself. "Excuse me," he said, coughing into his hand.

McGaney excused himself as well and headed for the door. Again, I followed him.

"Martin," Casper implored. "What about . . . " he nodded at the woman.

McGaney took his arm and whispered loud enough for her to hear: "Take Miss Clark's statement and make sure she gets home. Then drive over to WKKK and find out where the Reverend Hoppe was Friday night."

Casper nodded and smiled.

"Thank you, Miss Clark, you've been very helpful," McGaney said. "And I want to see a report," he told Casper.

Casper stopped smiling.

While we waited for the elevator, a file folder McGaney was carrying slipped from his fingers and fell to the floor. "Oh, damn," he said. "Confidential information on the Lamb case. I must be more careful."

I stooped to retrieve the folder. It was McGaney's working file. I was glancing at the contents when the elevator doors slid open; McGaney punched the button marked B for basement.

The first page was labeled TIMETABLE—LAMB MURDER, TUESDAY, OCT. 8. It was virtually the same as mine, except it omitted C. C. Monroe. The second page, a list typed on Ramsey County Medical Examiner stationery, was headed WOUNDS CHART, AMY LAMB. There were six by the ME's count, all carefully and clinically identified. I skipped over them, stopping at the part that suggested the wounds were caused by .9mm bullets fired at a distance of three to five feet. Most of the other pages were handwritten and barely legible. From what I could make out from McGaney's scrawl, a door-to-door canvass of the neighborhood had proved fruitless—no witnesses, no gun. Nothing had been taken from Amy's apartment. Nor was there any evidence of forced entry, no jimmy marks on the door jambs or windowsills, no scratches on the perimeter of the locks. The front and back doors had Yale deadbolts that must be locked with a key both inside and out. The front door was locked; the landlady had let me in. The back door was not; the key was still in the lock, on the inside.

"Killer went out the back," I assumed.

"Wouldn't you?" McGaney asked.

"How did he get in?"

Still another page contained notes taken during an informal discussion McGaney'd had with the ME: "Preliminary examination reveals no evidence of sexual assault." "No evidence of sexual assault" was circled three times.

"She knew her killer," I volunteered. "She let him in."

"Or her," McGaney reminded me.

I leafed through the rest of the file, asked about physical evidence, hair samples, skin tissue. "Did you check the sinks like Anne suggested?"

"Of course."

"Well?"

"C'mon, Taylor. It hasn't even been two days yet."

"I've seen more information on a dog bite complaint," I said, handing back the file.

"I'm expecting a report from the lab this afternoon," McGaney replied almost apologetically, but not quite.

Amy Lamb. I closed my eyes and there she was. I tried to see her as the young woman eating Vietnamese and talking about Starbuck. Instead, it was her blood-splattered body that I saw, her hands clenched in fear and rage and pain, her fingernails cutting bloody half moons into the palms. I shook my head, but the image would not disappear.

"A couple of things that are not in this file," McGaney said as the elevator doors slid open. "Thoreau and Brown were not killed by the same gun; Thoreau was shot with a twenty-five and Brown with a nine. So far there is no evidence to suggest they were companions except your girl's message."

"When was Thoreau killed?" I asked.

"Between nine and midnight Friday night."

"Friday night? Are you sure?"

McGaney shrugged. It wasn't his job to fix postmortem intervals.

He continued. "We speculate he was entertaining; we found female pubic hair and secretions in his bedroom and on his genitals; the lab is working them. No suspects. The neighbors claim they saw no women going in or out, claim they saw nothing and heard nothing."

"You sound surprised," I told him.

"When I was a kid, the neighbors saw and heard everything. My parents always knew what I did on a Saturday night two hours before I got home."

"Yeah, the same with me," I said. "Now no one wants to get involved. Twenty-five years ago you couldn't stop them. How 'bout Brown?"

"A single shot, close range, like this," McGaney said and poked a finger in my ear.

"Had to be someone he knew to get that close," I volunteered.

"Not necessarily," McGaney said. "He was bombed; toxicology report says his blood alcohol content was point-two-one. The assailant could have walked up to him carrying a bazooka and he wouldn't have noticed."

"Witnesses?"

"A gas station attendant remembers a man matching Joseph Sherman's description coming in around midnight. The man asked to use the john, and the attendant lent him the key."

I let "That fits" slip out and McGaney jumped all over it.

"What do you mean, 'That fits'? That fits what?"

I didn't answer and McGaney pushed me up against the wall of the corridor.

"Let's get something straight," he said, jabbing a finger at my face. "I ain't your buddy, I ain't your pal, I ain't your ex-partner. I don't give a damn if you're sleepin' with some college kid or playin' poker till dawn . . ." He noted my surprise at the last statement and added, "Do you think I'm stupid?"

"No, I never . . ."

"I'm cooperating with you because I think you might be able to help me. And the lieutenant. If you can't or won't, I'll cut you off at the knees. Got it?"

"What do you mean, help the lieutenant?"

"Something's bothering her. Originally, I figured it was her old man. But that remark you made about obstructing justice, it has to be something else."

"You don't miss much, do you, Detective?"

"Not a helluva lot, no," McGaney admitted.

I appraised him for a moment, realizing for the first time that he closely resembled one of my favorite actors, Paul Winfield—when Winfield was thin—even down to the smile that he wasn't using just then. He let me look.

"There are an awful lot of cops who get their pensions without ever leaving this building," I told him. "They work nine to five for twenty years and figure they've accomplished something with their lives. And then there are cops with a fire in their belly and a . . ."

"Yeah, yeah, I heard the speech when I was a rookie. Get to the point," McGaney said.

"A *real* cop, you tell him a certain thing and he might feel he has to do something about it; he can't just let it slide. He'll tell himself he has to do something because it's his job, because it's important. So maybe, you don't tell him . . ."

Now it was McGaney's turn to study me; I wondered if I reminded him of a favorite actor. Probably not.

"So, where does that leave us?" he asked after coming to a decision he preferred not to share.

"I give you my word of honor: If I uncover any tangible evidence that identifies the killer of Thoreau or Brown or Amy Lamb, I'll give it to you, no matter who it implicates."

"Your word of honor doesn't mean jack shit to me," McGaney said and jabbed his finger at my face again. "I'll be watching. I'll be watching real close."

"I appreciate that," I said.

"One more thing. If I have to bust the lieutenant I will," he said. "I won't like it, but I'll do it and I won't lose any sleep over it later."

Sergeant Alexander Mankamyer, the St. Paul Police Department's forensic firearms expert, was sitting on a stool at a high workbench and examining the disassembled parts of a sawed-off 16-gauge shotgun with a cut-down stock. He did not look up when we entered the cluttered room. He did not say "Hello" or "What do you want?" or "Who are you?" or "Get lost." Instead he said, "Had a gang shoot-out last night and a couple of uniforms took this off a juvvie. Now the CA wants to know if it can be fired. Shut the door."

I did.

"Can it be fired?" I asked him.

"What? You the CA?"

"You brought it up," I reminded him, leaning on the edge of the bench. Mankamyer frowned at me. "Sorry," I said and pushed myself upright.

How Mankamyer functioned in this laboratory of violent death was a mystery to me. There were hundreds of firearms hanging from hooks along two walls, and plastic envelopes containing bits and pieces of evidence stacked on desks and tables and shelves all around.

"You guys slumming?" he asked.

McGaney gave Mankamyer the bullet. "What kind of slug is that?" he asked.

"It's not a slug," Mankamyer told him. "It's a bullet. A slug is round and flat and has a hole in it and kids use them to rob vending machines."

"Bullet, then."

"Probably a nine; I'll weigh it to be sure."

"I need to know if the weapon . . ."

"Gun, gun," Mankamyer repeated, obviously annoyed. "Anything can be a weapon. A can of whipped cream can be a weapon. Remember the woman with the Pine-Sol?"

McGaney took a deep breath. "I need this bullet checked against the bullets taken in the Brown and Lamb cases; I need to know if they were fired from the same *gun*."

"How much time do I have?"

"Lieutenant Scalasi wants it right away."

"You still a cop, Taylor?"

"No, I left about . . ."

"At least the bullet is clean. I remember once they took a thirty-eight out of this guy's brain and stuck it in a plastic bag. Only thing, no one bothered to clean it and the guy's bodily fluids destroyed most of the markings. Later, they bring me the gun and ask for a match. Yeah, sure. Amateurs, I'm telling you. Amateurs. That Scalasi, though, she knows her forensics."

"How long?" McGaney asked.

"How long what?"

"How long before I get a report?"

"What is this, takeout? Do I look like I'm frying chicken here? These things take time. I remember once we had this bullet from an S and W . . ."

"Mankamyer, how 'bout I start putting goldfish in your firing tank again?"

"You were the one who did that? You sonuvabitch."

"Mankamyer!"

"Friday, end of the day," Mankamyer promised and then shook his head. "You people must think I live for this."

McGaney and I started for the door.

"Taylor, what are you doing here?" Mankamyer suddenly asked. "I thought you pulled the pin months ago."

TWENTY-ONE

Louise turned her head abruptly away and pretended not to see me pass quickly through the campaign headquarters to the office in back. Marion Senske was not happy about my presence, either. She was sitting behind her desk, observing while an image consultant instructed C. C.

The consultant was tall, with shoulder-length auburn hair. She was wearing a conservative two-piece, double-breasted blue suit with gold earrings and a thin gold chain around her throat. She looked like she should be running for governor.

"As I said, there are two things to remember," she told C. C. "Use the right grip—two firm pumps, yes?—and maintain a pleasant facial expression. It's important that you look interested. I know that will be difficult. You shake, what, a hundred hands each day?"

"More," C. C. said, rolling her eyes.

"That makes it even more crucial that you leave a positive impression. Most of us make assumptions about a person's level of success, trustworthiness, credibility, economic standing, education, social position and sophistication based on that first meeting—within seconds in fact. And consider: The vast majority of the people you meet during the course of a campaign will never shake your hand again. Therefore, the first impression you make is the one they will carry with them, quite possibly forever."

I was leaning against the doorframe watching the show, when the image consultant noticed me and decided I would make a good prop.

"Smile when you approach the voter," she instructed as she moved toward me. "Extend your hand." She did. So did I. "One hand. No limp-fisted fish, no bone crushers, no two-handed sandwiches." She took my hand and, true to her word, gave it two firm pumps. "Hi, I'm Deborah Dixon."

"Will you marry me, Debbie?" I asked. C. C. giggled. Even Marion cracked a smile. Deborah was not amused.

"You will occasionally have to deal with inappropriate behavior," she told C. C., turning her back on me.

"Ms. Dixon, could you and Carol Catherine continue your instruction in the next room, please? I must speak to Mr. Taylor."

Deborah agreed and moved past me. C. C. extended her hand. "Hi. I'm Carol Catherine Monroe and I would be happy to marry you," she said smiling broadly.

"I'm sorry, Miss Monroe. My heart belongs to Debbie. It was the first impression that did it."

C. C. giggled some more and followed Deborah outside.

"Close the door," Marion told me. I did. "What are you doing here?" she asked.

"I had a rather disagreeable encounter with an associate of yours last night," I told her.

"I know. He called me."

"Did you have a pleasant conversation?"

"We did not."

"Pity."

Marion did not waste any time. "I could see to it that you lose your license, that you never work as a private investigator again," she said.

"Is that what you told Freddie?"

"I mean it."

"I know you do and if you and C. C. had already won the election I'd be plenty worried. But since you haven't and since I'm in a position to help see that you don't . . ." I shrugged.

Marion pursed her lips and tapped her toe. "How?" she asked.

"There's something you should know about Freddie," I replied. "He'd *love* to see his name in the newspaper."

Marion leaned back; the chair creaked under her bulk and I wondered what advice Deborah would give her.

"All right, how much?"

"There you go," I told her, "making assumptions based on a first impression. Tsk, tsk, tsk."

"Goddamn it, Taylor! How much?"

I've never had a lot of money, so it's easy for me to get along without it, easy for me to put my hands behind my head and say, "Marion, I'm for rent, but I'm not for sale."

"Ten thousand dollars," Marion bid.

I shook my head knowing full well that, like everyone else, I probably did have a price. I just didn't know how high it was . . .

"Fifteen," Marion said.

And I didn't want to find out. "I don't want your money," I told her.

"What do you want?"

"Information."

"What information?" Marion asked, obviously preferring to give me money instead.

"Where were you and C. C. Friday night between nine and midnight?"

"Mankato," she answered without hesitation.

"Witnesses?"

"About twenty-five hundred, not counting those who saw us on TV."

"Mankato is an hour's drive," I said, thinking out loud.

"More like an hour and a half," Marion volunteered. "Galen

Pivec drove us there and back in the Buick. Why?" she asked, then answered herself. "That's when Thoreau was shot, wasn't it?"

"Yes," I admitted.

Marion smiled. I smiled back.

"Of course, we have no idea where Freddie was, do we?"

"Mr. Taylor. If I had wanted to kill Dennis Thoreau or have him killed for the videotape, I would have the videotape. I certainly would not have called you or . . ."

"Your friend in the police department," I volunteered.

"Exactly."

"You never spoke with Dennis Thoreau yourself, did you?"

"What are you suggesting?" Marion asked.

"Nothing much," I shrugged. Then I added, "You told me that Joseph Sherman never contacted C. C."

"That's what I said."

"That's what you said," I repeated. "Only I know for a fact that Sherman spoke with C. C. on Thursday."

Marion opened her mouth but nothing came out.

"Didn't she tell you?"

Again Marion had nothing to say.

"You once told me that you were in charge around her," I said as I rose from the chair. "I'm beginning to doubt it. I'll be seeing you, Marion."

I was halfway to the door when I had another thought. "Why didn't you have Freddie deliver the money to Thoreau?"

"Freddie was hired to expose secrets, not keep them," Marion answered without looking up.

Made sense.

TWENTY-TWO

To look at Randy you would never guess that he cleared over a quarter million dollars a year, drove a Volvo and owned a brick house in Mendota Heights. Instead, you would look at his out-of-date clothes, his sleep-starved face, the nicotine stains between his fingers and the quirky-jerky way his eyes moved and assume he was probably just a seedy little bookie— which, of course, is exactly what he was.

He was waiting outside my office. "Where have you been?" he wanted to know.

"What's new?" I asked him.

"What's new is I haven't got my money is what's new. Where's my money? I want my money."

"If you don't mind my saying so," I told him as I unlocked the door, "you really ought to get a hobby."

"Always with the cracks, Taylor. Where's my money?"

"It's not Friday yet," I reminded him.

"I know what day it is. Jeezus Christ, don't you think I know what day it is?"

"Calm down."

"I'll be calm when I get my money."

I never gambled when I was on the force and I'm not a big gambler now; one hundred bucks—a honey bee—is my weekly limit, and only when I have it. Randy likes me because I'm not hard to find when I lose and I don't camp on his doorstep when I win. And because I once kinda-sorta saved his life.

We were leaving Donahue's on a bright summer afternoon nearly three years ago when a middle-aged man, well dressed in a thousand-dollar suit, pushed Randy against the wall and called him a sonuvabitch. He had one hand in his jacket pocket, pretending it was a gun, pointing the pocket at Randy's head. Randy flattened against the building in absolute terror and slid slowly to the sidewalk, bringing his knees to his chest, never taking his eyes off the pocket.

"You have a problem?" I asked the assailant calmly.

He motioned with the pocket. "You too. Up against the wall."

"You watch too many James Cagney movies," I told him.

"Move or I'll shoot," he said.

I reached under my own jacket and unholstered the Beretta, letting it hang at my side. "You won't . . . but I might," I said. The man took his hand out of the pocket. It was empty. "On the sidewalk, next to him," I ordered. The man sat next to Randy. Randy tried to get up but I shoved him down again.

"Maybe you two should talk."

They did, but not to each other.

"He owes me five K," claimed Randy.

"He threatened my children," the man protested.

"I did not."

"He did, too. He had someone call my office and when I said hello all the caller did was recite the names and ages of my two girls and where they went to school and what they were wearing when they left the house."

"It wasn't me," Randy protested.

"Of course it was," I agreed. Randy would never hurt anyone. But threaten? That's easy and Randy likes what's easy. I looked down at the gambler. While I holstered the Beretta I told him, "So, now you know what kind of people you're dealing with. Do you have what you owe?"

"Yes."

"Then pay it and get out. Get yourself in treatment if you have to. Don't ever let me see you again. Go."

The man scrambled to his feet with as much dignity as he could muster and walked quickly away.

"As for you," I said to Randy, "you don't mess with a guy's family. What's the matter with you? Families are off-limits."

"I wasn't going to hurt anyone."

"No, neither was he."

"Why do I hang out with you?" I asked Randy as he paced my office.

"We're friends," he answered casually.

"No, we're not."

"Sure, we are. And let's face it, you don't have many friends; you're just not that likable."

"I have lots of friends," I protested.

"No, you don't. You just know a lot of people."

"Go away, Randy," I told him and he did—after reminding me yet again that he wanted his money.

I told Randy I would get him his money and I meant it. Only I was embarrassed. I was a detective, for God's sake, a finder of things. Yet I had found nothing during this investigation, things had found me: John Brown, Dennis Thoreau, Amy Lamb. I had been shot at, pistol-whipped, mugged, threatened, manipulated, lied to and generally snookered. And all the while I'd just stood there with my mouth hanging open. *Well, those days are over, pal.* It was time I took charge. Randy would just have to wait.

I sat down at my PC. I could do this one of two ways. I

could call up directories myself and drag Dennis Thoreau's name through them; find out what this guy was about, maybe learn enough to start asking a few intelligent questions for a change. Or I could access an information service and have them do it for me. Both options were expensive and time consuming, only with the latter it wasn't my time. I typed a list of questions I wanted answered into my disk drive, a standard deep-background investigation, and zapped the questions to a national information service based in Austin, Texas. I informed the service I wanted the answers delivered to my electronic mailbox. Some of them would take a while. DMV information usually takes twenty-four hours. A complete financial history often takes forty-eight. As for the rest, I told the service I wanted what they had when they had it.

In the meantime . . .

Heather Schrotenboer answered her doorbell on the third ring. When she opened the door, I went inside without asking permission. She didn't seem surprised to see me.

Finding her address was easy enough. I simply did a song and dance for the University of Minnesota registrar and was directed to an off-campus apartment building near Lake Nokomis in Minneapolis. It was a nifty apartment in an attractive neighborhood—not at all what you would expect from the average graduate student. But then, Heather Schrotenboer was anything but average.

"Hi," she said, like I was the boyfriend she'd been expecting for brunch. "Want some eggs?"

"No," I told her curtly.

"Juice?"

"Listen, kid," I said, trying to sound casual, trying not to give her the pleasure of an overt threat, "I realize you're having a real swell time with this, but I just had a visit from

Guido the Killer Bookie and if he doesn't get his seventy-two fifty-five tomorrow, he's liable to shoot you."

"You wouldn't let him do that, would you?" she asked, doing a near perfect Kathleen Turner impersonation as she sashayed across the room toward me. She lightly fingered the lapels of my jacket and tilted her head up expectantly. I leaned down. When our lips were nearly touching I said, "Yes, I would," and stepped away.

"But why?" she asked, playing the dumb blonde. Only she wasn't dumb. Reckless, maybe; careless, certainly, but most definitely not dumb. I was angry now, a parent angry with a small child who simply will not listen.

"Why did you call McGaney and tell him I wasn't with you Saturday night?"

"McGaney? Oh, the cop. Taylor, I was frustrated and angry. I thought you loved me and then you . . ."

"Huh, what? Wait a minute . . ."

"You do care for me, don't you? Maybe just a little?"

"No."

"You say that, but you don't mean that. I know something happened when we met, something wonderful, I could feel it. I've been naughty, I admit it. Only you and I . . ." A solitary tear slowly trailed down her cheek.

She was good, I had to give her credit, trying to confuse my loyalties, playing to my middle-aged vanity. There was a time when her stratagem might have been successful. Times change.

"Heather, you know all those psychology textbooks you've been studying? I read them, too."

She had no response to that.

"Tomorrow," I said. "Seven thousand two hundred and fifty-five dollars. I'll be here at noon to get it."

I left her alone in the middle of the room, watching me. She was one of those few people whom you could actually see think. What she was thinking I had no idea.

TWENTY-THREE

IT WAS SURPRISINGLY quiet in the claustrophobic waiting room outside the U.S. Trustee's hearing room in Federal Bankruptcy Court. Everyone spoke in whispers, as if they were attending a funeral—everyone except a lawyer dressed in a two-thousand-dollar Armani who moved from one group to another, asking questions and collecting money. "Do you have a check for me?" he asked a woman who was unable or unwilling to make eye contact. She handed him a check and he gave her a receipt, writing something on the corner of her file envelope and tearing it off. "How about you? You have any money for me?" he asked the next man, who was sitting ramrod straight.

"I've already paid in full," the man informed him.

"Let me shake your hand," the Armani said and he did. The man grinned; he wasn't like the others, he wasn't a deadbeat.

All the chairs lining the walls had been taken and knots of people stood nervously, filling the remainder of the available space. It took a while before I spotted Cynthia Grey sitting in the corner and holding the hand of a woman who looked like a corpse. I caught her eye and she nodded. I juked and jived through the crowd toward her, brushing the shoulder of the Armani.

"You looking for Sam Halvorson?" he asked.

"No, is he lost?" I said in reply and he turned back to a file he was reading.

"Livestock?" I heard him asking a couple fidgeting in their chairs before him.

"Three cows, eight hens and a goat," the husband answered.

"Well, you'll be able to keep the animals," Halvorson told them. "Also, Wards and the bank are willing to let you keep your credit cards if you agree to pay off your debts. I recommend against it. Do you have a check for me?"

Cynthia patted the hand of the corpse, then stood and crossed the room, meeting me halfway. "Who is this guy?" I nodded toward Halvorson.

"Samuel A. Halvorson, attorney at law. When it comes to bankruptcy in Minnesota, he's the best," Cynthia said.

"Best or biggest?"

"Is there a difference?"

"Hell, yes."

"The court is running late," Cynthia told me. "We'll be up in ten minutes and then we can go to lunch. Will you wait?"

"Forever," I said.

"Oh, cut it out," she told me and went back to the corpse. Cynthia was grinning.

I moved back to the door and waited. Halvorson was arguing with a client, an older woman who insisted on paying off her VCR. "Why do it? We're here to eliminate your debts, that's why we filed for bankruptcy." When the woman kept insisting, Halvorson offered a solution. "If you don't want to give it back, you could offer to pay for it at ten cents on the dollar," he said with a wink. "Believe me, they'll take it." The woman agreed.

Cynthia's client was named Mary Thomas. When the bailiff called her name she jumped three feet. Cynthia led her into the hearing room. The U.S. Trustee started asking questions even before she reached the debtor's table.

"Have you ever filed bankruptcy before?"

"Oh, no," Mary answered in a pitiful voice that nearly cracked. "I was raised in a family where you always paid your debts, always. You don't know how I suffered over this."

The judge nodded without looking up. He said something but I couldn't hear him. Halvorson was standing behind me, counseling a client.

"You're going to get a formal notice saying your case has been discharged," Halvorson advised. "It'll come in the mail in about sixty days. That's your diploma. It means you can use a checking account, a savings account. Only don't go back to your old bank, they're liable to be nasty. And don't fret about any telephone calls. Just tell them that you've filed and that Sam Halvorson is your lawyer. If you get an unpaid notice in the mail, just write them a note saying the same thing. If you get another, toss it. If you've forgotten any creditors, just mail the name to me along with twenty dollars and I'll take care of it. Okay?"

"Okay," the client said.

"Be sure to tell your friends about me," Halvorson reminded him. The client said he would.

Mary Thomas's hearing took five minutes. She was crying when Cynthia led her past Halvorson and out of the hearing room. Halvorson chose not to notice.

"I hate bankruptcies," Cynthia told me as we walked down Marquette.

"Then why do them?" I asked.

"People need help," Cynthia said. "This economy, over a million people will file this year."

"That's discouraging."

"It'll probably get worse," she said, then added, "I'm not hungry. Is it okay if we just walk?"

"Sure."

She took my hand. Yeah, walking was fine. We strolled down the avenue hand-in-hand, looking in the windows, not speaking, comfortable in our silence. Eventually we reached Orchestra Hall and then crossed over to Peavy Plaza, where we sat on the stone steps and watched tourists tossing pennies into the fountain. There were maybe three dozen people gathered around the fountain, most of them brown-bagging it. Cynthia leaned back against the stone, her eyes closed, her chin pointed up at the noon sky. After a few moments she said, almost sadly, "Did you know I made eighty thousand dollars last year?"

"Really?" I asked.

"I'll probably gross even more this year," she said. "It doesn't seem fair."

"Then why do it?"

"It's an identity thing, it's being able to say, 'I'm a successful attorney.' That can mean a lot. Especially to a woman."

"I understand," I said.

"No insult intended, Taylor, but I doubt it. I really do."

She was probably right.

After a while, she said, "I wonder where Joseph Sherman is."

"Someone is hiding him," I speculated. "If he's still in the state, most likely someone is hiding him. But he'll turn up. After a few days he'll become bored with the hole he crawled into and come up for air; he'll try to make a life for himself. When he does, the cops will take him. It's just a matter of time."

"Can you find him?"

"Probably. Give me enough time. Only I doubt that it's worth the effort. If he wants your help, if he wants mine, he'll find us. That's the only way it's going to work."

"Do you think he killed John Brown?"

"He had opportunity. Motive? Hell, I've busted guys who killed people because their radios were too loud. The important question is, did Sherman also kill Amy Lamb? My gut tells me no, but my gut has been wrong before. There's also Dennis Thoreau to consider. I'm conducting a computer search even as we speak to see if there's something, anything—a name, an address—that links the two men. You can bet the ranch the cops are doing the same thing."

"I know why the police care. Why do you?" Cynthia asked.

"About Brown and Thoreau? I don't. But whoever killed them probably killed Amy Lamb and I do care about that."

"Why?"

"I feel partly responsible."

"Do you want to talk about it?"

"Not particularly."

"You're not one of those macho guys who keep all their emotions inside, are you?"

"I show my emotions," I reminded her. "I showed them just the other night outside Le Chateau. If I recall, you weren't too happy about it."

"Don't remind me," she said.

We did not speak for a long time after that, not until Cynthia asked, "Are you really a strong, silent, hard-boiled character, or are you just posing for me?"

"Posing?"

"Gary Cooper, Humphrey Bogart, Robert Mitchum."

"Robert Mitchum? I don't think so."

"Time will tell," she said.

I reached out my hand and Cynthia took it. We retraced our steps, walking back to the office tower that housed the Federal Bankruptcy Court. This time the silence was awkward; we were both waiting for the other to speak.

Finally, Cynthia said, "Will I see you tonight?"

I thought she'd never ask. "That can be arranged," I answered.

She nodded. "We are going to get involved, then."

"We already are involved."

"One night isn't involvement," Cynthia said. "It's exercise."

"You're very cynical, you know that?"

"If a woman doesn't want to see a man, she has to tell him

not to call and usually that's not enough; she also has to give reasons. It's easier for a man. You don't want to see a woman, you just stop seeing her, stop calling, no explanations. After a few weeks the woman realizes she's been discarded. That happens to a woman often enough, yeah, she becomes cynical."

"I understand," I told her and she shook her head—there I went again, saying I understood when I probably didn't. Only this time, I did. Absolutely.

I let go of her hand when we reached the office building. We stood outside the revolving door and kissed each other and pressed our foreheads together and I asked, "Do you really make eighty thousand dollars a year?"

"See, now that's the kind of sweet talk a woman likes to hear."

TWENTY-FOUR

MOST OF THE INFORMATION I wanted on Dennis Thoreau was already in my e-mail when I returned from lunch. There was a time when I hated computers, when I looked upon PIs who used them with utter contempt. Now I don't know how I managed without one.

A quick skim gave me an outline of Thoreau's life and times.

NAME: Thoreau, Dennis Reese.
SSN: 473-00-8118 is valid; subject has not used other SSN.
SEX: Male.
PARENTS: Raymond and Alice (Reese) T.
FAMILY: Married Meghan Chakolis; divorced after eight
    months; no children.
EDUCATION: H.S., Irondale, New Brighton, MN;
    Attended University of Minnesota; no credits.
CRIMINAL: Dis. Con., Prescott, AZ, fine & time served; DUI,
    Modesto, CA, fine.
CIVIL LITIGATION: No record.
DRIVER'S LICENSE NO.: Info to come.
DRIVING RECORD: Info to come.
VECHILE REGISTRATION: Info to come.
CURRENT EMPLOYMENT: Salesman, AAA Printing,

91000 Washington Ave., Minneapolis, MN 55402.

PREVIOUS EMPLOYMENT: Info to come.

FINANCIAL: Current credit cards—Info to come; Chapter Seven Bankruptcy, Federal Bankruptcy Court, Salina, KS.

REAL PROPERTY: Info to come.

CIVIC/POLITICAL ACTIVITIES: No record. Still searching.

MILITARY: No record.

GROUPS/CLUBS/ORGANIZATIONS/AWARDS: No record. Still searching.

POLITICAL/RELIGIOUS AFFILIATION: Subject is not registered to vote; raised Methodist.

CURRENT ADDRESS: 24889 Dayton Ave., St. Paul, MN 55105 (rental property, Stephen J. Kirkus, private owner).

PREVIOUS ADDRESSES: 1127 Desnoyer Dr., New Brighton, MN; 25026 27th St. S., Minneapolis, MN; 881 Gondola Blvd., Enid, OK; 98½ President St., Prescott, AZ; 11600 Hempstead, Salina, KS; 170 Eureka Curve, Modesto, CA.

(List of six neighbors with names and phone numbers for each address above available upon request.)

"I'll be damned," I said aloud.

I went back to the PC. This time I did the work myself, accessing a national information service that specialized in biographical data. I input my instructions and waited, listening to the clicks and whirls of my machine.

Scanning, please wait . . .

Scanning, please wait . . .

Scanning, please wait . . .

　　Scan completed.

Press (return) to see your results . . . ->

Biographical Information scan results for: MEGHAN CHAKOLIS

PRESS TO SEARCH RESULTS

Format　Source　Type

Academic American Encyclopedia 0 full text directories
American Men & Women of Science 0 full text directories

EduDATA 1 full text directories

Everyman's Encyclopedia 0 full text directories

Marquis Who's Who in America 0 full text directories

S&P Register–Biographical 0 full text directories

H Database descriptions

M Main Menu

SOS on-line assistance

System is now searching the EduDATA database, copyrighted 1991

by EduDATA Education Data Service, Chicago, IL

Accessing network .... Completed

Accessing Database Host .... Completed

Logging on .... Completed

Logging on (second step) .... Completed

Selecting Database .... Completed

Submitting Search .... Completed

Retrieving the only full text article available on that subject.

^S/^Q: stop/start; ^T: Paging ON; ^C/(esc):

interrupt (^=CTRL/CONTROL key)

00093478 WA42, WA43, WA44 Record

provided by: EduDATA

Chakolis,*Meghan* (Chakolis, Meghan Marie)

OCCUPATION(S): public relations practitioner.

BORN: New Brighton, MN.

PARENTS: Thomas and Carolynn (Pivec) C.

SEX: Female.

FAMILY: married Dennis Thoreau, divorced, children—none.

EDUCATION: B.A., U. Minnesota, degree journalism, theater.
    M.A., U. Minnesota, degree journalism. Summa Cum
    Laude, Phi Beta Kappa, National Honor Society.

CAREER: Assistant public relations director, St. Catherine
    Memorial Hospital, MN; Public relations director, Con-
    cern HMO, Minneapolis, MN; Director House Informa-
    tion Office, MN House of Rep., St. Paul, MN.

CIVIC/POLITICAL ACTIVITIES: Campaign director Carol
        Catherine Monroe (elected House of Representatives).
POLITICAL/RELIGIOUS AFFILIATION: Methodist.
ADDRESS: 1237 Glendale St., Brooklyn Center, MN.

"Taylor," I said aloud, "you are the dumbest human being alive."

TWENTY-FIVE

"**W**OULD YOU LIKE some coffee, Mr. Taylor?" Dot Ladner asked.

"Thank you."

"Decaffeinated all right?"

"Yes, ma'am."

"I can't drink the other stuff no more. I get nervous."

"Yes, ma'am."

Dot filled a generous mug, set it in front of me and waited for me to taste it. I did. It wasn't anything special.

"Delicious," I said.

"Cookies?"

"No, thank you."

"It's no trouble."

"Thank you, no, ma'am." I patted my stomach. "Have to stay fit."

"Oh yes, of course. I'm sorry, what did you want to know?"

"How long has Ms. Chakolis been residing here?"

"Eight years come January."

"And you've been caretaker the entire time."

"Oh yes. Like I told you before, the building is owned by my nephew so I have plenty of job security."

"Was she living alone during the incident with Joseph Sherman?"

"Meghan? Yes, except when her husband was visiting."

"Her husband?"

"Uh-huh."

"Dennis Thoreau?"

Dot shrugged. "Dennis was his first name, I didn't know his last name. I always figured it was Chakolis. You know, when I was a girl, you took the husband's name and you kept it."

"Yes, ma'am. However, my information suggests that Ms. Chakolis and Dennis Thoreau were divorced in March of 1980."

"Mine, too."

"You knew that?"

"I knew they were divorced, I didn't know when."

"Yet, Thoreau stayed with her?"

"Personally," the old woman said, leaning close, "I think he was trying to patch it up with her." Then she leaned back and added, "Very nice boy, well mannered."

"When was the last time you saw him?"

"Oh, six years ago. Back, like you said, when that business with Joseph Sherman took place. He left right afterward. I was sorry to see him go, too. I could have used his help."

"You and Dennis were friends?"

"I don't want you to get the wrong idea, Mr. Taylor."

"No, ma'am."

"Dennis was young enough to be my own son."

"Yes, ma'am."

"Although he was as cute as the dickens."

"Yes, ma'am."

"We would talk is all and watch the soaps together. Sometimes he would bring doughnuts. He was very concerned about Erica."

"Erica?"

"Erica Kane. On 'All My Children.' Are you sure you won't have some cookies?"

"No, thank you. Why did Dennis leave? Did he tell you?"

"Meghan threw him out."

"Is that what he said?"

Dot took a bite of cookie and answered through the crumbs, "That's what she said."

"Did she say why?"

"No, but I think it was pretty sudden. One day they were a happy couple, the next he was packing."

Meghan Chakolis led me down the tunnel that connected the State Office Building with the capitol. The tunnel was brightly lit with video cameras and emergency call boxes every hundred feet.

"Tell me about Dennis Thoreau," I told her.

"Why?"

"You were married to him."

"Is that a question?" Meghan asked.

"No. You were married to him."

"And divorced. A long time ago."

"Have you seen him since?"

"Many times."

"When was the last time?"

"The night he was killed. I went to his place after work, we had sex and I left. Is that what you wanted to know?"

"Flabbergast" is an interesting word. It's eighteenth-century slang meaning "to make speechless with amazement; astonish." And boy, was I flabbergasted. I stopped dead in the middle of the tunnel and gawked at her like she was the Eighth Wonder of the World.

"I have nothing to hide," she told me.

"Apparently not."

"I didn't kill him."

"Can you prove that?"

"No," she admitted. "Fortunately, I don't have to."

She had me there.

"Anything else you want to know?" she asked. The smile told me she was more than willing to cooperate. Why shouldn't she?

"Tell me about you and Thoreau," I said.

"Dennis and I were married right after high school graduation," Meghan volunteered. "It was a foolish thing to do, to get married so young. We went on a glorious honeymoon, rented a cozy bungalow in Minneapolis, bought a lot of stuff we couldn't afford, began fighting and divorced. Dennis took off—I think he went to Oklahoma that time. I went back to school. He returned and I discovered that I still cared for him. Men like Dennis, you can't stay angry at them. It's like carrying on a vendetta with the rain. Besides, he was so much fun. The most fun I've ever had in my life. So, he would come and he would go and that's the way we lived."

"If you don't mind my saying so, you don't seem very distraught over his death."

"I do mind, Mr. Taylor. I mind very much."

We were standing at the capitol end of the tunnel, where the State Capitol Security Force was headquartered. Through the window I could see a bank of TV monitors and a uniformed officer scanning them. Conan stood next to the officer. But he was watching Meghan and me. I nodded at him and led Meghan past the window.

"Dennis was living in your apartment while you were managing C. C. Monroe's first run for the House," I reminded her.

"For a time."

"You threw him out."

"Yes."

"Why?"

"He was cheating on me," Meghan said.

"With whom?"

"Carol Catherine."

Lord, she was just full of surprises.

"Yet you're still her friend."

Meghan sighed. "Carol Catherine and I always will be friends no matter what happens, no matter what one does to the other. Don't you have a friend like that?"

I thought of Anne Scalasi. "One or two," I said.

"Well, then . . ."

We walked some more.

"We were roommates at the University of Minnesota," Meghan said. "We shared everything, even boyfriends. It didn't surprise me that Carol Catherine thought the arrangement also included husbands. I don't blame her. I blame Dennis. Besides, Dennis and I weren't married at the time. What is it they say in basketball? No foul . . ."

"No harm, no foul."

"'No harm, no foul,'" she repeated. "Anyway, quitting Carol Catherine would not have been in my best interest." (There was that phrase again.) "I agreed to manage her campaign for the House of Representatives for the same reason she agreed to run: to make contacts. As luck would have it, we were both very successful. She won the election and I was appointed to this position."

We were standing in the rotunda beneath the State Capitol's massive dome, near the center where a huge, eight-pointed star was imbedded in the marble floor. A troop of Cub Scouts leaned against the second-floor railing and looked down, half listening to a tour guide with a red, white and blue tie. Above, huge murals depicting various saints earning their sainthood graced the dome walls. Below, battle flags from the Civil War and miscellaneous Indian campaigns unfurled behind glass. Included among them was the bullet-torn flag of the First Minnesota Infantry Regiment, the regiment that saved the Union's bacon on Cemetery Ridge at Gettysburg, losing two hundred fifteen out of two hundred sixty-two soldiers in the process. It was displayed next to Frank B. Kellogg's

Nobel Peace Prize, earned for his work as coauthor of a pact renouncing the use of war as an "instrument of national policy." The pact was signed August 27, 1928, by sixty-two nations. All sixty-two participated in the World War just eleven years later. Well, at least Frank had tried.

"I'll miss this place when I leave," Meghan said.

"Are you leaving?"

"Eventually, I suppose. I guess I'm more like Dennis than I care to admit. I like to move around."

"You could stay and get an appointment from Carol Catherine if she's elected governor," I suggested.

"You mean when, don't you?" Meghan asked, and then shook her head. "Marion is Carol Catherine's chief of staff and she doesn't like me much; she thinks I'm a bad influence on Carol Catherine. When we were in school, we used to party pretty hard."

All right, I decided, now's a good time to let her have it, to kick down the wall of indifference she was hiding behind. "Did you know that Dennis and Carol Catherine made a pornographic movie together?"

"Sure."

You really know how to shake up a client, don't you, Taylor?

"Carol Catherine told me about it six years ago."

"You weren't upset?"

"Of course I was upset. That's why I showed Dennis the door. But like I said, it was six years ago. It requires too much energy, too much concentration, to stay angry over something that happened six years ago."

"Have Dennis and Carol Catherine been together since they made the tape?" I asked.

"Absolutely not!" Meghan's answer was vehement to the point of startling me.

I had to wait a few beats before asking my next question, "Are you aware that Dennis . . ."

"Attempted to blackmail Carol Catherine? Of course. Carol

Catherine told me everything. And in anticipation of your next question, Mr. Taylor, no, I do not believe she had anything to do with his death."

"What do you believe?"

"I believe the newspaper's explanation that Dennis was killed over drugs. I could see him getting involved in that; he was foolish enough."

Meghan Chakolis was starting to annoy me the way Barry Bonds annoyed National League pitchers: She was getting good wood on everything I served up. I decided to throw her an inside curve, see if I could move her off the plate. "Dennis was endangering Carol Catherine's campaign for the governor's office. Perhaps Marion Senske had him killed."

"Oh, Mr. Taylor. I'd hardly think so," she said, smiling at my suggestion. Then she glanced at her watch and told me it was time she returned to her office. Her heels made a pleasant echo on the marble floor as she walked away; I listened to them long after she was out of sight.

TWENTY-SIX

I STOPPED AT A hardware store for a can of putty and a pane of glass cut to fit my front window, the one the bullet had gone crashing through. Across the street from the store was a park with four softball diamonds, all of them idle. My friends and I used to play softball. We were pretty good, too; won a few tournaments, won a few league championships. Most of us had known each other since we were five years old and playing T-ball at Linwood Park. The game kept us together for nearly thirty years and while we played there was always time for dinners and parties and just hanging out; always time to have a few beers and talk it over. But families and jobs and the responsibilities of age eventually took their toll and one day there simply weren't enough of us left to field a team. Soon after that there wasn't enough time for anything. Now we get together once a year, at Christmas. I drove home depressed.

I stood on the aluminum ladder outside my front window, fumbling helplessly with the glass, trying mightily—and unsuccessfully—to seal it securely in the frame without smudging it with putty. As I worked I reflected on the identity of the person responsible for the shattered window and realized that if anyone wanted to shoot me in the back, now would be a good time.

"Hi, Taylor," a voice called.

I dropped the glass and putty knife and dived into the hedge that ran under the front windows.

"Did you fall?" the voice asked, concerned. It belonged to twelve-year-old Tammy Mandt.

"Don't ever, ever do that again," I yelled at her.

"Do what?" she yelled back. Tammy was tough; she didn't like to be pushed around. Yet she also was insecure; she looked down, away and over my head, but never directly at me.

I gave her a hug. "I'm sorry. You startled me."

"I'm sorry," she said and hugged back.

"No, I'm sorry," I insisted.

"No, I'm sorry."

"No, I'm sorry."

By the seventh "sorry" she was laughing.

"May I take Ogilvy for a walk?" she asked.

"Help yourself. His harness is on . . ." She didn't wait for my directions but scampered into my house. I went back to the window. The job took twenty minutes more—constantly looking over my shoulder slowed me down—and when I was finished I wondered why I had even bothered; the glass was so badly smudged you could barely see through it. Still, it kept out the rain and cold. I stood under it, admiring my handi-work, as Cynthia Grey drove up. She was wearing a high-neck blouse with a lace-trimmed collar under my sweatshirt; a pretty woman dressed in lace can sell me anything she wants. I walked toward her and she walked toward me, but before we met, Tammy came out of the house calling my name.

"Taylor, I'm going to take . . . Oh, hi," she said to Cynthia.

"Hi," Cynthia replied.

"I'm taking Ogilvy for a walk in the park now," Tammy informed us.

"Really? You can take rabbits for walks?" Cynthia asked with incredulity.

"Well, yeah," Tammy answered, apparently wondering why adults were so dense. She set Ogilvy on the grass and attached a fifteen-foot-long red leash to his harness. Cynthia knelt next to the rabbit and scratched his nose. Tammy regarded her suspiciously for a moment and then asked, "Are you Taylor's new girlfriend?" Kids say the darnedest things.

Cynthia blushed. She glanced at me and then back to the young girl. "Yes," she said.

"Okay," Tammy said. "C'mon, Ogilvy," she told the rabbit and gave his leash a tug. Ogilvy bounded off toward the street, Tammy hanging onto the red ribbon. They didn't get far. Kids have a radar for this sort of thing and before Tammy and Ogilvy had made it to the boulevard, a half-dozen urchins appeared out of thin air and crowded around, petting the rabbit, asking questions, allowing as to how they always wanted a rabbit, too, and conspiring to get one from their parents.

Cynthia watched with intense interest. She was smiling broadly when she came to me and wrapped her arms around me, hugging me tight.

We played miniature golf and Cynthia beat me three games straight, but the sun was in my eyes and my head still hurt and besides, I let her win. We roamed the shops on Grand Avenue and she bought me a bookmark that said: BE ALERT; THE WORLD NEEDS ALL THE LERTS IT CAN GET. I bought her a double-scoop French-vanilla ice cream cone. She bought me a sixteen-ounce T-bone at a pretty good steakhouse on West Seventh Street. I paid for the drinks at a jazz joint near Como Park where they know me; the woman fronting the house quartet dedicated a song to us from the stage, Hoagy Carmichael's "I Get Along Without You Very Well."

It was past one when we pulled into my driveway. I invited

Cynthia inside. She declined, saying she had to get up early. So, we necked in the front seat for about fifteen minutes. I invited her inside again, she wavered, but finally pushed me out of the car and drove off. Damn. Maybe I should have hired someone to shoot at us.

The digital display of my AM/FM clock radio with snooze alarm read 5:11 when the sound of my ringing telephone woke me from a Technicolor dream in which Cynthia and I were . . . Well, never mind that. The phone rang. It was Detective Martin McGaney.

"Meet me," he said.

TWENTY-SEVEN

IF YOU STOOD on your toes, you could see the black roof of the Ramsey County morgue across the river from where Joseph Sherman fell; you could follow the meat wagon as it climbed Hill Street to Kellogg Boulevard, took the Wabasha Bridge across the Mississippi River and turned into Harriet Island where Sherman lay facedown on the dry earth.

A tip was called into 911 about 2 A.M. The tipster, a man who suffered from a sudden, unexplained bout of amnesia when asked his name, said he and his girlfriend had discovered a body below the cliffs across the river from downtown St. Paul. A car was quickly dispatched, an officer located Sherman's body and the mechanism that is a homicide investigation was shoved into gear.

By the time I arrived the machine was humming along. The techs were already at work. One of them used a can of white spray paint to circle a .9 mm-casing found several feet from the body. Another took photographs; a strobe flashed like lightning across the graying sky, illuminating Sherman's shattered skull and the dark liquid running from his nose.

A large-caliber bullet had made a dime-sized entrance wound in the roof of Sherman's mouth and destroyed his brain before leaving a baseball-sized hole in the back of his head. A

.9mm Beretta was clasped tightly in his right hand. His left hand was between his knees, the palm turned outward. There were bloodstains on the front and back of Sherman's red-and-white shirt and jeans. His shoes were splattered with mud.

"Well, that's that," Casper said. "Suicide."

"Give me a light here," I requested, bending close to the body, looking hard at Sherman's wrists. I found contusions on both of them, just below the worn cuffs of his shirt.

"See it?" I asked.

"Yeah," McGaney replied.

"What? What are you looking at?" Casper stammered.

I left the scene and moved to a bench about three hundred yards away to watch as the rising sun turned the city from gray to gold. McGaney joined me some time later and together we followed a taconite barge as it drifted lazily past, following the river to St. Louis or Kansas City or New Orleans or a hundred other places we would rather have been. Finally, McGaney said, "Talk to me." And I did. I told him I had met Sherman at Le Chateau. I told him what he said to me and what I thought of his words. I told him Sherman had been carrying a Taurus.

"Are you sure?" McGaney asked. "They're very similar in appearance, a Taurus and a Beretta."

"I'm sure," I said.

We were soon joined by Casper, who seemed puzzled. "I just spoke to the lieutenant," he told McGaney. "I told her we identified the body. I told her it looked like a suicide." Casper shook his head.

"What did she say?" McGaney prompted.

"She said to be sure."

"Good idea," McGaney told him.

"It's suicide," Casper insisted. "Isn't it?"

"Maybe," McGaney said.

"What 'maybe'? What did you see that I didn't?"

"Start with the gun," McGaney told him. "He was still holding it; a man who shoots himself usually isn't able to do that."

"Cadaveric spasm," Casper protested. "I've seen suicides who go into spontaneous rigor mortis, who grip the gun so tight it leaves an impression in their hand. Haven't you?"

"I suppose," McGaney said.

"Yeah," Casper grunted, waiting for more. "Yeah," he repeated when none came.

"Look at his wrists, goddamn it!" I shouted.

"What about 'em?"

"The marks on his wrists," McGaney answered.

"Yeah?"

"They're the same marks handcuffs leave when you struggle against them."

"Hold the phone, *hold the phone,*" Casper demanded. "Are you saying he was murdered? By a cop?"

"Don't jump to so many conclusions," McGaney told Casper.

"Anyone can get handcuffs," I said.

"Are you saying a cop did this?"

"Keep your voice down," McGaney warned.

"Are you saying a cop did this?" Casper whispered.

"Maybe," McGaney answered.

Casper pondered the possibility with great solemnity, weighing it carefully, considering its consequences to the department, to himself, and said, "No. It's a suicide. No doubt about it. Suicide. The sonuvabitch killed two people, knew he was going down for it, couldn't bear to go back to prison and did himself. I'll bet a month's pay that the gun he used was the same one that killed Brown and the Lamb girl."

"I'd be surprised if it wasn't," I said, but Casper wasn't listening.

"Suicide. That's what I'm going to say in my report; you can say what you like."

I'd heard enough. I walked slowly back toward my Monza. If it came to it, Casper would be some defense attorney's best friend.

"Hey, where are you going?" Casper wanted to know. "The lieutenant said she wants to talk to you."

"She knows where to find me," I shouted over my shoulder and kept walking.

I sat in the car, listening to the engine idle. The cops couldn't find Sherman; I probably couldn't have found him even if I had looked hard. So, how had the killer? Maybe the killer hadn't. Maybe Sherman found the killer. I had a thought. I shut down the Monza and went looking for McGaney. I found him standing just inside the yellow tape imprinted POLICE LINE DO NOT CROSS. The ambulance jockeys had loaded Sherman onto a gurney.

"Just one second?" I asked, gesturing at the corpse. McGaney nodded and I asked the jocks to unzip the black vinyl bag. I checked Sherman's wrists again. And smiled.

"What?" McGaney asked.

"His shirt," I answered. "It's old."

It was still early, but I swung over to Heather Schrotenboer's apartment, anyway—I had things to do and I wanted to get her off my plate. I found her sitting on the stoop in front of her apartment building, cradling a coffee mug in her hands. "Beautiful day, isn't it?" she said. "The weatherman said it would get up to seventy-five degrees. Not many days like this left before winter."

"Do you have the money?"

"Nope," she said.

I didn't have time for this. "Good luck to you," I said.

"Don't worry about me."

"I won't."

I found a telephone that you can dial from your car in the parking lot of a minimart two blocks away. I called Randy.

"Heather Schrotenboer," I said and gave him the address. "One thing, though," I told him. "I will be very, Very, VERY displeased if anything nasty should befall her."

The halfway house hadn't changed much since I had been there last. Its concrete steps were still crumbling, it still needed paint and J. T. was still on the porch looking as surly as ever. Only this time he made no attempt to punch me out.

"I'd like to see Elliot Seeley," I told him.

"Hey, Elliot, some guy to see ya!" he shouted through the screen door without moving.

"Thanks," I said.

A moment later Seeley appeared. "Mr. Taylor, isn't it?"

"I have a couple of quick questions and then I'm out of here," I assured him.

"All right."

"When Sherman left last Saturday, what was he wearing?"

Seeley shrugged. "Sports jacket, shirt, black slacks . . . "

"What color shirt?"

"White. Cotton, I think. Why?"

Seeley had described what Sherman was wearing when I met him at Le Chateau. But not what he was wearing when he died.

"Did he take clothes with him?"

"Saturday? No, of course not."

"Have you seen him since Saturday?"

"No, as I keep telling the police . . ."

"Could he have come back without your knowledge, come back for some of his belongings?"

"No. But he could afford to buy new ones."

"Maybe not. If his money was in a bank . . ."

"It was."

". . . he might have been too frightened to go near it. He would only have the money he had on him."

"He was flashing a pretty big wad," Seeley told me. "Maybe a thousand."

Six hundred fifty of which he spent on a gun. "Thank you," I said and headed back toward my car.

"Pussy," J. T. called as I walked away. I ignored him.

Dot Ladner was not happy to see me.

"I want to see the locker where you kept Sherman's belongings," I said. When Dot didn't respond quickly enough to suit me, I started toward the basement. She followed after me. We stopped in front of the wooden locker with BUILDING stenciled across the front. I pulled on the lock. It was still secure, but the base plate wasn't. The screws had been removed. I pulled on the handle. The door swung open easily and smoothly, taking the lock with it. I stepped inside, yanked the string that operated the overhead light and found assorted pieces of furniture, most of them stacked on top of one another. Everything was covered with dust—everything except a large carton. I opened it; it was filled with clothes. The top layer had been tossed in anywhichway, without consideration for wrinkles, yet the clothes on the bottom of the carton were neatly folded. In between I found a wrinkled white cotton shirt. The shirt smelled of body odor. I left the clothes where I found them, closed the carton and then the door, and warned Dot to leave things just as they were.

I had Cynthia's office telephone number but not her address, and the news I had to give her you give in person—whether you want to or not. I found her firm in the phone book. Hers was an understated ad. It said simply: Grey & Associates, Attorneys at Law and listed her address, suite and telephone number. No punctuation. The ad on the facing page, however, had enough punctuation for a dozen law firms:

ACCUSED OF A CRIME?
DON'T TAKE IT LYING DOWN!
CALL TOM CROWDER!
FREE CONSULTATION! ANY TIME! ANY DAY!
Experienced Criminal Defense Lawyers!
DRUNK DRIVING—DRUG CHARGES
SEX CRIMES—ASSAULTS
MISDEMEANORS—GROSS MISDEMEANORS
FELONIES OF ALL KINDS!
"We're in Your Corner Fighting for You!"

Certainly inspired me to trust.

So many of the lawyers I've worked with over the years are pompous, self-absorbed, litigation-happy nitwits who do little more than clog the system with niggling actions in a never-ending search for the mother lode—a deep, deep pocket that's held in low regard by a jury. They're not attorneys, they're prospectors: They measure success not in cases won or lost, nor in justice served, but rather in the amount of damages awarded, in billable hours, in nuggets of gold. Even then I wouldn't mind so much except that there are so damn many of them and so comparatively few legitimate cases. As a result, lawyers are forced to create work for themselves by encouraging ordinary citizens to litigate over every little thing. This fosters an environment in which people take no responsibility for their own actions, where every problem or slight—real or imagined—can be blamed on a second party or a third or a fourth, who often is required to pay and pay big.

I have a grudging respect for criminal attorneys, even those who have attempted to make me look silly on the witness stand. And I give little credence to critics, who, in their anger

241

and frustration, often accuse them of corrupting the law, of using obscure technicalities and loopholes to pluck hardened thieves, rapists and murderers out of prison so they can pillage the nearest day-care center. Criminal attorneys, after all, are doing a job necessary to the survival of our civilization—they are providing equal representation under the law. If that means defending loathsome scum as if their own lives depended on it, well, that's certainly what I would expect from my attorney. As for civil lawyers, it's like they all took ancillary courses while studying the law: Litigation 101—How To Get Rich by Accident.

Cynthia Grey had offices in one of the oldest buildings in downtown St. Paul, a former convent remodeled to serve lawyers, accountants, advertising agencies and other small businesses. Its six floors were all adorned with marble ceilings, huge windows and hardwood—plenty of hardwood—most of it carved, projecting an image of permanence and style. The conference rooms, with their fireplaces and grand pianos, polished chandeliers and book-lined walls, only enhanced the image.

"Grey & Associates" was actually just Cynthia, two legal secretaries and two freelance attorneys who occasionally helped out when the workload got too heavy for Cynthia to carry. The secretary who greeted me at the door was obviously not pleased to see me—just drop in, unannounced, without an appointment, without even calling first? What was I thinking? She was ultracool, ultramodern, with sharp features and black hair that fell to the middle of her back. She wore a teal silk blouse. At least I think it was silk. It was shiny, anyway. She did remarkable things for the blouse; the designer would have been pleased. I shouldn't have stared but how often do you see teal?

As I was appraising her, she was appraising me, though with a lot less appreciation. She made one pass over my white Nikes, blue jeans, Irish tweed jacket and white shirt and probably decided I was a high school teacher accused of molesting a student. SEX CRIMES—ASSAULTS—FELONIES OF EVERY KIND.

"May I help you, sir?" she asked, clearly hoping I would say no and leave.

"I would like to see Miss Grey, please."

"May I say who is calling?" I gave her my name. She repeated it into her intercom like it was a disease that required treatment with penicillin. When Cynthia emerged from her office and hugged me, she pretended not to see.

"What's her story?" I asked Cynthia when we were safely inside with the door closed.

"She thinks most men are sexist pigs."

"That's ridiculous."

"Did you stare at her chest?"

"Well, I, you know . . ."

"So, go back out and tell her that it's not true, that most men aren't sexist pigs."

"Pass."

"Uh-huh."

After we sat down, Cynthia told me, "I'm actually very glad to see you."

"Even if I am a sexist pig?"

"We'll have to work on that. Anyway, let me tell you what happened. A man came into my office this morning, wants to take action against his former employer for age discrimination. What happened was, he became a grandfather for the first time; he was pretty excited about it. A couple of days after the child was born, he cruised the office showing pictures, telling everyone the boy was named after him. He showed the picture to his boss. The boss says, 'I didn't realize you were that old.' The next day, the boss takes him aside. My client thinks he's about to get a bonus, maybe even a raise. After all, he was the firm's sales manager and in the previous nine months had quadrupled the office's sales volume. But instead of the bonus, he was fired. His boss said the decision was 'based on the numbers,' that the office 'simply wasn't doing well.' My client, who is fifty-eight, was then replaced by a man in his early thirties, a man my client had trained."

"Are you taking the case?"

"Age discrimination is complicated," Cynthia replied. "Very difficult to prove. You are not going to find a signed memo stating, 'Get rid of the old geezer.' It's much more subtle than that. Plus, you have to file in federal court, which has a backlog that stretches into the next decade. Hours upon hours of depositions have to be taken, massive amounts of paper . . ."

"I didn't ask you that. I asked if you're going to take the case."

"Of course I am. You don't fire people because they're old any more than you fire them because they're black or gay or female. It's wrong. It's illegal. I'm going to get these guys. Want to help?"

"Help?"

"It'll be fun, working together," she assured me. "What I need is to find former employees, anyone who has been fired by the company in the past five years. That's first. Then . . . What's the matter?"

"Nothing," I told her. "Listen, you're right, working together would be fun, but . . . not right now. I have a few things I need to do, first."

"A few days probably won't make any difference," Cynthia said cautiously.

We spent the next half minute listening to the ticking of her antique clock. Finally, Cynthia asked, "Why don't we talk about the reason you came?"

"I just wanted to see you, say hi. Can't I do that?"

"Since the moment you walked in you've been waiting to tell me something. Now's a good time."

"Have you had any contact with Joseph Sherman since the other night?"

"At Le Chateau? No. I . . ."

"None at all?"

"What's happened?"

I took a deep breath and let her have it. "He's dead."

Cynthia reacted to my news by not reacting, by not moving a muscle.

"I see," she said finally, quietly. "Did the police . . ."

"No. When the cops found him he was already dead. He either committed suicide or was murdered; the cops aren't sure yet."

My expression must have told her something because, in a flat, lifeless voice, she said, "But you're sure."

"I'm sure."

"He was murdered."

"Yes."

"C. C. Monroe."

"Possibly."

"What are you going to do about it?"

"Go after the killer."

"When?"

"When I'm ready."

"I see," she said as if she actually did, then added, "Sunday?"

"Maybe before then."

"No, I mean . . ." Cynthia took two tickets from the top drawer of her desk and handed them to me. "Do you want to go to the Vikings football game with me?"

"Sure."

"They're playing the San Francisco 49ers," she said. "Are they any good?"

"They've been known to win a game or two," I answered, convinced that Cynthia was doing exactly what she once accused me of: posing. Only I didn't pursue the issue.

"I'll pick you up at your place," she said. "When would be a good time?"

"Eleven?"

"See you then," she answered and returned the tickets to the desk drawer. "I have to get back to work."

I went to the door and opened it; she stopped me with her voice.

"You seem to handle it so well," she said, looking at me, her eyes pleading.

"So do you," I told her.

She turned to the papers scattered on her desk and I stepped through the open doorway. What choice did either of us have? So much violence. It'll mess your mind if you let it. At best, it leaves you with a numbing awareness that the world is often very dark and very cruel. Occasionally, it goes beyond that, squeezing your heart and scrambling your brain and making you want to scream to high heaven. I've seen it burn out a lot of good men; it almost got me. But there's a trick. The trick is not to fight it and not to linger over it. The trick is just to let it happen. The trick is to take it for what it is—a part of life— and let it go.

As I was leaving the office, I heard Cynthia's voice plaintively delivering instructions over the intercom to her secretary. "I don't want to be disturbed," she said.

TWENTY-EIGHT

I HAD STOPPED outside my office door, my hand in my pocket fumbling for my keys, when I saw them approach: two men, their suit jackets unbuttoned, one on either side of me. They moved deliberately down the corridor, trying to act casual, almost pulling it off. They stopped six feet away, keeping their distance, keeping their edge. I looked from one to the other.

"Minneapolis Police Department," the man on the right said, fishing a shield out of his outside jacket pocket and holding it up for me to inspect. I looked at the other. He showed me his shield, too.

"What did I do?" I asked.

I couldn't figure out what crime I had committed and the detectives who picked me up were no help at all. I only knew it was big, capital *B-I-G*, because they took me to Room 108 in the Minneapolis City Hall. Room 108 is Homicide.

"What's it all about?" I asked, but Sean O'Connell, chief of the Minneapolis Police Department's Homicide unit, wouldn't answer me, either; wouldn't even look me in the eye. The young Hennepin County assistant attorney who sat next to him had no trouble with eye contact, however; no sir. He stared fiercely at me without blinking, like he wanted to burn a hole through my skull. His name was Paul Aasen and he didn't like me at all. He got right to it, a police stenographer taking down every word.

"Do you know a Mr. Randy Sullivan?"

"Possibly."

"I will ask the question again: Do you know Mr. Randy Sullivan?"

"I do."

"He is a gambler, a bookie?"

"If you say so."

"What do you say?"

"I don't."

"It would behoove you, sir, to cooperate with this office."

"Fuck you."

"Jeezus, Taylor," O'Connell moaned.

"You, too, Sean," I told him. "You drag me off the street, drag me down here, no explanations, no nothing. I don't need this. If you want to arrest me, arrest me; read me my rights, I'll call my attorney and we'll take it from there. Otherwise, you tell me what's going on or I'm leaving."

Nice speech, I thought. Gritty, loaded with defiance. But Aasen had a speech prepared, too. It went like this: "Mr. Taylor, this is a field investigation; you are not in custody. Therefore, we are not obliged to advise you of your rights. However, you will answer my questions. You will answer them here and now, without further obfuscation. If you refuse, I will subpoena you to appear before the grand jury and you will answer them there. If you refuse again, you will be held in contempt." Aasen smiled, slipped a piece a paper out of his folder, glanced at it, returned it to the folder and smiled again. "Your license comes up for review in January," he added.

"So it does," I admitted and sat up straight, folding my hands neatly in front of me, a model of decorum. The additional threat to my livelihood hadn't been necessary. Bullying me with a contempt citation was more than sufficient.

"Do you know a Mr. Randy Sullivan?" Aasen asked.

"Yes."

"Is he what is considered a bookie?"

"Yes," I answered, telling myself I wasn't telling him anything he didn't already know; Randy had a jacket, after all. I helped hang it on him.

"Were you employed by Mr. Sullivan?"

"Yes."

"In what capacity?"

"Why do I have the feeling that you already know the answers to these questions?"

"In what capacity?"

"Mr. Sullivan believed he had been cheated during a recent poker game and he engaged me to determine who the cheater was," I answered, taking on Aasen's speech patterns.

"And did you discover the identity of this alleged card cheat?"

"I did."

"Who was the card cheat?"

"I am not at liberty to say," I told him. Now it was my turn to play. "'No license holder shall divulge to anyone other than the employer, or as the employer may direct, except as required by law, any information acquired during such employment in respect of any matter or investigation undertaken or done by such employer.' Subdivision four, section thirteen, Minnesota statute three-two-six-point-three."

"Randy Sullivan was killed this morning," Aasen said, just like that.

"What?"

"Do you have problems with your hearing?"

"You sonuvabitch! You bastard! You little pimple-faced bastard!"

"Was he your friend?"

"Yes!" I answered the sonuvabitch. Randy was my friend; I realized it the moment I knew he was gone. Goddamn it. "Who killed him?"

"I will ask the questions."

Goddamn sonuvabitch . . . "Who killed him?" I yelled and lunged at him. As I tried to go over the table, Sean met me, pinning my arms to my sides.

Aasen didn't even flinch. "What was the name of the alleged card cheat?" he asked calmly, looking down at his file.

"Heather Schrotenboer," I answered without thinking.

Aasen nodded but did not look up. "Miss Heather Schrotenboer made a statement earlier today, freely, without compulsion, in which she admitted that she'd won—without cheating—seven thousand two hundred and fifty-five dollars off Randy Sullivan—and you—in two separate card games . . ."

"She said that?"

"She claims Mr. Sullivan was infuriated by losing to a woman, that he demanded she return her winnings and sent you to collect them."

"Not true," I said.

"Is it true that you told Miss Schrotenboer, several times, that if she did not return the money Randy Sullivan would harm her? Is that true?"

"Randy wouldn't hurt anyone. He's all talk . . ."

"Did you tell Miss Schrotenboer that Mr. Sullivan would harm her if she did not return the money?"

"I suggested it."

"Did Miss Schrotenboer agree to return the money?"

"No."

"Why not?"

"She didn't say."

"I see," Aasen said. "And did you inform Mr. Sullivan that Miss Schrotenboer refused to . . ."

"Yes."

". . . Return his money?"

"Yes."

"Did you give Mr. Sullivan the home address of Miss Schrotenboer?"

"Yes."

"I see," Aasen said again and stood up. "Thank you, Mr. Taylor. I will have a transcript prepared for your signature immediately. Please wait." He nodded to the stenographer, who switched off her machine and carried it by its tripod out of the room.

"You didn't tell me what happened," I reminded him.

"When Mr. Sullivan arrived at Miss Schrotenboer's apartment at approximately eleven-fifteen, he was carrying a baseball bat," Aasen answered, making a production number out of gathering his papers. "Miss Schrotenboer shot him six times in the chest."

"She murdered him," I muttered.

"I agree," Aasen said. "But I doubt there is much I can do about it."

That caught my attention.

"You gave her an ironclad case for self-defense," Aasen said when he saw the expression on my face. "You told her Mr. Sullivan was coming, you told her he was dangerous. She will go into court looking like a ten-year-old and sob and weep and tell that to a jury. A sensitive young woman menaced by dangerous men simply for having the temerity to excel in a male-dominated activity, albeit an illegal one . . . I cannot beat her. She set up your friend and killed him and I cannot beat her in court. Nice job, Taylor. Well done."

Aasen gathered the rest of his papers and headed for the door. He called to me over his shoulder. "I will send a copy of the case file to the Private Detective Services Board. They will have plenty of time to examine it before your license comes up for renewal."

I stared at the door after Aasen slammed it shut. O'Connell pulled his chair next to mine and laid a heavy hand on my shoulder.

"What were you thinking?" he asked.

Heather Schrotenboer stood on the corner of Third Avenue and Fifth Street in downtown Minneapolis, waiting for the light to change. When she saw Sean O'Connell and me leaving city hall she smiled and waved. O'Connell grabbed my arm.

"It's okay," I told him but he didn't believe me.

Heather came over to where we stood on the city hall steps. "How are you?" she asked, like we were dear friends meeting by chance. O'Connell was right to restrain my arm.

"So, how *does* it feel to kill a man?" I asked.

"Interesting," she answered, giving O'Connell a weary once-over.

"Listen, they won't hit you now; they'll wait," I told her. "They'll wait a couple of weeks, a couple of months, maybe even a year. But they'll do it. Count on it. They'll come at you like this: A man pulls up next to you at a stoplight and looks over; maybe he has a gun, maybe he doesn't. Your doorbell rings, a college kid says he's collecting for the Clean Water Act; he could be telling the truth. You walk across the street and hear a car engine accelerate . . . You know how easy it is to kill someone, don't you?"

"What are you talking about?" Heather demanded.

"The Mafia."

"What?"

"You think you can run a book in this town and not be connected? Randy worked for the Mafia and you killed him instead of paying your debts. That's bad for business—it gives other gamblers the same notion. Yeah, the Mafia will have to do something about you."

With that, O'Connell and I walked past Heather, her mouth hanging open; I brushed her aside with my shoulder. She got off on fear? I just gave her a few months of it. Perhaps more.

"There are probably two hundred full-time bookies working the Twin Cities," O'Connell told me after we were out of earshot. "I don't think any of them is tied to organized crime."

"I know," I admitted.

O'Connell began to laugh, a deep, rich Irish laugh that shook his whole body. "The Mafia. I don't believe it, the Mafia . . ."

TWENTY-NINE

I STOOD ON THE free-throw line I had painted across my driveway and faced the hoop attached above the door to my garage. I was poised to shoot, a Kevin McHale autograph-model
basketball raised slightly above my head. Yet, I did not shoot.
It was my habit when I was alone with too much on my mind
to crash the boards, even in winter. Shooting baskets helped
clear my head; it brought me comfort. Only now it seemed
absurd, what with Amy dead and Sherman and now Randy.

And the men I've killed . . .

Four men, all of them with a lifetime of priors: one hundred seventeen arrests, eleven convictions, twenty-two years
served, combined. Two had been shot, one killed with a knife,
one blown to hell-and-gone with a hand grenade. The oldest
was forty-two; the youngest seventeen; their average age was
twenty-four. One was married, the others were single; they
had five children among them. Three were black, one was
white. Three of them were trying to kill me when they died,
and the fourth . . . The fourth died because I could not think
of a reason, any reason, for allowing him to live.

And that was how I chose to live with my sins, reducing
them to mere statistics, notations in a box score.

In each case I was exonerated by a review board for "acting

within the course and scope of my employment." How nice for me. And each time the verdict had come in, I'd crashed the boards.

I let the ball bounce to rest on the asphalt and sat against the garage door. *Maybe it would be better all around if I just quit the business and became an appliance salesman for Sears; Lord knows I don't seem to be very good at this job.* I had let a twenty-four-year-old college kid play me like a flute and now Randy was dead. And it was my fault. I had let C. C. Monroe and Amy Lamb and all the rest distract me. I would have seen it coming if I hadn't been distracted; I would have been able to deal with the problem properly. Randy had depended on me and I had let him down.

"Do one job, do it well, and then move on." Who said that? Probably my father. He was always saying things like that and I always ignored him. I wondered what he would say if he were here now. "When the going gets tough, the tough get going." *Yeah, that's what the tough do. But Dad, tell me, what if you're not tough? What do you do then? Shoot baskets?*

I was sitting there feeling sorry for myself when Anne Scalasi drove up. She stopped her car at the end of the driveway and walked toward me, pausing to retrieve the basketball. She dribbled it.

"Did I ever tell you about the time I set the Minnesota State High School League record for assists in a single game?"

"Frequently," I told her.

Anne set and fired. The ball banged off the rim and caromed onto the lawn. From the expression on her face, Anne had needed that shot. She sighed and sagged down next to me.

"Sean told me about Randy," she said.

"What was it he used to say? 'Easy come, easy go'?"

"That's what he used to say."

"He was a big boy, he knew the risks of his profession."

"Yeah, he did," Anne agreed. "No sense getting upset about it."

"None at all."

"It was probably inevitable," Anne ventured.

"Remember the time the uniforms saved him?" I asked. "He cut off this guy's line of credit, claimed the guy was into him for something like twice his yearly salary. The guy punched his lights out; nearly killed him. If the squad hadn't happened by Randy would have bought it right then and there."

"True, that's what would have happened and then we would've had to solve the case."

"I've been thinking about that, too," I said. "You know, we didn't solve crap."

"What are you talking about?"

"Ninety percent of the murders we investigated were so dumb, we usually knew who did it before we even arrived at the scene. How many times did we find the killer standing over the body, covered with blood, practically begging to confess? We got guys who killed people over ice cream cones, over which program to watch on TV, over whose turn it was to take out the fucking garbage. Yeah, we needed to be real detectives to solve those."

Anne took my hand and gave it a squeeze. We were friends again, just like that. All that was required to repair our relationship was to simply ignore the events that had damaged it in the first place. We could do that easy.

"We've been through a lot, you and I," Anne reminded me.

"Too much.

"Way too much."

"Speaking of which, how are you and your domestic associate doing?"

"We've decided to go our separate ways."

"I'm sorry to hear that."

"It's been coming for a long time now."

"I'm sorry," I repeated.

"Me, too."

"How are the kids taking it?"

"They actually seem happy, especially my oldest. She thinks

it's the smartest thing her father and I have done in years. Who knows? I tried to talk to them, but I think they're hiding their feelings, trying to put the best face on things. Either that or they don't know what they feel yet. I certainly don't."

"Anything I can do . . ." I volunteered.

Anne squeezed my hand again. "You can pay the fifty bucks you owe me."

"What fifty bucks?"

"The bet you made," she reminded me. "The nine you dug out of your wall *did not* match the bullets that killed Brown or Amy Lamb."

"You're kidding."

"I never kid about bullets."

"Then who was shooting at me?"

"Damned if I know," Anne answered as she stood and walked to the basketball. She fired it from the lawn. Swish. An honest three-pointer. I rebounded and dished off to her. Swish. Another three-pointer.

I said, "Double or nothing you miss the next shot."

"You're on," she replied and put it up again. The ball banked high off the glass, caught the front of the rim and fell in. "In your face, Mama!" Anne exclaimed, pumping her fist.

"Luck, all luck," I said and passed the ball back to her. She missed her fourth attempt. I rebounded, dribbled away from the hoop, spun and dropped a ten-footer. Anne rebounded for me.

"It looks like Sherman's suicide is going to hold up," Anne said, bounce-passing the ball to me at the line.

"No way," I told her.

"The medical examiner believes the wound, the area where the body was found, the fact that Sherman was a fugitive— he believes it all fits a pattern of a self-inflicted type of thing."

"The ME is nuts."

I took a jumper and missed.

"He said it was a problem of interpretation," Anne said. "He said the evidence could support suicide a lot more easily than murder. If I'm going to persuade him it was a killing, I need to give him more."

"What about the gun?"

"It fired the bullets that killed Brown and Amy Lamb."

"Surprise, surprise, surprise."

"My sentiments exactly."

"What about Amy's tape?"

Anne's skyhook hit nothing but net.

"The ME figures she could have been referring to Sherman; there's nothing to suggest she wasn't."

"So that's it?"

"That's it," Anne said, holding the ball.

"There's always Reverend Hoppe," I said without much hope.

"He has no alibi for Thoreau, but the good reverend claims he can prove he was in bed when Brown took it."

"Witnesses?"

"Yep."

"Vivian Olson?"

"Nope. Brenda Clark."

" 'Hell hath no fury . . . ' " I quoted as Anne passed me the basketball. The foibles of man and woman never ceased to amaze me.

"I wish I'd found C. C.'s videotape when I searched Thoreau's house," Anne said. "I don't know if it would have made any difference, but I wish I'd found it."

"You mean you didn't?"

"I told you I didn't," Anne reminded me, shooting a layup and passing me the ball.

I froze at the line and pondered her words. They didn't make sense. If Anne really hadn't found the tape, hadn't left it for me to find . . . I started dribbling the ball.

"Taylor?" Anne called. "Taylor!"

I stopped dribbling.

"You're zoning out on me."

"Sorry. I have a few things on my mind."

"Don't we all."

THIRTY

AFTER I SHOOED Anne out of my yard, I called Paul Aasen. He picked up, answering smoothly, "Hennepin County Attorney's Office, this is Paul Aasen. May I help you?" He hung up when I identified myself. I called back.

"You have sixty seconds," he barked after I begged him to listen to my story.

"Answer this question first: Heather's gun, was it a nine-millimeter?"

"Yes, it was. She claims her father gave it to her several years ago, that she never used it before, that as far as she knows it has never even been fired. You have fifty seconds."

"All right, consider this: Heather shoots Randy in her apartment, claiming self-defense. Physical evidence at the scene, the presence of a weapon, for example, seems to corroborate her story . . ."

"You have forty seconds."

"Plus, there's testimony confirming her claim that Randy was, in fact, threatening her over a considerable sum of money."

"Thirty seconds."

"Now, perhaps she can explain why she made no effort to return the money. Perhaps she can explain why she did not call the police when she knew he was coming; why she waited for him in her apartment; why she shot him six times."

"Twenty seconds."

"However, can she explain why she tried to kill me and another woman two nights before?"

"What are you talking about?"

"How much time do I have left?"

"Forget that. Repeat what you just said."

"Late Wednesday night someone shot at me and a lawyer named Cynthia Grey in my home. At first I thought the shooting was connected to something else I'm involved in. Now I know better."

"Can you identify Miss Schrotenboer as the assailant?"

"No."

"Can the lawyer . . . Miss Grey?"

"No."

"Quit pulling my chain, Taylor . . ."

"I have something better than an eyewitness. Something unshakable."

"What?"

"I have a bullet fired from her gun."

That stopped him. After a few moments of thought Aasen asked, "Where is the bullet?"

"Sergeant Mankamyer of the St. Paul Police Department has it."

"He is their forensic firearms specialist?" Aasen asked.

"Hmm. Did the St. Paul PD recover the bullet?"

"No, I pulled the bullet out of the wall myself and brought it to them."

Aasen said, "The constructive-possession rules . . ."

"They don't apply," I insisted, cutting him off. "Maybe you can't prove that the bullet came out of my wall. But you certainly can prove that the bullet came from her gun. Put her in front of a grand jury and ask her how that's possible if her gun was never fired before, if it never left her possession. I'm curious to hear her answer."

"So am I."

"Something else. Heather once told me she wondered what it was like to kill a man. Question her friends, her classmates. I bet you'll find she made the same kind of statement to others."

"I don't know if that is enough to convict her for killing Mr. Sullivan."

"Probably not. But it's enough to arrest her and once she's in custody, you know how it works, we might find out that she's not as smart as she seems."

"I will arrange to secure the bullet from St. Paul and have our own forensic experts compare it to the bullets removed from Mr. Sullivan's body. If there is a positive match we will proceed from there."

"Sounds reasonable to me."

"Thank you, Mr. Taylor."

"Thank you, Mr. Aasen."

Freddie slept in a king-size bed with a Victorian canopy and silk sheets; both were the color lingerie manufacturers call peach though it doesn't resemble the fruit at all. Still, the color contrasted well with Freddie's complexion. I sat at the foot of his bed and watched him sleep, playing with the Colt Commander he had left on the small marble-topped table next to the bed. Freddie owned a condominium in Uptown Minneapolis, not too far from Lake Calhoun; you could see the lake from Freddie's balcony. The condo was on the eighth floor of what was advertised as a "security building," but Freddie and I both knew better and I found myself wondering why a man in his line of work wasn't more careful. On the other hand, my house wasn't exactly Fort Knox, either.

"Hey, Freddie," I said, tapping his foot with the barrel of the gun, amazed that anyone could sleep this late into the day. He did not respond so I tapped harder. "Hey pal, the sun is shining, the birds are singing . . ."

"Go 'way, Taylor," he mumbled and rolled over. That got me laughing and my laughter must have shot a load of adrenaline through him because he popped up, wide awake, looked me in the eye and said, "Oh, shit."

"Man, it's late afternoon. What are you doing in bed?"

"I was partyin' last night."

"Hanging out with your journalist friend?"

"What you want?"

I waved the Colt in his general direction.

"This ain't your style, man," he grumbled.

"You asking or telling?"

Freddie pulled the sheet tight around his throat like it was bulletproof and repeated, "This ain't your style, man."

"You never know," I told him. "A man with a large bump on his head is liable to do anything."

"I'm really sorry about that, Taylor."

"Sure you are."

"What you gonna do?"

"Depends, Freddie. Depends. I have a few questions to ask. You going to answer them?"

"Ask me no questions, I'll tell you no lies."

I smashed the toes of his right foot with the barrel of the Colt.

"Motherfucker!"

"Tell me about Dennis Thoreau."

"Who the fuck is Dennis Thoreau?" he squealed, rubbing his foot.

"He's an asshole, just like you."

"Man, I don't know no Dennis Thoreau."

"I didn't think so," I said. I didn't even bother asking him about Brown, Sherman or Amy Lamb. Freddie was a goon, a leg-breaker, a head-basher, maybe a killer, too. He killed the three Filipino thieves. But he could have killed me and he didn't, which meant he probably hadn't killed anyone. At least not recently. Something else. Freddie would not have kept the gun after doing Brown. Keep evidence? Of murder? Freddie was just not that careless.

Of course, I could be wrong.

"Pick up the phone," I told him.

Freddie hesitated.

"Do it," I said softly.

When he uncradled the receiver I asked him if he knew Marion Senske's private number. When he nodded, I told him to dial it.

"Man, I don't work for that bitch no more."

Freddie's statement infuriated me, although I couldn't tell you why. I thumbed back the hammer on the Colt and screamed, "Call her or I'll blow your fucking head off!"

Freddie proceeded to set the Olympic record for the seven-digit dial. The phone rang five times before Marion answered it. "Yeah, this is Freddie . . . No, man . . . Listen . . . I know that . . . Would you fuckin' listen?" Freddie yelled. "Taylor's here . . . Yeah, Taylor. He's got a gun. He wants to talk to you." I shook my head no. "He doesn't want to talk to you . . . How the fuck should I know? . . . Yeah . . . Yeah, a gun . . ."

"Tell her the police found Joseph Sherman this morning," I said.

"Who's Joseph Sherman?"

"Tell her."

"The cops found Joseph Sherman this morning," Freddie repeated.

"Tell her he's dead."

"He's dead . . . No shit?"

"Is that what she said?"

"No, that was me," Freddie admitted.

"What did she say?"

"Nothin', man."

"Tell her it looks real good that the cops will pin Amy Lamb and Brown on Sherman and close the case."

"Taylor figures the cops will . . . She heard you," Freddie told me.

"Tell her that leaves Thoreau."

"That leaves Thoreau."

"Tell her I'm willing to make a deal."

"He says he's willing to make a deal . . . She wants to know for what."

"She knows for what."

"You know for what . . . How much?"

"I'm a reasonable man. Make me an offer."

"He's a reasonable man . . . Ten thousand?"

I shook my head no.

"He don't like that," Freddie said into the phone. "Fifteen?"

I shook my head.

"He wants more . . . Twenty is as high as she'll go."

"She'll go higher," I said.

"You'll go higher . . . Twenty-five," Freddie told me.

I shrugged.

"Yeah, he'll go for that . . . Where? When?"

"Thirty minutes. C. C.'s office in the State Capitol."

"He says thirty minutes . . . She says that's unacceptable; she and Monroe are leaving for a fund-raiser in thirty minutes."

"Hang up the phone, Freddie."

Freddie hung up the phone.

"Now what?" he asked.

I gave him a telephone number and told him to dial it. He did. While it was ringing I had him pass me the receiver.

"They're selling you out, honey," I told the woman who answered.

"What are you talking about?" Meghan Chakolis asked.

"Looks like the governor's office is worth more to them than you thought."

"I don't understand."

"C. C.'s office in forty-five minutes," I said and flipped the receiver back to Freddie, gesturing for him to hang it up.

"Aren't we having fun now," Freddie said.

I briefly contemplated the incredible damage I could inflict on his body. I could fix it so Freddie never walked again, never bent his elbow to raise a glass, to feed himself. Ahh, hell. Now we both knew how vulnerable we were.

"I don't figure we're even Freddie," I told him. "I figure you still owe me big time. But I'm satisfied and I'm willing to let it go at this—busting your pad, letting you know I can take you out anytime I want. You don't agree, you know where to find me." Freddie watched me suspiciously, until the realization of what I said hit him. He smiled. Then he laughed.

"You got 'em," Freddie told me. "You got 'em, that ain't no lie. They may be white, but you got stones like a brother."

"I have a few things to do, Freddie. I don't want to see you around when I do them. Understand?"

He didn't say if he did or didn't. He just kept laughing.

THIRTY-ONE

THE ONLY SOUND I heard in the State Capitol Office Building was the noise I made myself. I took the elevator to Blue and padded quietly down the corridor to C. C.'s office. C. C. was sitting in a chair in front of her desk. Marion Senske was sitting in C. C.'s chair behind C. C.'s desk, a shaft of light from C. C.'s desk lamp giving her face a hard edge to go with the scowl. She did not speak when I arrived, acknowledging my presence instead by sliding open the top desk drawer, withdrawing a thick, oversized envelope and tossing it on the desk. I went nowhere near it.

"I'm disappointed in you," C. C. told me, turning in her chair. She was wearing a black silk shirtdress with a shawl collar, a long slim skirt that closed with four gold buttons and a jeweled belt. She crossed her legs, giving me a good look at her thighs. She was grinning.

"Marion letting you dress like a grown-up tonight?"

C. C. shot a hurt look at her mentor.

Marion ignored her. "We don't have time for this," she reminded me.

"Make time," I said.

She nudged the envelope toward me. "Twenty-five thousand dollars," she said between clenched teeth. "Not a penny more."

"I don't want your twenty-five thousand dollars," I told her. "You said . . ."

"There must be some mistake. All I want, let's see, five days multiplied by four hundred . . . you already paid me for two days, plus expenses . . . You owe me, let's call it twelve hundred bucks."

Marion was confused as she ever hoped to be and admitted it.

"You hired me to find a blackmailer," I reminded her. "I succeeded." During the drive over I had planned to do a drumroll before making the announcement in a loud voice. But once I was there, I thought better of it. I merely pointed at Representative Carol Catherine Monroe and said, "Here's your blackmailer. That'll be twelve hundred dollars, please."

"What are you talking about?" Marion demanded.

I cast an accusing glance at C. C., who uncrossed and crossed her legs again.

"Carol Catherine Monroe, Dennis Thoreau and Meghan Chakolis made the porno flick together. They did it to cause a scandal that would force C. C. out of the campaign."

"But why?" Marion wanted to know.

"Yeah, tell us why," C. C. added.

"My guess? They did it for two million dollars, for the money in the campaign fund."

"I don't think I want to hear this," Marion moaned.

"I don't blame you, Marion," I told her. "Your protégée and her comrades made the tape and planned to release it to the media—anonymously, I assume. They made it last week, not six years ago like C. C. claimed. It was made between the time C. C. frosted her hair and you made her change it back.

"Once the tape was made public, the ensuing scandal would have forced C. C. to withdraw from the race. And, as you know, any money that remains in a campaign fund after the candidate's bills are paid becomes the property of the candidate. She can do with it as she pleases—give it to other candidates, give it to her party, keep it for herself. C. C. was going to keep it. Weren't you C. C.? And nobody would have bothered her about it, either. Hell, it's unlikely that anyone involved in local politics would have even admitted to knowing her. Probably including you. She and her friends would have walked away . . . rich."

Marion was watching C. C. now. Her expression did not change.

"How do you know all this?" she asked softly.

"The videotape. I was supposed to find it. That's why I was sent to see Thoreau."

"You were sent to pay off a blackmailer," Marion insisted.

"Thoreau was already dead when C. C. said he called your campaign headquarters with his blackmail demands. My guess is that Thoreau was going to release the tape using the original cover story, that he was C. C.'s ex-boyfriend. Only someone killed him first. When C. C. and Meghan discovered he was dead, they decided to hell with it, they'd go through with the plan anyway. The blackmail nonsense was just a ruse to get someone over there to find his body and the tape— or to call the cops and let them find them."

"Why would they want to become involved in a murder investigation?"

"Why not? They wanted scandal, remember? Besides, the tape wouldn't have been much use as a motive for murder. Why kill Thoreau for the tape and then leave it? No, they weren't worried about that. They just wanted to keep their hands clean. That's why they came to you, so you would take charge. They wanted you to send someone over there to discover the body. If not your friend at the St. Paul Police Department, a private investigator would do just fine. There was only one problem."

"The tape is missing," C. C. said, rubbing a smudge of dirt off the toe of her shoe. "I put it in the camera. I figured that was the best place for it. I was really surprised when neither you nor the police found it. You think it could still be there?"

I shook my head no and C. C. sighed heavily.

"It was Meghan who found Dennis. She said the house had been ransacked and she was worried about the tape. Only I had it." C. C. shrugged. "I was kinda watching it at home. She said we should put it back and let nature take its course. So I did, Saturday night, after I did the speech for the Teamsters."

"Tell me something," I said. "When Thoreau turned up dead, what did you think? Who did you think killed him?"

C. C. shook her head—there was a lot of head shaking going on. "We figured it was maybe one of Dennis's girls from California."

"What girls?"

"When he was down there he made movies of himself having sex with women without them knowing it—mostly married women. Then he would sell the movies back to them. He told us about it when he came back; that's what gave us the idea in the first place."

"Nice guy," I said.

"Actually, he was kinda funny," C. C. volunteered.

Marion slumped in her chair as if all the weight in the world had been dumped on her shoulders. I actually felt sorry for her. But not too sorry. Finally, she slowly rose and walked around the desk to C. C.'s side. The slap was lightning swift and fell on C. C.'s cheek so hard it knocked her to the floor.

"Oooo, I bet that hurt," I told C. C.

"Have you any idea what you've done?" Marion asked C. C. in measured tones. "Have you any idea how badly you've hurt the movement, the state?"

"Fuck the movement, fuck the state and fuck you," C. C. replied, baring her teeth like a dog. "I never wanted any part of this election. *I only wanted to be left alone.*"

"Yeah, left alone with two million bucks," I said.

"Carol Catherine, what do you think paid for the campaign headquarters and the telephones and the Buick?" Marion asked her. "What do you think paid for the flyers and the mailers and the signs and the bumper stickers? What do you think paid for the TV spots and the radio spots and the newspaper ads and the billboards? Why do you think we were attending a fund-raising dinner tonight? The two million dollars is gone! We spent it! You did all this for nothing!"

"Nothing? There isn't any money left? There has to be! How about the money we're supposed to take in tonight?"

Marion left her to puzzle it out, going back to the chair behind the desk.

"I can't believe you spent all of it! I told you not to spend all of it! Didn't I say that?"

"I'll be damned," I muttered.

"I didn't do anything wrong," C. C. insisted.

"No, of course not," I said.

"I didn't!"

Marion sighed audibly. "You have the tape, don't you, Taylor? That's why you know so much."

I shrugged.

"So, now what?"

I'd shown them the stick, now it was time to give them a good whiff of the carrot. "No one needs to know about the tape or what C. C. and her friends intended to do with it. You can still pull off the election."

Marion eyed me suspiciously. Then her gaze fell on the envelope. "How much?" she asked.

"You never listen, do you? I don't want your damn money."

"What then?"

"I want C. C.'s testimony . . ."

"Testimony?" Marion repeated.

"And let me tell you what happens if I don't get it."

"What are you talking about?" C. C. asked.

"I'll see that she's charged as an accessory to murder," I told Marion.

"What?" C. C. screamed, panic in her voice.

I turned on her. "You didn't kill Thoreau. We know that. You were in Mankato at the time he died. But you know who did. And a pretty good case can be made that you sanctioned the killing."

"That's ridiculous."

"Is it? Thoreau was trying to blackmail you, wasn't he? That's what you told me. That's what you told Marion."

"But he wasn't . . ."

"To protect your political career you had someone kill him."

"No, I didn't . . ."

"Sure, that's what you say now."

"But you said yourself . . ."

"Did I?"

C. C.'s eyes grew wide with confusion. "I don't understand," she said at last, shaking her head.

"I understand," Marion said from her seat behind the desk. We both turned to her. "I'm a lawyer, remember?"

"I forget," I told her.

"Sometimes I do, too."

"What?" C. C. said again.

"He wants you to roll over on your friend."

"Roll over?"

"He wants you to testify against your friend. He won't hurt us if you give up your friend."

"What friend?"

I did not answer. Neither did Marion. Instead we waited while C. C. worked it over in her brain. It took a long time. Finally, she said, "Meghan did it. Yeah, Meghan Chakolis. She was always jealous of me, even when we were in school, because the boys liked me best. She must have thought I was after her husband. I wasn't. I didn't want him. I didn't care about Dennis. But everybody, they think because I'm beautiful I want all their boyfriends . . ."

"Oh, don't be ridiculous, Carol Catherine," Meghan Chakolis said from the doorway. I glanced at my watch. She was early.

C. C. looked away when Meghan entered the room. "How long were you listening?" she asked.

"Long enough," Meghan said.

"I didn't mean to say *you* killed Dennis."

"Oh, Carol Catherine," Meghan muttered, not surprised at all.

I moved over to the desk and sat on the corner. "So, what's your side of the story?" I asked Meghan.

"I'm pretty sure Joseph Sherman did it."

"Why?"

"He figured out that Dennis was the one who killed Terrance Friedlander with his car."

"No. Sherman didn't even know Thoreau existed until I told him. And that was four days after Thoreau was dead."

Meghan didn't answer.

"My God, my God, my—Oh my God, you killed Terry," Marion muttered from behind the desk.

"We didn't. Dennis did. It wasn't our idea," C. C. assured her.

"No, we knew we were going to lose the election," Meghan added. "We knew we were going to lose when we started."

"We wanted to lose," C. C. said.

"Dennis thought he was doing us a favor."

"That's why you threw him out," I said to Meghan.

"I thought it would be best if he disappeared for a while until everything blew over."

"Until Sherman was convicted of a crime he didn't commit."

"Sherman was a drunk," Meghan said contemptuously. "Who cared about Sherman?"

"Oh my God," Marion muttered again.

"Don't be so melodramatic, Marion," Meghan snapped. "Taylor can't prove anything. So what if the tape thing didn't work out? Carol Catherine can still be governor. You can still run the state."

"Maybe they can," I agreed. "But you? You are going to spend the rest of your life in prison."

Meghan smiled. "Give it up, Taylor. You have nothing," she insisted.

"I have motive—your jealousy of your ex-husband and your best friend. A motive your friend will testify to, won't you C. C.?"

C. C. said nothing.

"And I have opportunity. You already told me you were with Thoreau the night he was killed, testified that you had sex with him. Semen, hair samples, fingerprints . . . forensics will put you in the house right at the time Thoreau was killed.

"Something else," I added. "You're about to become part of the bureaucracy. When the civil servants who work in Homicide come in in the morning, you're going to be on their list of things to do; they're going to be thinking of catching you. It's nothing personal. It's a job. It's what they do for a living, like assembly-line workers who put nut A on bolt B. They may get bored, they may get frustrated, but they're not going to quit. They are not going to shrug and say, 'Aww, I think I'll do something else today' because what they do every day is catch killers. That's why, of all the crimes committed, murder has the highest clearance rate. You think you've gotten away with something, but you haven't. Your time is coming."

"You're not trying to bluff me, are you, Taylor?" Meghan asked, a smug grin on her face.

"Bluff you? Do you know what the cops are doing right now?"

"What?"

"They're showing your photograph to Thoreau's neighbors, asking them if they saw you there Friday night," I lied.

"But I didn't do it," Meghan insisted.

"You look awful good for it."

"But I didn't!"

"I don't give a damn," I told her. "You're going down for it just the same."

"You're trying to frame me."

"Am I?"

"I'll show them the videotape . . ."

"What videotape?"

Fear began to creep over Meghan's face at the realization of what I was doing to her.

"You can't do this."

"Sure I can."

"But why? What was Dennis to you? You didn't even know him."

"I don't give a shit about Dennis. For what he did to Terry Friedlander, he got what he deserved."

"Then why?"

I leaned in close, giving her a good whiff of my breath. "Amy Lamb."

She hesitated. "I didn't kill Amy Lamb . . ."

"John Brown."

"John . . . I don't know any John Brown."

"Joseph Sherman."

"Joseph Sherman killed Joseph Sherman."

"No, he didn't. He was murdered—murdered with the same gun that killed Amy and Brown."

"You can't prove that."

"He changed his shirt," I told her. "He went back to his old apartment building—your apartment building—to get his old clothes. I'm betting that's when he figured it all out. I'm betting he went to your apartment—the one across the hall from his—and pounded on the door. Yeah, he was just dumb enough for that. And when you opened the door, he recognized that you were the woman he saw in the parking lot the night Brown was killed. Only you were too quick on the draw for him."

"You can't prove any of this," Meghan claimed and she was right.

"I know," I admitted. "But it doesn't matter. Not to me. When you go down for Thoreau, you'll go down for the others, too."

"No, no, no!" she repeated. "I didn't do these things. Why

would I kill Amy? Why would I kill this Brown person? Why would I . . . Oh, Jeezus . . ."

The man had knocked softly on the door frame. "Ms. Senske," he said, "do you still want me to wait with the car?"

Meghan went silent and we all turned to face the newcomer. It was Conan. He took us all in, uncomfortable with our stares, until his eyes fell upon Meghan. "Oh hi," he said.

He was wearing the dress uniform of the State Capitol Security Force. The name tag above his pocket read GALEN PIVEC. I froze on the name. "Meghan," I whispered, more to myself than to her, "your mother's maiden name is Pivec."

I sprang at him. "Galen!" Meghan screamed, but it was too late. I hit him. I hit him harder than I've ever hit anyone in my life. I executed a hook kick to his head, catching him above his eyebrows. Without setting the kicking leg down, I followed with a roundhouse to his face, smashing his cheekbone with the blade of my foot, then, just because I was pissed off, I hit him in the temple with a ridge hand. He went down like he'd been shot by a howitzer. For a brief moment I contemplated stomping him to death. But the words came back to me: *When hand go out, withdraw anger; when anger go out, withdraw hand.*

I reached under his coat. He was carrying. I pulled the gun, de-activated it, unloaded it and tossed it on Marion's desk. "Don't touch that," I warned her. It was Joseph Sherman's Taurus.

I turned on Meghan. "Galen Pivec is your cousin, isn't he? I ran a computer check on you. Your mother's maiden name was Pivec. How many Pivecs can there be?"

Meghan's eyes were ablaze with anger; C. C.'s were glazed over with confusion. Only Marion seemed to be seeing clearly but all she had were unanswered questions. "What does Galen have to do with this?" she asked.

I ignored her. I turned my back on the room and went to the window, turning everything over in my head, seeing how the pieces fit so neatly, wondering why I hadn't seen it before.

"Amy told Conan everything," I said to the window, using my nickname for Marion's chauffeur and security guard. "They're sitting together with nothing to do and she told him everything, told him about Thoreau and Sherman's calls. No doubt Conan took his job as campaign sheriff seriously. He killed Thoreau . . . No, that's not right. He was in Mankato. But there's no doubt he set up Sherman and killed Brown by mistake. The gun proves that. Amy must have figured it out. Read about the killings in the paper, figured it out. She came here, to the capitol that morning, confronted him. So, Conan killed her. The gun again. Later, Sherman went back to his old apartment building, where his belongings were stored . . ."

I turned back to the room. No one had moved. All three women were watching Conan, his breathing irregular. I didn't know if he was conscious or not. I didn't care.

"Was I right? Did Sherman confront you? Meghan!" I shouted when there was no reply.

"Yes," she said. "I tried to talk to him, gave him a drink, some vodka. While he was drinking I went into the bedroom and called Galen. He came over and took Sherman away. Put his handcuffs on him and took him away. Sherman was alive when I last saw him. I didn't know. I didn't know . . ."

We all watched Conan some more. Only Marion wasn't thinking about the boy. She was sizing up the situation in a way only a trained politician could.

"Carol Catherine was not involved in the killings," she said, more than asked. "She had nothing to do with Terry's death or any of the others."

She smiled. Honest to God, she smiled.

"It's over, Marion," I told her. "Get used to it."

Conan pushed himself to a sitting position. His face was bloody and swollen; his breathing was heavy and labored. He moaned pitifully, trying to speak. "I'm sorry," he whimpered at last—to whom, I do not know.

Conan was choking back tears along with the blood. "I

couldn't let them hurt you." He was speaking to C. C. now.

C. C. smiled. "How sweet," she said.

"For God's sake, Carol Catherine," Marion said.

"Is that why you killed them, to protect C. C.?" I asked.

He nodded. "I had to. Don't you see?"

"And Amy Lamb?"

"She was going to tell."

I turned away. If I hadn't, I would have killed him. *Perspective, perspective,* I kept telling myself. Except I couldn't find any. Then I heard the collective gasp of the three women. I wheeled about. Conan's pant leg was hiked up, a small holster was strapped to his ankle and a .25 caliber Iver Johnson was in his hand.

I can't explain it, but I was not frightened when I saw the gun. I was merely annoyed with myself. I remember thinking, *Taylor, how can you be so careless?* and then making plans to move closer to the gun so I could do something about it. I inched toward Conan. His hand was trembling from fear or pain, I couldn't tell which.

"That's far enough, Taylor," he warned. He learned fast. I stopped. "Put up your hands."

I put them up. "Is that the gun you used on Dennis Thoreau?"

"I don't know no Dennis Thoreau."

"He was trying to hurt Miss Monroe, too," I told him.

"Is that right? Someone else was trying to hurt you?"

C. C. rolled her eyes.

"Kill him," Meghan told Conan, recovering her voice at last.

"No, wait," Conan protested, confused.

"Kill him!" Meghan insisted.

"Don't be stupid," Marion said.

"I'll make it easy for you," Meghan told her cousin. "Look." She stepped over to C. C. and ripped the woman's bodice, exposing soft, full breasts supported by white lace; tore the buttons on her skirt, tore the white lace slip underneath, used her fingernails to scratch C. C.'s legs and run her stockings.

"Don't do that!" Conan yelled. "Leave her alone!"

"Now shoot him," Meghan repeated again.

"Meghan!" Marion shouted.

"We'll tell the police that you heard screaming. You came to investigate. When you arrived you saw Taylor raping Carol Catherine. The two of you fought, the gun went off and you killed Taylor."

"Oh, pleeeze," I said.

"It's perfect," Meghan insisted.

"Wait, wait, let me think," Conan said. From the look on Marion's face, she was thinking, too.

"Hey, Meg? I don't think this is such a good idea," C. C. said.

"How the hell would you know?" Meghan screamed, turning on her. "You're so stupid . . ."

"Meghan, don't!" C. C. cried.

Meghan slapped her once, twice, three times, all the while shouting, "Shut up! Shut up! Shut up!"

"Leave her alone!" Conan cried. I moved closer to him. "Quit it, Meghan! Quit it . . ."

"Shoot, you dumb sonuvabitch!" Meghan shouted at Conan. And he did.

He shot Meghan in the face. She was dead before her body hit the floor.

Conan spun and fired at me, but I was already moving. I dived across the desk, taking Marion down with me. I heard two more shots as my head hit something hard, setting off an explosion of light and sound followed by darkness.

When the dark fog lifted, I found myself next to the credenza behind C. C.'s desk. There was a smudge of blood on the corner and much more matting my hair to my head in the exact spot where Freddie had cracked my skull. I used the credenza to pull myself vertical. I stood leaning on it until the dizziness passed and the nausea subsided. My head throbbed and there was a stabbing pain in my lower back, but other than that I was in one piece.

I couldn't say the same for Marion. A bullet had hit her high in the left shoulder, near the collarbone. She was conscious and holding the wound with a bloody right hand. "Help her!" she pleaded. I glanced around the office. C. C. was gone. So was Conan.

"You need help," I told her and reached for the telephone. "I can help myself," she replied.

I handed her the telephone, then went through the office door and down the corridor, not even bothering to glance at Meghan's lifeless body. I stopped at the elevators and listened. All I could hear was my own breath coming hard. I used the stairway, going down, my Nikes squeaking with each step. I stopped at Green and listened. Nothing. I stopped at Maroon. The same. I went down to the next landing, the lobby. Two people stood talking just inside the door, a man and a woman, their backs to me. I hit the stairs again and descended to the next level. That's when I heard them. I followed the sound. It led me to the tunnel, brightly lit, with video cameras and emergency boxes every hundred feet. I activated one of the boxes as I moved along.

I found Conan and C. C. in the middle of the tunnel. C. C. was on the floor, her back pressed against the tunnel wall, trying to disappear into the wall, a broken heel a few feet away. Conan was pulling her arm with one hand and holding the Iver Johnson with the other, holding it like he knew how to use it. C. C. pleaded with him: "Please, please, please . . ."

"Galen!" I called. It was probably the only time I used his rightful name.

He whirled toward me and snapped off a shot, missing me by three feet. An Iver Johnson .25 holds seven. He had two left.

C. C. regained her feet and tried to run, but Conan grabbed her, wrapping a beefy arm around her throat and pushing the muzzle of the gun into her ear. "Don't move," he ordered.

I stopped, leaning against the wall for support. "Let her go," I said.

"No, I love her."

"Yes, that's why you have a gun pressed to her head."

"I have two bullets left," he told me; apparently he was keeping track, too. "One for her and one for me."

"Put the gun down!" I yelled.

"Why should I? Why shouldn't I kill her and then kill myself? Give me one good reason. C'mon! Just one! You know what they're going to do to me. So, c'mon. Give me a reason."

"Because they'll make fun of you," I told him, not knowing where the words came from. "They'll say you're insane."

Conan thought as I poured it on.

"They'll say you killed sweet, innocent Carol Catherine Monroe because you were some kind of nut, like Jeffrey Dahmer and John Hinckley Jr. C. C. will become a political martyr and they'll profile her in *People* magazine and write quickie books about her and make TV movies—and in every one you'll be portrayed as a homicidal maniac. Do you want that? Or do you want to tell your side of the story? I think you should tell the world your side of the story. What do you think?"

I was fairly amazed when Conan slowly released his grip and C. C. slid to the floor. He turned to face me, reaching out the hand holding the Iver Johnson, like he wanted me to take the gun. Then a loud *crack* rocked the tunnel and Galen Pivec's chest exploded as a bullet bore its ugly hole through it, exiting above his heart. The force of impact slammed him against the wall. He bounced off and fell down dead on top of C. C., who pushed and clawed and kicked herself free of him, all the while screaming, "Please, please, please . . ."

The security officer called John came cautiously down the tunnel from the opposite end, his gun trained on Conan. "I saw it all on the TV," he said, gesturing toward the cameras.

C. C. crawled to the officer and yanked on his trouser leg. "Did you see, he was going to kill me, he was going to kill me for no reason, did you see?"

I had nothing to say to either of them. As the guard attempted to half carry, half drag C. C. to the tunnel's State Capitol entrance, I went in the opposite direction, toward the State Office Building. "Where are you going?" the officer questioned.

"Send an ambulance and officers to C. C.'s office," I answered.

By the time I reached the office, Marion was standing and leaning over the desk, drops of blood soaking the blotter. She was barking orders into the telephone. "Do it now!" she shouted at someone as I arrived.

"Carol Catherine?" she asked me after she hung up the phone.

"She's fine," I said. "Galen's dead. The Capitol Security cops got him."

Marion smiled. "It's all going to work out after all," she said.

The dead body on the floor didn't bother her one damn bit.

THIRTY-TWO

I<small>N NO TIME THE</small> joint was crawling with the blue uniforms of the State Capitol Security Force, the maroon uniforms of the Minnesota State Patrol, and the dark suits of the Minnesota Bureau of Criminal Apprehension. One of the suits escorted me from C. C.'s office to the State Capitol Security Center. We went through the tunnel. A photographer was snapping shots of Galen Pivec's fallen body. I refused to look.

When we arrived at the Security Center, a disheveled C. C. Monroe—looking as if a Hollywood makeup artist had mussed her hair and a costume designer had artfully ripped her clothes—was charming nearly a dozen uniform and plain-clothes officers; they pressed around her, hanging on her every word. One of them handed her a cup of water and she smiled at him. He smiled back. Another draped his coat over her shoulders and she smiled at him, too, while all the others looked on enviously. C. C. told her story calmly and quietly while absentmindedly trying to brush Conan's rich red blood off her dress. One officer sighed, actually sighed. Oh, if only he were a glove on that hand . . .

As I predicted, in C. C.'s version of the events she and Marion were innocent victims of a psycho villain.

"Bullshit," I said.

"Mr. Taylor, I'm so glad you're all right," she said, smiling. "I thought he killed you, too."

"No such luck, honey," I said. The officers were greatly offended by my remark. Call Carol Catherine Monroe "honey"? I half expected one of them to grab a rope.

"Galen shot Mr. Taylor in the head," C. C. told the officers and they looked at me skeptically.

"There's nothing wrong with my head," I countered. But one of the suits touched the side of it with his handkerchief, sending a bolt of lightning through my brain. He held it up for the crowd to see. The cloth was stained with blood. My blood. The officers all nodded and decided to forgive my boorishness.

The suit took me into a separate office and I gave him my statement, complete and unabridged; gave it to him while a paramedic performed maintenance on my skull. They made me wait after I'd finished. I waited a long time. I fell asleep waiting. When I woke, a man was standing in the doorway, the light streaming past him. He was calling my name. When I answered he introduced himself as an assistant to the attorney general. He did not give his name, only his title.

The assistant AG wanted to review my statement. He said he had a few problems with it. He asked me questions about the statement for well over an hour. By the time he was finished, I didn't believe a word of it either. Eventually, he suggested that I should go home and rest for a few days, rethink my story. In the meantime, I should keep my allegations to myself—at least until I was in a position to produce corroborating evidence to support them. And as a personal favor to me, the assistant AG would contact the Department of Public Safety and inquire as to the status of my license. He was sure that with his recommendation, my application for renewal would sail through without any problems. I nearly started laughing. Here was another guy threatening to take away my license, my livelihood. Well, get in line, pal. Get in line.

I thanked the assistant AG and left. No one paid much attention as I walked through the Security Center. Outside the center, Marion Senske, her arm in a sling, was conducting a hushed conversation with the attorney general. He smiled at me. He looked like a man who made his living playing cards and right now held a fistful of aces. Marion did not smile. She had already used up her allotment for the day.

"I believe you have something that belongs to me," she said.

"What could that be?" I asked her.

Marion came forward and whispered so the AG couldn't hear. "Twenty-five thousand dollars," was her bid.

I glanced sideways at the AG. "No sale," I said.

"We'll talk," she called to me as I walked past her and down through the tunnel. The tunnel was clean; there was no indication at all that Galen Pivec had been killed there. There wasn't even a chalk outline to show where he had fallen.

It was very late or very early, depending on your point of view.

I found Louise's address in the telephone book. She lived not too far from Amy, in a small, unassuming white house on a dead-end street near a park built for small children, a park with swings, sandboxes, monkey bars and a merry-go-round. I woke her with my incessant pounding. She opened the front door after identifying me through the spy hole.

Louise was wearing a tired blue robe that she held closed at the throat with one hand. The robe covered a white cotton nightgown that brushed the top of ridiculously large slippers made up to resemble alligators, their long red tongues flapping up and down as she moved.

"How do you feel?" I asked as if she had been ill and I was bringing her Tupperware filled with chicken-noodle soup.

She didn't answer.

"I'm sorry to bother you so late," I told her.

She turned away from the door and I followed her inside.

The living room was immaculate; you could eat off the floor if you didn't mind blue and white carpet fibers with your food. Pillows were placed at exact angles on the chairs and sofa, magazines were fanned evenly on a highly polished coffee table, even sections of the newspaper were stacked neatly on the sofa where she had been reading them. On an end table was a photograph framed in silver, a photograph of an old, white-haired woman and a much younger, much livelier woman who was dressed in late-sixties style: bell-bottoms, tie-dyed T-shirt, long hair that fell to her waist. The young woman was beautiful. The young woman was Louise. What had happened? I wondered. What had transformed that vibrant flower child into the woman she had become, a woman who refused to walk barefoot in her own home for fear she would leave a mark?

Louise pivoted toward me. The neck of her robe fell open but she quickly closed it again, pinching the lapels together with her right hand. She patted her hair with her left hand. She did not speak.

"The man who killed Amy Lamb is dead," I said.

She did not respond. Maybe she was afraid of interrupting me.

"Galen Pivec did it," I continued. "He was shot to death this morning by the State Capitol Security Force after he killed Meghan Chakolis and wounded Marion Senske. You'll read all about it in tomorrow's paper."

Louise nodded. Other than that, she did not move.

"I'm telling you about it now because the paper won't say anything about Amy," I added. "It's possible that Pivec will never be accused of Amy's murder. Joseph Sherman had already been blamed for it and the attorney general . . . Anyway, Pivec did it. He told me so before he died. I just thought you should know."

Louise nodded again.

"Sorry to bother you so late," I repeated.

"Do I owe you anything?" Louise asked. "Money?"

285

I shook my head and for the first time realized it was un-likely I would be paid for any of this.

"Thank you," she said and drifted toward me, dropping her hand, letting the top of the robe fall open to reveal the un-adorned neckline of her white gown. "Would you like to stay a while? I can make coffee." Her voice was hopeful.

"Thank you, I can't."

"You were right, what you said, about being lonely," she said. "I'm not a homosexual. When I kissed Amy . . . I was just pretending."

"I understand."

"Do you? Do you know what it's like to be someone like me? When I come through that door each night, I know I'll be alone. I know I'll eat alone, I know the phone won't ring. When I go to bed at night, I'm alone. When I wake up in the morning, I'm alone. That's the worst part, waking up alone. Sometimes I whisper 'I love you' even though there's no one to hear me. Sometimes I pretend there's someone else saying the words to me. I just want to belong to someone. Can you understand that?"

I flashed on Laura's face. And Anne Scalasi's. And Cynthia Grey's. "Yes, I can," I said softly.

Then I said, "Tell me why you killed Dennis Thoreau."

Louise did not seem surprised by the question. She merely shook her head and moved to a walnut desk shoved up against the wall next to the kitchen door. She opened a drawer and took out a videotape. She handed it to me.

"He put something in Amy's drink. Then he made this movie. He offered to sell it to her for one thousand dollars. Amy didn't have the money. She came to me. She told me about the movie because . . . because she didn't have anyone else."

That's pretty much what I had figured. I knew C. C. didn't kill Thoreau and Meghan had convinced me she hadn't done it, either, although I had every intention of framing her for it. Conan had claimed he didn't know Dennis Thoreau and I be-lieved him. He was in Mankato when Thoreau was killed, playing chauffeur for C. C. and Marion. And Sherman hadn't known Thoreau even existed until I told him. That left Louise. A wild guess? Not really. She had come after me when she thought I hurt Amy. Why not Thoreau? Besides, McGaney said Thoreau was killed with a .25, the same caliber as the gun I took off Louise in my office.

"Sometimes, the people we love, we just want to protect them in the worst way," I mumbled and I slipped Louise's Ruger out of my pocket; I had kept it in my trunk. I set both the Ruger and the video on the coffee table and told Louise, "If I were you, I'd get rid of these."

"You're not going to tell the police?"

"No, I'm not."

"Why not?"

"I'm just too damn tired to argue with them."

"Thank you, Mr. Taylor."

"Don't thank me, Louise," I told her, recalling my own sleepless nights. "I'm not sure I'm doing you a favor."

"Thank you, Mr. Taylor," she repeated.

"Good-bye, Louise. I hope you find what you need."

She did not answer. I left. The door closed softly behind me.

THIRTY-THREE

ANNE SCALASI put her hand up, shielding her eyes from the headlights of my car as I swung into the driveway. She was sitting on my front steps, waiting for me. Apparently she had been waiting a long time.

"Where have you been?" she asked.

I eased myself next to her. "I had an errand to run."

She looked at her watch. "A little late, isn't it?"

"I was about to say the same to you."

" 'Eternal vigilance. We never sleep.' "

"I thought that was the motto of the Pinkertons."

"Yeah, well, it goes double for homicide cops."

I leaned back against the steps, looked up at the stars. Anne did not look up or down, just straight ahead. After a moment she said, "The state claimed jurisdiction. I can't get near the place."

"The capitol?"

"No, the fucking moon."

"Let it go, Annie," I told her.

"I'd like to, I really would."

I watched the stars some more, then told her what she wanted to hear. "C. C. and Marion did not kill Dennis Thoreau. They had nothing to do with it. Brown, Sherman,

Amy Lamb: They had nothing to do with them, either."

"They're innocent?" Annie asked.

"Well, I wouldn't exactly say that."

"Tell me," Anne said.

"Galen Pivec killed John Brown; thought he was Joseph Sherman, thought he was trying to blackmail C. C. Amy Lamb found out, so he killed her, too. Then he finally caught up with the real Sherman. End of story."

"Thoreau?"

"Meghan Chakolis," I answered, lying.

"Why?"

"It was a crime of passion. He was her ex-husband. She still loved him. He was playing around. Want a beer?"

"Bullshit," Annie said.

I gave her a hard look; I didn't know if she could see my eyes or not. "What happened to Thoreau and the rest, who killed them and why, had nothing to do with what you did or didn't do, Annie. I wouldn't kid you about this."

"I have the feeling there's a lot you're not telling me," she insisted.

"Yeah, there is," I admitted. "But giving you the details won't make any difference. We can't prove anything."

We both stood. I unlocked the door, opened it, held it for her. "What about the videotape?" she asked, brushing past me.

"I'm sure it'll turn up," I said, following her inside.

I switched on the lights and went into the kitchen to fetch two Summit Ales from the refrigerator. The phone rang. I looked at the clock. *Not even the telemarketers call this late,* I thought, betting myself a quarter it was Marion Senske with another offer. It wasn't.

"I didn't wake you, did I, Taylor?" Lieutenant O'Connell asked.

"What did I do?"

"Nothing, nothing at all. What makes you think you did anything?"

"It is kinda late, Sean," I reminded him. "This isn't a social call, is it?"

"Well, lad, as a matter of fact it is. We're just finishing up here and I thought I should tell you what happened before you read it in the papers."

"What happened?"

"I killed Heather Schrotenboer tonight."

"What?"

"Me or Adzick. You know Pete Adzick."

"What are you talking about?"

"Aasen sent us over to pick her up; he wanted to ask her questions about a bullet fired from her gun. We knocked on the door. She asked who it was. I answered, 'The police.' She said, 'Come in, the door's open.' That sounded a little queer to me, so we each took a side and I pushed the door open with my foot. She fired on us . . ."

"What?"

"Put three rounds into the wall behind us, across the hall. I went in high, Adzick went in low. We fired about eight rounds between us, hit her twice. Forensics said they'd tell us which one did the job if we wanted to know. I don't want to know. Why would I want to know?"

"Jeez, I'm sorry, Sean," I said, meaning it.

"I never killed anyone before," Sean confessed. "Never even fired my gun except on the range."

"I'm so sorry."

"Can't figure out why she did it, though, started shooting at us. Why would she do something like that, Taylor? Hmm? Was she frightened? Did she think we were out to get her? Did she think we were, maybe, the Mafia or something?"

I didn't answer.

"I think she thought we were the Mafia. Isn't that crazy? Why would she think something like that?"

I didn't answer.

"I never killed anyone before!"

I had nothing to say. Apparently, Sean didn't either. After a minute or so I hung up the phone.

"What happened?" Anne asked, sipping on the beer.

Did Heather Schrotenboer belong to me?

Did she?

No, I decided. Randy, maybe. But not Heather. I had a lot of sins to answer for, a lot of penance to do. But not for Heather.

"I'm going to the football game Sunday, Vikes and 49ers," I told Anne.

"Oh?"

"A friend of mine has tickets."

THIRTY-FOUR

T HE BANNER STORIES on the front pages of both the *St. Paul Pioneer Press* and the *Minneapolis StarTribune* Sunday newspapers told the tale of the crazed gunman who had kidnapped Carol Catherine Monroe, killed her best friend and wounded her campaign manager before he was killed himself after a brief but tense standoff with State Capitol Security Force officers Friday evening. Both newspapers were quick to point out that the popular member of the Minnesota House of Representatives was unharmed and would continue her campaign; that she hoped to prove by example that people need not be afraid. "We need not allow ourselves to become victims," the heroic gubernatorial candidate was quoted as saying. "We need not walk in fear, one of another."

Jeezus, now she was stealing from Edward R. Murrow.

I read the stories three times and they didn't mention my name once. Obviously the attorney general hadn't given my statement to the press, which meant he was sitting on it—assuming, of course, it hadn't already been shredded.

In a separate, six-paragraph article in the St. Paul paper, it was announced that the Ramsey County Medical Examiner had concluded that Joseph Sherman, the subject of a week-long manhunt by local law enforcement agencies, died of "self-inflicted gunshot wounds." The article said the ex-convict had been sought for the brutal murders of John Brown and Amy Lamb. It was not explained why he had wanted to kill either of them.

No mention was made of Dennis Thoreau and his videotape. I wasn't surprised.

Cynthia Grey read the story over my shoulder. "This is a travesty," she claimed. "We should file suit on behalf of Sherman's family, make sure the truth comes out."

"Does Sherman have a family?"

"I don't know."

"It's probably best to just forget about it," I said.

"Is that what you're going to do, forget about it?"

"Eventually," I answered. I made a production out of folding the paper and dropping it in the recycle bin. "Ready to go?"

"I guess," Cynthia answered with a sigh. Then she smiled. "Do you realize this is the first football game I've ever seen in person?"

"You'll enjoy it," I said, tucking a videotape-sized package wrapped in brown paper and addressed to Hersey Sheehan, c/o *The Cities Reporter,* under my arm.

"I need to stop at a mailbox first," I said. "It'll only take a minute."

EPILOGUE

SIXTEEN DAYS LATER the mayor of St. Paul was elected governor of the state of Minnesota, defeating the former governor by less than one percent of the votes cast. Carol Catherine Monroe was a distant third—scandal had forced her to drop out of the race three days before the election, but the secretary of state's office had not had enough time to remove her name from the ballot.

It was reported that she had a campaign debt of nearly a half million dollars.

Fewer votes were cast in this gubernatorial election than in any other in Minnesota's history—this in a state that regularly ranks first in the nation for per capita voter turnout.

I was one of the voters who stayed home.